2

DRAGON BETRAYED

OPHELIA BELL

Dragon Betrayed
Copyright © 2016 Ophelia Bell
Cover Art Designed by Dawné Dominique
Photograph Copyrights © Fotolio.com, DepositPhotos.com, CanStock.com

Published by Ophelia Bell
UNITED STATES

ISBN-13: 978-1537284835
ISBN-10: 1537284835

ALSO BY OPHELIA BELL

STANDALONE EROTIC TALES

After You
Out of the Cold

OPHELIA BELL TABOO

Burying His Desires

•

Blackmailing Benjamin
Betraying Benjamin
Belonging to Benjamin

•

Casey's Secrets
Casey's Discovery
Casey's Surrender

Love thyself.

TRIGGER WARNINGS

Beloved readers, this book is a little beyond the ones I've written so far. Like many writers, I like to stretch my boundaries, and this is one of those books. Hopefully it won't be something you can't read, but you need to be warned that there are some extreme kinks present later on in the book.

The sex itself is as steamy as always (I think steamier, in some scenes), but there are details you should be prepared for. These include rough bondage and edge play, including erotic asphyxiation (breath play) and blood play taken to the extreme. Every scene is 100% consensual.

It's one thing for an immortal dragon who literally *can't die* to try these things—Belah is at least old enough and experienced enough to know her limits and to test them. She can't die. If she could, she'd be a lot more choosy about her kinks, but then this would be a very different story.

Please always do your research and learn your limits before attempting new things, and always, *always* make sure you are with a skilled partner who respects those limits, too.

Be safe, sane, and consensual.

-Ophelia

CHAPTER ONE

Nile Delta, About 3,300 Years Ago

Belah the Queen. Belah the Empress. Belah the Goddess.

Belah had a slew of other titles, but none fit the role she filled now. She strode through the muddy battleground of the Nile Delta, pondering all her titles, resigned to the fact that one was also Belah, Priestess to Dying Men.

Mud squished through the toes of her sandals and she left the shoes behind, irritated more by her impeded progress than the mud clinging to her feet. The war she'd orchestrated had been a success. She'd conquered an entire kingdom with only a breath. One word uttered and thousands had died, securing her place as Empress of yet another land filled with more human subjects.

She didn't need to be out here, in the wake of one of the most impressive victories she'd overseen, and she had overseen thousands in the past several centuries. Her commanders had already come to her to report their success, along with a list of casualties, and her proxy would see that the dead were given honorable funerals and their families taken care of.

All but one of her commanders had reported to her. The man who had secured this victory, whose troops had been the vanguard, had been too gravely wounded to attend her in person. His healer didn't think he'd live through the night, and his last wish was to lay eyes on his Queen, his Goddess, before he died.

Belah had watched the battle unfold from the skies. Her presence in her true form—that of a huge, blue dragon—was seen as a good omen by the soldiers and often turned the tides. The enemy would see her flying over and cower in fear, often surrendering entirely. This particular enemy, however, was led by a young upstart of a dragon who had to be put in his place.

She and her siblings had to fight to maintain order in the world. The more their descendants bred, the more they fought, and the more entitled they became, each of them believing they were worthy of having a bigger share of the plentiful treasures available.

Human followers were the greatest treasures in all the world, besides a dragon's own offspring. Belah had more than she needed, but she wasn't about to let a power-hungry youngster encroach on her territory. She would have to have a talk with Gavra and tell him to keep his progeny in line. What was it about the Red dragons in his line that were such troublemakers?

The mood around her was subdued as she made her way through the encampment, cloaked in drab robes with no retinue to give away her status. Morale was positive, but exhaustion and grief still prevailed. They had lost many, but nowhere near the amount their opponent had sacrificed. That didn't diminish the value of the men who had died or the cause they'd died for.

They believed they'd fought for the glory of their Empress, and were proud enough of that cause, but glory wasn't Belah's end game. Keeping the ever-growing population of dragons in line was the purpose for every battle she fought. This one had been hard-won, and she wondered yet again whether the outcome was worth it.

When she reached the wounded commander's tent, she paused. From beneath her hooded cloak, she met the eyes of the pair of guards posted at the entrance. They recognized her instantly, and without a word, they bowed at the waist and pulled the flaps aside for her to enter.

The interior was dim and stuffy and smelled of acrid medicinal balms, blood, and smoke. A linen-robed figure bent over a narrow cot, unwinding bloody bandages from an unconscious shape.

"Meri, I have come. How is he?"

The young healer only shook her head, her back rising and falling with a heavy sigh.

"See for yourself, mistress. This wound is mortal, yet he clings to this world. When he is conscious, he only has breath to beg for you." She cast a fleeting, accusatory glance over her shoulder at Belah, then lowered her gaze to her task again.

Belah caught a brief impression of the thoughts that bubbled under the surface of Meri's mind. Her physician was loyal and deferential, but not without her opinions. At the moment, she assumed Belah and her commander had a far more intimate connection than they did.

"We've never been lovers, Meri. I need to know my commanders are following my orders for the right reasons.

3

Nikhil is the best of them. In spite of being new to his rank, he's ruthless and adept at breaking through an enemy's defenses. But I assure you, if I inspired him somehow, it was his spirit and not his cock that was the recipient of that inspiration."

Meri made a noncommittal noise that Belah might have read as insubordination if she hadn't known the woman for her entire life.

Meri wasn't that far off the mark where Belah's effect on her subjects was concerned. Even though Belah had a dedicated harem, a night with her was often considered one of the highest honors she could bestow on a subject who had pleased her. And she was nothing if not generous.

Meri discarded the soiled bandages and moved to pour clean water into a bowl from a ewer on a small table by the bed. When she moved, Belah stepped closer to inspect the soldier's wound. A deep gash stretched across the right side of his abdomen, just under his ribcage. It had been neatly stitched, but the flesh around was proud and red, warning of infection. The skin around it was clean, but the rest of him was still covered in dried blood and dirt. Other, smaller lacerations covered the areas that would have been bare in battle. This cut must have been from an incredibly sharp spear. Glancing around, she saw his discarded armor, the blood-soaked rent through the side confirming her thought.

She pulled a small stool close and sat by his side, pushing back her hood. Reaching for the bowl of water, she said to Meri, "Were the internal wounds as grave as this looks?"

"Very grave. I repaired what I could, but the trauma is more than most men would survive. His channels still may not be clear. I prayed to Sekhmet to ease his pain, at the very least. If a fever sets in tonight, he is unlikely to see daybreak."

Belah nodded. Meri was more than capable, but the man's survival would likely require more than the divine intervention Meri had prayed for. Sekhmet was capable of healing him, but Belah knew her sister was too far away to hear that prayer. Sekhmet had as many names as Belah did in this age. In her own land, she was known as the Great Sky Goddess. In Belah's kingdom, she was Sekhmet. In their siblings' kingdoms, she had other names entirely. To Belah herself, her sister's name was Numa. None of those identities could answer Meri's prayers today. Belah, in her guise as Isis, would have to answer them herself.

The other woman watched her expectantly. In a low voice, she said, "I also prayed to you because it comforted him. You answer more prayers than any of the other gods and aren't afraid to sully yourself to do it." Meri regarded Belah's muddy hem and her dirty feet peeking out beneath.

"If a walk through a muddy camp will save the man who ensured the safety of my people, I would do it a million times. Whether or not I can answer anyone's prayers now will remain to be seen. Will you go fetch more hot water, please?"

Meri retrieved the empty ewer and left the tent with a grim set to her mouth.

Alone with the soldier, Belah took a breath and exhaled a lungful of magic smoke. The blue-white cloud swirled around Nikhil's torso, spreading out and settling onto his skin. It shimmered in the lantern light inside the tent, seeping into his pores, some of it trickling into his nostrils with his shallow intake of breath. Belah closed her eyes, letting her mind reach out for the magic, using it to sense the gravity of his injuries. She couldn't heal him with her magic, at least not physically. Without sharing a sexual bond with him, her abilities were limited to healing of the spiritual or mental variety. Two of her brothers and one sister could heal just about any physical damage with their breath, but they weren't available, so she would do what she could.

The first thing she did was dull the man's pain as she mentally explored his internal damage. Meri wasn't wrong—he'd experienced serious trauma, but the physician had done an excellent job piecing him back together.

There wasn't much else to do but make sure he was comfortable until he could heal—or die. Belah dipped a cloth into the bowl of cool water and pressed it to his fevered brow, then began to clean the dirt from his body. The remnants of her breath seeped into the wound and would at least prevent any kind of infection until the tissues managed to knit back together.

Nikhil was a strong, well-built man, youthful but battered from starting life as a soldier as young as he could. She had watched him from birth, and had been involved in his life peripherally for even longer. His mother was the widowed wife of one of the former commanders of the armies who fought to protect her kingdom. She had been young and newly pregnant when her husband was killed while defending Belah's subjects during a raid.

Belah had called on her brother, Ked, for a favor. Nikhil's pregnant mother was beautiful and bereft to the point that Belah worried for the unborn baby's health. Belah's brother, ever the secretive dragon, opted to visit the woman in the dead of night and seduce her while she slept, make love to her, and leave her unborn child with a blessing that would ensure he thrived and might ultimately rise to be the mate of one of their kind. It was an uncommon gift among dragons, but one Belah felt compelled to facilitate, considering the value of the commander she had lost. Soldiers died all the time, but skilled commanders were not easy to come by. If the child grew up to be even half as capable as his father, it would be worth it.

Afterward, the woman claimed her pregnancy was the product of a union with a god. Belah knew better, but didn't disavow the woman of her fantasy. In her kingdom, they knew Belah's brother as Osiris. In his own land far to the East, they called him Svarog.

Nikhil's troops believed his mother's story about his origin and followed him like he was a demi-god. Judging by the scars he carried, he'd survived a lot during his time as a soldier. It wouldn't serve the fantasy for him to die now.

The strong chest beneath the damp cloth she held rose more sharply than before and fell, a ragged breath escaping Nikhil's throat.

Belah glanced at his face, raising an eyebrow when she saw his dark eyes flutter open. He blinked a few times, barely able to focus.

"*Tilahatan,*" he said, struggling to rise up on his elbows and immediately gasping when his abdomen rippled with agony. He fell back again with a groan.

She wrung out the cloth, pretending to ignore the name he'd given her. He'd just called her "goddess" in his own language, and the very utterance of the word left her jittery in spite of being accustomed to that level of deference. Something about hearing it from this man affected her strongly. She clutched the cloth, working to still her shaking fist before raising it up to wipe across his sweat-drenched brow.

"Not goddess, just Belah. You earned the right to my true name today. You called for me and I came."

Nikhil lay back, his eyes wide and staring. "Are you real?"

Belah reached out and gripped his hand where it lay on the blanket beside him. She squeezed and leaned closer, letting a bit of her breath seep out when she spoke, along with the calming magic that accompanied it.

"I am very real, Nikhil. You've spoken to me at the palace when you and the other commanders reported in."

"You should lead the armies yourself," he said. "You are smarter than all of us combined."

"A good empress knows how to command from the throne. If I displayed too much of my own power to my enemies, they would all be trying to kill me. I give you the power, and you execute the orders. You were the one who showed your greatness today, Nikhil. I had nothing to do with it."

He answered slowly, his voice strained. "You gave me the idea. My injury was calculated to make the enemy think our army lost their commander. I fell, but stayed conscious as long as I could to command them to victory. The enemy was too cocksure, and our armies too skilled. We routed them."

Belah picked up the pot of honey and began dabbing the sweet, sticky ointment gently on his wound. Nikhil winced once but bore the pain. "You risked your life for the cause," she admonished.

"I risked my life for you," he said gruffly. With more strength and speed than she could've expected, he reached out and gripped her wrist tightly and held it.

"I live my life at your pleasure, *Tilahatan*. Every lie I tell is for you." His fingers dug in even tighter, to the point of pain.

She'd believed all along that she was immune to the touch of a Blessed human, but when his hand wrapped around her wrist, the pleasure of that simple contact made her entire body grow still.

It wasn't a simple touch, though. His fingertips dug painfully into the tender flesh on the inside of her wrist, while the warmth of his palm sunk into the back. Lightning seemed to charge through his hand and up her arm.

All she could do was stare down at his fist gripped around her wrist, dumbfounded. As quickly as he'd grabbed her, he released her and his hand fell to the bed.

Belah forced herself to regain her composure. Never in her life had another person ever made a threatening move toward her. Yet Nikhil's adoration was plain, and his touch… while rough, it had been exhilarating to feel her power seep away from the contact.

More than exhilarating, it had been a relief to feel—if even for a split second—that he might overpower her. Not that he could have in his state.

"I am sorry," he said. "I've displeased you."

"No, you didn't," she said. Her mind reeled at the tilting sensation she felt. Power was her element and had always been. That a single, desperate touch could make her feel something wholly new and amazing left her confused and scrambling to regain her senses.

His own innate power was what she'd felt in his touch, even as desperate as he'd been to make his point. He had power over so many. So much power that his soldiers would willingly die under his command. They loved him enough to carry out his orders even while he lay near death after inviting a fatal wound himself.

Belah fumbled with the damp cloth and was grateful when Meri returned with more hot water. She returned the basin to her physician.

"Make arrangements for him to be brought to the temple tonight. He's well enough to travel. You should stay to see to the other wounded. I can take care of Nikhil when he is with me."

When Belah left the tent, she glanced down at her wrist, her mind spinning at the sight of the four dark, finger-shaped bruises he'd left on her skin.

After a few steps, someone launched himself bodily at her, beseeching her to heal him. Mud splattered up her cloak and she stared down blankly at the man babbling at her feet, not even registering his words. Without thinking, she blew out a breath to calm him.

As he stood, smiling and thanking her, the other observers cheered.

Within a moment, guards surrounded her, one of them pushing her hood over her head.

"You should have let us know you were ready to leave, mistress."

Belah clenched her eyes shut. She should have been less of an idiot, but Nikhil's touch had done something to her.

Her guards urged her forward and she went, succumbing to their disciplined instructions. Their orders were to keep her safe.

She had very little control over her life outside the temple. Everyone bowed at her feet when she walked by, if they knew it was her.

Nikhil would have bowed as well, if he'd been physically able to. But his touch made her want to bow to him. Goddess or not, she'd loved the force of that touch. All she could picture in her mind now was what he might have done to her if he'd had more strength to follow through. Would he have had her bowing at his feet instead?

His feet. Even his feet had been beautiful after she'd cleaned them. Every inch of him was perfect. His body a finely honed weapon that had seen its share of battles. Even though he was still relatively young, the scars he carried mapped the journey he'd chosen. If he survived this wound he would return to that path, even though he was fated for something much greater.

"The Blessing," she said to herself, making her way past the last of the tents and into the litter that would carry her home. He was Blessed, thanks to her. Blessed by her own brother and fated to mate a dragon. Perhaps she would be that dragon. If only that could be true—if she mated him, he would lose that spark like every one of her past mates had, if they even managed to survive the first few weeks after being marked.

Nikhil… Belah took a deep breath. All her senses focused on the memories of him. His dirty, bloody scent, the bruising grip of his hand on her arm, the desperate sound of his voice.

The adoration in his eyes and that sound he'd made when he apologized.

"Wait!" she called.

Her litter lurched to a stop and she hopped out.

"He's coming now," she said, charging back to Nikhil's tent. She didn't trust anyone but her own personal guard to carry him, and she needed him to be at the temple tonight. Even if she didn't dare destroy his will by mating him, she would have him in every other way she could.

CHAPTER TWO

It might have been a bad idea to turn her study into Nikhil's sick room, but she did it. Belah had a bed brought in and set by the window where the clear air could come in. It was the closest she could get him to her own room without raising suspicion. He was her honored commander, living out his last days in luxury rather than on a muddy battlefield, as far as everyone else was concerned. Not that anyone would have questioned her decision either way, but her façade could still be broken, even as powerful as she really was. She'd rather rule by love than terror.

She occupied herself irritating the cooks with a new schedule, trying to ignore the huge man that was being deposited in her personal space.

She made it back up to his new bedroom when he arrived. He let out a soft groan as her guard lay him upon his new bed, and she came to attention at the signal of pain.

A second later she was at his side, aching to alleviate his pain, but now that he was awake she couldn't use her power without giving away her secrets.

Instead, she simply sat and swabbed his fevered brow with a damp cloth.

"You are my goddess," he whispered before drifting off again.

The second he was unconscious, she bent low to his mouth and exhaled a slow breath, making sure the magic went where it was most needed. Then she closed her eyes and reached out with her mind, seeking any impression of his deeper feelings, yet finding only a sense of exhaustion and relief when his pain finally abated.

He would feel no pain tonight.

When she returned to her own room, she found herself too restless to settle down. Normally her late-night itch could be alleviated by a visit to her harem where she had her pick of virile male flesh or supple female curves. But her well was full and she rarely took her full pleasure from those in her service. Their pleasure was what sustained her. She preferred to take her own pleasure alone, when she needed the release. Giving up too much of her magic to another would form a bond deeper than she was willing to have with a human she had no desire to fully mate. So what was she thinking, bringing Nikhil here? She wanted his commanding touch too much not to share her magic with him in the way she only could by allowing him to share her bed. A bond would be inevitable, but at what cost if she didn't dare mate him?

The question made her wings itch, so in the dark, she stepped out onto her balcony and surrendered her body to the wind. Under the caress of the breeze blowing through the delta, her skin shimmered and transformed into sapphire scales. Heavy horns erupted from her forehead and her body grew large and elongated with a tail sweeping back through her open doorway. Then she launched herself into the moonlit night.

Belah soared for hours, trying to shake the feeling that Fate had grabbed her by the tail and was once again twisting her life into knots. She hadn't craved a mate in more than a century, and never one quite so much as this man. The past six mates she'd chosen out of necessity to breed, not out of true desire or even love. They hadn't even known the truth of her nature and had been too weak to endure the magic, all of them dying either instantly or within days of her mark.

They had been pets as much as the members of her harem were her pets. Treasured possessions that she considered not much more than status symbols to compare with her siblings. She and her immortal brethren each had their own particular preferences where their collections were concerned. Belah was known for her menagerie of docile, accommodating males, but enjoyed females who were more direct. The combination was what pleased her the most, since most often she was an observer while her pets played with each other.

Her brother, Aodh, had a penchant for virgins. Ked preferred to take in the lost and damaged, and Belah wasn't even certain he sated himself with them as often as the others did with their own harems. Gavra, by contrast, habitually exhausted his pets and borrowed from his siblings. Both her sisters had wildly disparate preferences—Numa's collection were the most fertile and nurturing, and Aurum's the most wild and carefree.

They all treasured and spoiled their pets, as did most dragons. Belah cared for hers like any of the belongings she'd accumulated over her long life, and she grieved when one of her pets grew too old and died. Immortality was a gift she could have given to all of them, but the cost would be too great. It would mean divulging her true nature, and she and her siblings had an unspoken rule to never reveal what they were to their subjects, much less their most prized possessions. Only their mates could know what they were.

The rising dawn came too quickly for her to completely shed the itch brought on by the presence of the wounded soldier she'd taken in. Still, she had no choice but to return. Flying all night had depleted her energy reserves, and she would have to take advantage of her harem before day's end or risk inadvertently shifting in public.

With a graceful sweep of her wings, Belah shifted just as her talons touched down on the edge of her balcony. Inside her chamber, she admitted her servants and allowed them to prepare her bath, bathe her, then clothe her.

She made her way down the long hallway to the lower-level chamber where her pets spent their days. On her way past her study door, she hesitated, her curiosity drawing her gaze to the elaborately carved and polished wood barrier between her and the man who lay beyond.

How had he slept the night before? Was he in pain now? Perhaps she should see him before he woke and infuse his body with another breath to ensure he remained comfortable. Her mind reached out, found him conscious and comfortable, albeit sore and still groggy. Meri was already attending to him.

She had her own needs to see to now, and Nikhil was in no condition to help her with them. She swiftly walked on, fleeing the image of how his beautiful body would perform were he inclined to fulfill her daily requirement for energy. Would he be as insistent and passionate as that single grip of her wrist had suggested? She reached down and wrapped her hand around the same place he had, the memory of his fingertips digging in as vividly as if the bruises hadn't already healed and the physical reminder still marked her.

Once in her harem chamber, Belah relaxed a little. The room was dim, the early morning light barely peeking through the closed curtains that covered the windows. She closed the door gently to avoid waking those of her pets who still slept. She rarely visited so early in the day, so she waited, closing her eyes to reach out to the variety of sleeping minds and find the ones who were closest to waking.

One entire side of the chamber was filled with luxurious beds, curtained with gauze, and strewn with comfortable furniture, richly appointed and covered in cushions. Incense meant to aid sleep burned in the corners, but would be replaced by a more enlivening scent by her servants in anticipation of her morning visit. One entire wall was comprised of carved wooden panels that let bits of the daylight stream through the gaps in the designs. During the day, those panels would open onto the temple's vast courtyard where there was a pool and a garden for her pets to spend their days in.

She never wondered about their level of contentment because their emotions were transparent. Occasionally if she neglected to visit for too long, she could sense a level of competition among them, and perhaps slight resentment from the ones who she considered her favorites. Each one desired her as much as she desired them, and she made sure they continued to. If one of her pets ever wavered in their adoration, she simply released them from their obligation to her. They had each other when she wasn't there, however, and were encouraged to indulge themselves in her absence. It wasn't uncommon for two to fall in love and wish to carry on their married life outside the temple, though even the committed couples sometimes chose to remain her pets.

Even now there was a bright spot of energy pulsing from one of the many curtained beds. Lush moans carried to her ears from within. Belah made her way to the bed on quiet feet. Through a gap in the canopy, the ebony curls of one of her newest pets, Nyla, moved over the taut flesh of a man's torso as she kissed her way down his stomach.

Belah tried to see who was the lucky recipient of the young woman's attention, but his head was obscured by the round swell of Nyla's backside. Only his broad shoulders and large, tanned hands were visible, stroking up and down the backs of Nyla's thighs.

Belah watched, unnoticed, while Nyla took the man's thick erection into her mouth. Her eyes closed as though savoring him, her lips sliding down and encompassing his length. At his urging, she repositioned her hips to straddle his shoulders and let out a soft moan when he gripped her ass, drawing her closer to his mouth.

Over the curve of Nyla's ass, a pair of dark brows raised, and brown eyes blinked at Belah in amusement.

Belah smiled at Zeb and simply motioned for him to continue pleasuring his new partner. She had always liked Zeb's easy manner and had been drawn to him more frequently for sustenance than many of the other males in her harem.

Nyla sucked and stroked Zeb's cock enthusiastically, moaning louder and louder from his attention between her thighs. Their auras bloomed brightly around them, and Belah enjoyed the crackling energy that tickled her skin from being in close proximity. The undercurrent of something more sweetly potent made her smile broaden.

They were in love.

Still, they were her pets, and their purpose was to serve her. She almost regretted interrupting their fun when she rested a hand on Nyla's shoulder and squeezed to get her attention.

Nyla slid her mouth off Zeb's glistening cock with a soft pop and stared at Belah in a daze. Her cheeks were flushed and her lips wet; her pink tongue darted out and swept across her lower lip. After a second, comprehension struck, her eyes widening.

"Stop, my sweet," Nyla said, looking over her shoulder and reaching back to still her lover's steady licks. She turned back to Belah, a fresh glimmer of excitement in her eyes. "Mistress? May we serve you this morning?"

Belah moved to sit on the bed near Nyla's head. She cupped the young woman's chin and bent close, taking her mouth in a slow, languid kiss that Nyla returned eagerly. Belah hummed in appreciation of Zeb's salty flavor clinging to his lover's tongue. They had both been so close to climax, their auras still pulsed vividly around them, but that would have to wait until the magic had doubled.

Belah's pets were nothing if not eager to please. The delay in satisfaction might have been torture to some, but every member of her harem had been well-trained to hold back until their mistress was ready. Belah made sure never to disappoint them.

She reached toward the bedside table and opened a wooden box that rested there, one of many beside every other bed throughout her harem's quarters. From within, she lifted an earthenware bottle and uncorked it, releasing a spicy aroma into the air. Both her pets breathed in deeply, and Nyla shifted as if to move off her lover's torso.

"Don't move yet," Belah said. "Just sit up for me." This was one of the many little rituals she enjoyed with her pets, and one she hadn't done with Nyla yet. She tilted the bottle over Nyla's chest and a stream of oil drizzled out, gleaming gold in the morning light. It landed on the upper swell of one breast and ran down over Nyla's dark nipple. The young woman closed her eyes and smiled, her nipple hardening.

Before the liquid could drip off the tip, Bella cupped her hand beneath the heavy globe of flesh, catching the excess in her palm and swirling it around Nyla's nipple. She set the bottle back down and focused her attention on smoothing the oil over Nyla's breasts and shoulders while Zeb watched, his torso twisted sideways to get a better view of the proceedings. Between them his cock still stood erect and glistening.

When the front side of Nyla's torso shone with the oil and her breasts heaved from desire, Belah gave both her nipples one last squeeze and stopped. She poured another bit of oil into her palm and reached between Zeb's legs, beginning with his smooth, supple balls and working her palm up the length of his shaft and back down.

Zeb let out a rough groan, his head falling back against the cushions. When his aura pulsed dangerously close to climax, she stopped.

"Down again, but don't touch him yet," she said to Nyla in a whisper. The young woman obediently lowered her torso so that her cheek rested on Zeb's hip, but she remained a breath away from the base of his shaft with her hands resting on his thighs. "Good girl," Belah said.

She stood and tipped the bottle of oil again, trailing a line down the woman's spine until it trickled between the round, firm cheeks of her ass. Nyla's bare cunt already flowed with her own juices, but her flesh quivered when the cooler oil reached it. She let out a small whimper when Belah cupped her ripe folds and swept back upward. She teased slowly through her cleft, moving higher and pausing to add another small dollop of oil between Nyla's cheeks. With her fingertips, she gently worked the oil in a narrowing spiral around the tight rosette of her ass.

Belah's own heartbeat had sped up in her chest and she was grateful for this delicious distraction from her thoughts of the night—of the man who now rested mere footsteps from her own bedchamber. A heavy, throbbing sensation began deep between her thighs, and she forced herself to focus again on Nyla.

Reaching back to the box, she retrieved a blunt, smooth piece of marble that had been polished to a silken shine. It was shaped like an elongated egg, with a flared base like a tiny pedestal.

As she anointed the dildo with more of the oil, Belah grew aware of the arousal of another nearby and glanced up. Through Zeb and Nyla's curtains, one of her other pets watched raptly.

The large, dark-skinned Idrin smiled sheepishly at her, but his awareness made the endeavor even more interesting.

She bent her lips to Nyla's ear. "We have an audience. Do you mind if he assists me?"

Nyla looked up at her curiously for a second, then turned her head in Idrin's direction.

"No," she whispered back, her response accompanied by a new flush.

Belah beckoned to the other man, who rose and strode toward them, his eyes downcast but still taking in Nyla's naked, oiled body. He paused a few feet from the bed, glanced between Belah and Zeb, and waited with his head down.

Belah met Zeb's eyes with a raised brow and was pleased to see the man nod his shaved head with a smile. They were nothing if not accommodating to her games, never once expressing an objection. Of course, she made a point to make sure they were satisfied every time she visited.

She had pleasured both these men in the past—sometimes at once—and knew they worked well together. They could easily bring her to the crest of her climax, but knew she rarely wished to be pushed beyond. When they reached that point, she merely had to give the command and they would release into her, both their seed and their energy flooding her in delicious waves. The inundation was as complete and almost as fulfilling as an orgasm, but she preferred to wait until she was alone to finish the job. These men weren't meant to be her mates, and she didn't want to risk the complication of becoming too closely bonded with either of them. Every time she climaxed, a measure of her energy would flood into them, so she had to be careful in order to preserve what freedom they still had in spite of their status. Every so often she would allow it, simply because sharing her energy on occasion helped maintain a level of health and happiness among them.

Nyla seemed nervous, gazing up at Idrin's large, sleek frame and the intense look in his eyes.

Belah stroked her hand down the woman's back and whispered in her ear. "He's gentle, I promise." Looking up at Idrin, she simply handed him the bottle of oil. He flashed a perfect, white grin and took over, pouring a small puddle into the hollow of Nyla's back and massaging it in, slowly working his way over her shoulders and sliding both hands around her torso to cup her breasts.

Nyla arched like a cat, allowing him access to her breasts. He teased and massaged languidly for a moment. Belah could easily sense Nyla's hunger by the way she stared at Zeb's cock, licking her lips but intent on not disobeying her mistress. With a sigh, Nyla turned away, only to spy Idrin's dark column right at eye level and within reach.

"May I?" she whimpered, her fingertips digging harder into Zeb's legs.

"Please do," Belah said, meeting Idrin's lust-filled gaze. His eyelids closed and his lips parted as Nyla lifted up just enough to take his thick tip into her mouth and swirl her tongue around the ridge.

Zeb's gaze had shifted, and he now watched enraptured as his lover hungrily sucked the other man's shaft deep into her throat. He turned his head to watch Belah slide her oiled palm back down over Nyla's round ass, which tightened slightly when she grazed her fingertips deliberately over her puckered opening. He licked his lips and took the proffered dildo. His eyes shone with lust when he pressed the rounded tip of it against her ass.

Nyla went completely still for a second, then let out a soft moan around Idrin's cock and pressed back into Zeb's hands. He clutched at one full cheek with his free hand, teasing his thumb up and down through her slick channel and spreading her juices up and around the tight orifice. With one smooth push, the polished stone slipped inside, only its carved handle remaining outside Nyla's body.

The young woman's entire body shivered with pleasure.

"Not yet," Belah whispered, her own aching inner muscles clenching with the craving to be filled the way Nyla was going to be before this session was finished. She moved back down to Nyla's head, sliding her oiled palm along the contour of her body. She cupped her chin and urged her off Idrin's cock.

Nyla obeyed and looked up at Belah imploringly. Silently, Belah guided her off Zeb's torso and urged her to turn and face him, straddling his hips. Zeb's hands immediately rose to Nyla's hips and she bent to kiss him—an impulsive act that should have begged Belah's permission, but she overlooked it. The pair seemed made for each other, and she only hoped they would choose to stay with her rather than seek out a private life outside the temple.

Opposite Belah, Idrin resumed his earlier slow caresses of Nyla's body, still focusing on her breasts, which Nyla seemed to have grown comfortable with and responded to with little sighs.

Still engaged in a passionate kiss, Zeb slid his hands down over Nyla's hips and around her ass and found the end of the dildo. He pulled it out of her and pushed back in, beginning to fuck her with it, to Nyla's apparent delight. She kept her hips poised above his cock, much to Belah's satisfaction—her pet wouldn't indulge herself without being commanded to.

With her thumb and forefinger of one hand she spread Nyla's sodden folds apart, and with the other she gripped Zeb's stiff cock, pressing his tip between the pink petal-like flesh.

Both her pets let out sharp gasps, but before they could get carried away, she motioned to Idrin, who climbed onto the bed behind Nyla. Belah took control of the dildo while he positioned himself, Zeb clutching tightly at Nyla's hips and holding her still.

When Belah removed the dildo, Idrin pressed the thick head of his cock in to replace it. Nyla let out a long, slow sigh as he slid easily to the hilt in one careful stroke. Nyla lifted her hands to grasp the headboard. Her breasts hung over Zeb's mouth and he cupped them together, sucking her nipples between his lips one at a time while his hips shoved up into Nyla's depths.

Belah watched for a few seconds, enjoying the way their auras built in intensity, merging together in a colorful bubble of light that only she could see. Soon all that energy that swirled and pulsed around them would be hers, and she could take care of her other growing need in the privacy of her bedchamber.

The auras shimmered and the tempo of their moans and their fucking increased. Their bodies glistened with sunlight reflecting off the oil and sweat, so enticing Belah couldn't resist touching them even if she'd wanted to. She slid an oily hand down Idrin's muscular back, his ebony skin the most sensual color, as unmarred and shining as her own tresses. His dark eyes regarded her from beneath lowered lashes and his lips quirked into a smile as her hand paused over the bunching tightness of his ass. She knew what he liked.

She shifted the dildo from her other hand and quickly poured more oil onto it, then pressed it between his clenching cheeks. He pulled out of Nyla just long enough to relax and take the hard, smooth object into him, then slammed back into the woman's ass with a harsh grunt.

They were creatures of lust now and little more. But one emotion Belah sensed overflowing from them was adoration for her. She reached up and pulled Idrin into a hungry kiss, sending just enough of her breath into him to trigger the silent, conditioned response: it was time for him to give his Nirvana to her.

His head flew back and his hips smacked hard against Nyla's ass, evoking a cry from her.

Belah slipped a hand around the base of each man's cock and squeezed, and they both yelled out, their shafts pulsing with the power of their orgasms. Belah's fingertips found Nyla's hard clit, and it only took the slightest brush for her to be thrown over the edge too.

Belah simply closed her eyes, holding onto her pets where they were joined together and soaking every bit of their accumulated magic into her hungry well.

CHAPTER THREE

On the way back to her bedchamber, a hot ball of arousal pulsed in Belah's core, wetness running slickly over the tops of her thighs. That had been one of the more enjoyable morning visits to her harem, and she smiled to herself at the memory of the sweet words Zeb had whispered to Nyla when they lay entwined moments after their orgasms had subsided and Idrin had retreated outside to the bathing pool.

Now she felt sated and would be able to make quick work of her other need with her own collection of toys, or maybe just her own fingers, once she made it back to her chambers. Then in the afternoon she would be energized and clear-headed enough to announce her army's victory to her people and bestow commendations on her commanders.

That thought, combined with the sight of the door of her study made her pull up short. Her best commander lay on the other side of that door, wounded. He was one of hers too, yet had never enjoyed the attention she gave the members of her harem. Would he even want what she'd given them?

She approached the door and pushed it open slightly, staring through the crack. He lay sleeping peacefully, his vast muscles relaxed, yet still he seemed too large for the bed he rested on. He could be a dragon, at his size.

Belah remembered choosing him as her commander. He'd been barely more than a boy then, for all his emerging masculine beauty. He was a man, by his human culture's standards, and he'd proven himself, but his body hadn't quite caught up yet the day she gave him that power.

He'd grown since that day. And he had never once failed her.

She wouldn't fail him either, she decided. Just a touch of her Nirvana would heal him more than her breath could, but she couldn't just climb on and fuck him. He was too damaged.

All she needed was a touch. Bonds be damned. He would live and be bonded to her until he healed, then she would let the bond fade once he resumed his position at the head of her army with a promotion to general.

Her craving to share her energy with him had nothing to do with the way he'd touched her earlier. No… that insistent grip on her wrist was a fluke.

She opened the door and walked in, closing it softly behind her.

His still form was so beautiful. If she couldn't see his chest rising and falling, she might believe he was a statue molded from gold. She stopped at the side of his bed and pushed the covers down to his feet. The room was warm enough that he didn't stir.

Every inch of him was beautiful, from his feet to his face, tilted toward her in slumber.

He was still sound asleep, his angular features made more stark by the few days' worth of short, black hair growth on his normally shaved head, as well as thicker stubble on his cheeks and chin.

Belah sank down into the comfortable chair by his bed and watched for a moment. Her core throbbed harder when she stared at him, but looking away didn't help.

His soft, bow-shaped lips entranced her, inciting fantasies of what they would feel like on her flesh. The hard edges and contours of his muscles were no less impressive in repose. Neither was the thick, sleeping column of flesh resting along the juncture of his hip and one bulky thigh.

Like any of her soldiers, he was almost entirely hairless, a conscious choice as both a signal of his status and to prevent infestations. The members of her harem often observed the same grooming techniques.

Belah had no opinion one way or the other. She kept her own body as hairless as her pets, aside from her thick mane of blue-black waves, but would have enjoyed taking in every inch of Nikhil's magnificent shape regardless.

His aura was a soft, comforting glow, clinging close to his body like a cocoon. She wanted to touch him, to please him and see that aura brighten and expand, but didn't dare disturb his slumber. Her kind had a strong distaste for coupling with any but the most alert and willing partners, though she didn't think she would mind if he roused her from sleep by fucking her.

The thought of being teased to arousal while half-asleep and then penetrated made her close her eyes and sigh in pleasure.

She leaned back in her chair and unfastened the belt at her waist, letting the panels of her gown fall open. She braced both her feet at the edge of his bed, her toes making the barest contact with his hip and thigh. Her knees spread apart and she gazed at him, imagining this man waking her with the stiff prodding of his beautiful cock as it slid deep into her. She drifted her palms slowly over her torso, cupping and caressing both her breasts, then pinching her nipples hard enough to cause pain. The sharp jolts made her gasp, and her already soaking cunt ached even deeper to be fucked.

He would be the one to pluck that pain from her body, to use those strong, brutal hands to overpower her, to command her submission. Belah was an expert at making use of others for her own pleasure and glory, but Nikhil would be the perfect man to use her, and oh did she want to be used by him. She kept her eyes open, flitting her gaze up and down his body as she slid one hand down between her thighs. All the while she imagined his large hands, both rough and tender, on her body, fingers digging into her soft flesh with bruising insistence, or teasing her to the point of begging.

She teased herself, sliding her fingertips through her wet cleft and rubbing her clit while her other hand continued to savagely pinch her nipples. The fabricated images of how he might make love to her were more than enough to send her over the edge. Her thighs quivered as the tension built, wetness flooding even thicker over her fingers. She plunged three fingers into herself, pretending they were the tip of Nikhil's cock, and pulled them back out slowly, spreading her wetness over every inch of tender flesh between her ass and her throbbing clit.

Eyes closed and head thrown back, she readied herself to plunge into that beautiful abyss. At the same time, a steel-hard grip wrapped around her ankle and her eyes snapped open.

A dark, feverish gaze met hers and her cry turned into a surprised exhalation of his name.

"Nikhil!"

"Don't stop, *Tilahatan*," he said, his voice grating like stone on stone. His gaze dropped to her hand and she realized she had slowed, though her body craved its release even more now that he was watching her.

Another movement caught her eye and she realized his free hand gripped his cock, now a thick and rigid staff jutting up between his thighs. He stroked himself once, never moving his gaze from her hand.

His fingers dug into her leg painfully, the jolt of sensation making her cry out. He ripped his hand away.

"I am sorry, I didn't mean to hurt you. But please, you are so beautiful. I have never desired anything more than conquering your enemies, but now I desire to see you break in that way women do in my bed. You will always be my *Tilahatan*. Just let me have this moment before I die."

Belah pushed her foot against his hip. "Put your hand back. I want to break for you, to hurt for you the way you have endured hurt for me."

His fingers closed around her ankle again. Her nod encouraged the tightening of his grip.

"Yes, like that. Like you've shackled me to you," she said, closing her eyes and resuming her stroking. "I am your goddess,

Nikhil. *Yours*. As gods we are slaves to our power, I am your slave now."

"Mine," he replied, the bruising pain of his grip emphasizing the word. The strokes of his hand up and down his cock quickened and the pink tip of his tongue darted out to lick at his dry lips. He looked thirsty, ravenous, but not for food or drink. As his aura bloomed brighter around him, the hunger that accompanied it was for her alone, not any other sustenance.

A look of determination crossed his face and he tried to rise once, but let out a sharp cry as the pain of his wound sent a spike of bright red through his aura. His arousal flagged briefly, but after a moment, the agony diluted with the pleasure until his aura had a reddish, throbbing tint lingering beneath the silvery glow. He was still in pain, but endured the discomfort for her sake, as though the experience gave him more power.

"I want to pin you down and feel you under me, feel the hot clutch of you around me, hear you cry my name again and again like you are praying to me as I pray to you. I would worship you by breaking you, *Tilahatan*, because that is what I know. It has always been my gift to you, to be the breaker of wills, of entire armies and kingdoms. To give that gift to you one last time before I die would lighten my heart. Had I the strength now, I would break you before I join your brothers as an honored god in the afterlife."

Belah almost stopped teasing her clit to climb on top of him, but no—when she first gave into him, she wanted it to be exactly as he described, pinned down with his hard length pounding into her.

Instead, she spread her legs wider and pinched her nipples harder. Her eyes stayed locked with his, that dark gaze owning every single movement she made, as though storing it away to take to the grave.

This would not be the last time for him, not if a taste of her Nirvana healed him. But she no longer wanted to merely give him a taste. She wanted to give him *everything*.

Her orgasm built again, more abruptly than before. With a rush of heat through her limbs, she called his name and the power inside her burst forth, surging through her body and into his in a shimmering current.

Nikhil's entire body tensed and his head fell back against his pillows, eyes widening. His back arched, his hips rising up off the bed. Pain caused his aura to flare bright red again, but was outshone by his cock erupting with a thick stream of semen, so powerful it fell in spatters across his pillows. Even as the pulsing flow subsided, more managed to stray to the side, hitting the hand that still gripped her ankle so tightly she'd lost almost all sensation in her foot. A few droplets landed on her lower leg, as hot as molten metal. Belah nearly came again with the accompanying surge of his energy.

Nikhil's hand slipped off her ankle and lay limp by his side. He closed his eyes and furrowed his brow, his other hand slipping off his cock to rest lightly over the bandage on his side as though it troubled him.

"What is it?" Belah asked, closing her dress and refastening her belt. She didn't bother cleaning his semen off her leg—it complemented the reddened skin and the growing bruise that graced her ankle, and she almost wished it had been hot enough to burn and leave a mark. She stood to pour fresh water into a bowl and grabbed a cloth to clean him with.

"Something's wrong," Nikhil said, opening his eyes to watch distractedly as she wiped the pool of his seed off his taut stomach. His fingers splayed wider over his wound. "Or no… something *isn't* wrong, and that's what's wrong."

"I couldn't very well let you die." Belah smiled at him indulgently as she continued cleaning.

Again his hand shot out and gripped her wrist, startling her.

"What did you do to me? I was meant to *die*. I was meant to become a god for what I did, to live beside Osiris and Ra." He ripped the bandage off his side, displaying a honey-coated wound that was swiftly sealing itself and leaving no trace behind. Not even a scar.

"Death isn't what you think it is," Belah tried to say, but his hand shot up and gripped her throat, his fingers digging into the flesh beneath her ears. The size of his hands had never been so apparent. She couldn't even swallow the way he clutched her neck. Breathing was problematic. Her entire body tingled at the sudden contact and her cunt screamed for more.

"What did you do to me?" He searched her face, eyes wild. She tried to ignore the surge of arousal that his violent outburst had incited, but the thrill of being so near such a volatile creature made her tremble. His face caught the glint of sunlight from outside, casting the other side in shadow. He shifted, and the sunbeam hit his face fully, illuminating his dark eyes so they seemed alight with inner fire.

Unlike her docile collection of human pets, this man was untamed. He may do her will on the battlefield, but he was made for violence and feral as a result. She wouldn't have him any other way.

In a strangled voice, she whispered, "I did nothing more than the sun does every day. I illuminated something great. Something meant to stay in this world and make it great, too. Let me help you, Nikhil. You can be better with me than you would be with Osiris, living in his shadow."

His fingers loosened, becoming a caress, then shifted to the back of her neck. He pulled her down and she relented, aching for a taste of his lips.

The connection destroyed her. Sharing her Nirvana with him was one thing, but a simple kiss was too much. It was a taste of a fire she knew could burn her like no other could. Now that they were bonded, that contact—that simple touch of skin on skin—sent her energy skyrocketing again.

It didn't matter that she wanted it. She wanted all of him. All of the hot, hard body that now lay beneath her, fully healed. She had lived so long already and could never die, but to be pushed against the edge of that abyss made her feel more alive than she had in eons.

He wrapped his arms tighter around her and moaned. "Did you mean what you said? You want to break for me?" He seemed so hesitant, so reverent, Belah sat back.

"Do you think you aren't worthy of the job?"

She found herself flattened to the mattress a second later, Nikhil hovering over her with his hand still at her throat.

"Is this what it means to be worthy? To overpower you?"

"If that's what it means to you."

His gaze held hers as his fingers idly caressed her skin. Slowly, he began to shake his head, as though the situation wasn't ideal.

"No," he said, trailing his fingertips down her chest and tugging the sides of her gown apart to bare her breasts to him again. "I can't be worthy if there is no challenge for me to meet."

"Conquering my enemy wasn't enough?"

Nikhil bent his head and hovered his lips over her breast, hot breath gusting over one nipple. As he did, he moved to kneel between her thighs, pushing her legs apart and shoving her gown up. He gripped her roughly by the hips and yanked her against him.

"You're no better than any other woman who comes crawling to my bed and begs me to fuck her," he said roughly.

Belah gasped in surprise at the hot, hard flesh that pressed against her pubic bone, the base of his cock rubbing at her orgasm-slickened clit. Pleasure burst through her, but not before she caught his meaning. She had decided she wanted him, and as was her habit, had gone about *having* him as though she were entitled. It didn't matter that she considered her attention a reward for his performance in battle and the near sacrifice of his life. True, he deserved everything she wanted to offer and more, but to suggest a man like him couldn't also *earn* the final prize belittled his abilities and his importance to her empire all these years.

She had to make him work for it, now that the offer was on the table.

Nikhil shifted his hips, the friction on her clit enough that she nearly gave in and let him fuck her. His desires were polarized, however, and she read every nuance in his eyes and his aura, without even sinking her powers into his mind to find out more.

Physically, he desperately wanted more—to bury himself in her and fuck her until she called him her master. But his reverence for her as his Queen, his Goddess, his *Tilahatan*, held him back. The strongest emotion she sensed in in him was his fear that she may not really be worth everything he had done for her over the years—that all the armies he had routed and the wounds he'd endured were at the behest of a woman who would simply spread her legs for him on a whim. He feared the power she had over her entire kingdom may have been nothing more than an illusion all along. He needed to work as hard for her bed as he had for her glory.

Belah's mouth spread into a wicked smile. If it was power he needed to see, that's what she would show him.

All it took was an ankle hooked around the back of his muscular thigh and her hands on his wide shoulders and she flipped them both with ease. She landed astride him with her hot, sensitive folds spread across the column of his thick shaft. With swift grace, she had his hands pinned above his head. She tilted her hips to slide up along his length, enjoying the rough groan that escaped him as much as she enjoyed the sensation herself.

She rarely had the need to make such a display of her basic physical strength. Goddesses didn't need to get their hands dirty, of course. But if this was what he needed to find her worth the challenge of conquering, so be it.

Hot lust rose up in her as she stared down at him. He pushed up against her, struggling and more than a little surprised that a female as slightly built as she was could keep him pinned down.

"I could do this with a breath, my love," Belah said, allowing a flash of her magic to show behind her eyes. The bright blue light she emitted reflected in his own dark irises, and his eyes widened for a second before narrowing again with pleasure.

"*Tilahatan*, you are so beautiful," he said, glancing up at his immobilized arms and then back at her, flashing her his own devilish smile. "I will enjoy this." He lifted his head and sank his teeth into her forearm.

Belah gasped at the bolt of pain, but didn't flinch. The hot spike only made her wetter, and she let herself sigh in pleasure when he released his teeth and simply sucked on the bite, teasing his tongue over the bruised flesh.

"Enough for today," she said, reluctantly releasing him and standing beside his bed while she straightened her gown again. She let her gaze slip down his body one last time. He left his hands up above his head and flexed his entire torso as luxuriously as a cat, with his hips rising up and his glistening cock catching the sunlight alluringly. She could already sense he was working out a scheme to subdue her the same as he would form a battle plan.

As much as she looked forward to being his toy, Belah decided she couldn't make it easy for him. Nikhil was her most devious army commander, after all. He would be her toy first, but she had no desire to break him—only to collar him long enough to remind him she was still in charge, and that he was only conquering her because she allowed it.

"You'll stay and continue your recovery until it suits me, and you will refrain from taking your pleasure with anyone else." She eyed his hand as he stroked his cock. "Including yourself. I don't give my orgasms away lightly, and neither will you."

Nikhil paused his stroking and let his hand fall to his side, his eyes blazing with even stronger lust. "Yes, mistress," he said gruffly, though his deference didn't extend to his expression. Those dark eyes and his hard-set square jaw spoke of the kind of determination she had only ever seen on him when he was preparing for battle.

She left the room with her skin tingling. If his history with her enemies was any indication, that look meant he would conquer her, plunder her, and leave her with no recourse but to fall at his feet and beg for mercy. He had never once lost a battle.

If he won this one, who would have the glory at the end?

CHAPTER FOUR

Belah deliberately left Nikhil alone the next day, and the day after. She urged a perplexed Meri to leave him alone too, telling her physician that Nikhil simply wished to spend the day praying that the gods saw fit to heal him, and that if they didn't he would gladly join them in the afterlife.

Meri had pursed her lips and narrowed her eyes, ever the skeptic, yet she held her tongue about her belief in the so-called gods. "You are as much a god as they are, mistress. Is he not praying to you, too?"

Belah laughed. "Perhaps he is, but I doubt his prayers to me have anything to do with his wound."

She kept her mind focused on his, even when she was on her throne hearing petitioners, eager for him to slip up so she could punish him.

Oh, did she long to punish him. To make him fall to his knees, begging her for release. To goad him into taking control of her in return.

As she heard petitioner after petitioner, that was all she could picture. The days wore on and she satisfied the worries of her people while still fabricating a fantasy in her mind of how Nikhil's submission might look. She decided she wouldn't make him kneel, after all. Instead, she would have him trussed up like a calf for slaughter, but she would slaughter him with pleasure, teasing him until he begged for her mercy.

At the end of the day a week after his arrival, Belah gritted her teeth and ignored him still, spending a restless night alone with only her toys for relief. She considered visiting her harem, but even the idea of her favorite pets had lost its allure.

The next day, she went to him and informed him that he could attend her with her other advisers during the day. Since he was still technically recovering from his wounds, she would appoint him to lead her war council.

His proximity to her throne that afternoon made her itch, particularly considering the amazement of the rest of her advisers when he took his seat among them. They said nothing, but she could read every astonished thought as clear as day. They had all expected him to die.

Nikhil sat silent and watched her smugly as the day wore on. She had more trouble reading his emotions, merely sensing that he was biding his time. Until what? Until he could figure out how to attain the upper hand? As much as she wanted precisely that, it irritated her that she hadn't taken advantage of his weakness when she had the chance. She should have fucked him that first day, but giving into her own lust would have given him far too much power over her.

When Belah dismissed her advisers at the end of the day, Nikhil remained behind, simply relaxing in his seat, his elbow on the armrest and his knuckles resting under his chin, regarding her with that dark, calculating gaze.

"What is it, Nikhil?" she asked without glancing in his direction. "You have fulfilled your duties for the day. You may leave."

"On the contrary, mistress," he said, his voice ripe with suggestion. "One of my duties is to make myself worthy of you. You have given me no new instructions as the leader of your war council, so I need to know what you desire. Shall I mount a new war against one of our neighbors? Should I conquer the world in your name? I would, if that would please you."

The suggestion made her entire body thrum. She didn't want the entire world conquered, but the idea that he would offer that to her thrilled her. She hazarded a glance over her shoulder to his seat.

His irreverent posture irritated her as much as it incited a fresh wave of warmth between her thighs. He was taunting her. She wanted him to conquer *her*, and they both knew it. After she'd offered the challenge, she felt compelled to shore up her defenses, but maybe it was time to go on the offensive and prove again to him how hard she wanted him to work for it.

She sneered at him. "Get back to your quarters, Nikhil. I'll see you tomorrow."

He shrugged and stood, chuckling as he sauntered through the door into the courtyard outside.

"Guards!" she called to the soldiers who made up her regular retinue.

They all stood at attention, their commander calling, "Yes, Empress!"

"The general has been impertinent and requires disciplining. Take him to my chambers and strip him, then bind him to the braces. I will see to him myself tonight."

The commander, a seasoned veteran who had chosen to retire to the court rather than languish without a post, looked confused for a second. He and Belah shared a glance. The quirk of her mouth and her raised eyebrow were enough to let him on to her intentions.

It helped that they knew their mistress had a nearly unquenchable appetite for sex and required their assistance, on occasion, to facilitate her pleasure. She did have dozens of pets in her harem, after all, some of whom were also retired veterans who often left the harem as quickly as they joined when they discovered that her pets sometimes worked as hard as any soldier. She never faulted them, but she always made sure they enjoyed themselves while they were there. She also avoided mentioning that they were the most pampered members of her harem when they *were* in attendance.

This act would make her guards believe that Nikhil had also become a member of her harem, which was one of the most honored positions in her court and very fitting of a wounded general. It was also a position that regularly involved her guard retrieving and securing members in her chamber for her later use.

She took her time making her way back to her room, stopping on her way to have a leisurely dinner with her physician. Meri was a friend, and a woman she respected enough to tell many of her secrets to.

"Let me give you more," Belah said after they'd finished their meal on the balcony of Meri's quarters, overlooking the torch-lit courtyard below and the tranquil sea beyond. "You have liberty with my harem, but I know that isn't what you want. So tell me, Meri. What is it you desire? If it's one of my brothers…"

"No, it isn't that, I promise you," Meri said. "I… I had a dream about you and I haven't been able to stop thinking about it."

"Tell me," Belah said, sensing Meri's hesitance. The woman was a skeptic and rarely gave credence to superstition, but she seemed rattled.

"I dreamed you had a child that turned to ashes. When you tried to gather them up, they turned into a bird made of fire and flew away. It made me so sad I woke up crying. You were sad in the dream too, but not as though you'd lost a child. You were filled with regret so deep it made me want to comfort you. Do you have such regrets?"

Meri reached out a hand, her eyes watering. Belah's skin chilled in spite of the warm breeze that blew through. Did she have such regrets? Only one, long past that no one but she and her closest brother shared. That particular secret was buried so deep, she rarely even thought of it herself anymore. That wasn't to say she wouldn't have other regrets, in time. Such was the burden of immortality.

Belah shook off the chill, refocusing her attention on her friend. She took Meri's hand and squeezed, sensing nothing more than deep love and caring from the woman. This woman deserved a gift only Belah could give, but she wouldn't push.

"I have no regrets, Meri. If I ever do, I will let you know. Please consider letting me give you a gift?"

Meri shook her head. "I know you are a special woman, but I serve you because I love what I do. I need no other reward than your friendship and the already ample compensation I get by living here."

Belah nodded. "If you ever need anything, I will not fail you, friend."

Meri laughed. "I know you won't. You never lie, even when it would suit you to do so. But you do like to hide your emotions. You're in love with him, aren't you? If you weren't, you would be telling me exactly how you feel."

Belah's eyes widened at Meri's display of intuition. But no… she wasn't in *love*. Was she?

"I…" She stopped and closed her mouth again, took a swallow of her drink, and looked at Meri helplessly. She couldn't lie to her friend, either. She wanted Nikhil on a visceral level, but he had captured her heart so deeply during his time as her commander that she couldn't deny it. "Yes."

Meri sat back and smiled dreamily. "You deserve it. I don't think I've ever seen you in love. It suits you. So, what are you going to do, woo him? He would probably be putty in your hands if you so much as winked at him."

Belah laughed, thinking about what she had waiting in her room now. What was she going to do? Oh, she had a multitude of ideas, none of which she would share with Meri.

"I might wink, but I want to see how he does in his new *position* first."

If her guards had done their job, Nikhil's current position was trussed up naked in her room, hanging in the doorway that led to her balcony.

With that thought, she said her farewells to her friend, wishing yet again that Meri would accept her gift. Belah would happily bond the woman just to keep her around longer.

CHAPTER FIVE

Belah stole into her quarters and paused just inside the shadows of her doorway. Nikhil was there, shackled across the room in the arch that led to her balcony, right where she'd commanded he be put.

He was glorious, his body framed by the moonlight outside and his tensed muscles highlighted by the lamplight in her room. He stared at her in spite of the caution she'd taken to keep silent. She could be as stealthy as the best thief, but still couldn't beat her brother.

He laughed when she paused. "I wondered if part of your challenge was to have me escape, but thought otherwise once I figured out where they were taking me," he said. "Tell Amun I am sorry for his nose, and tell Neb I'm sorry for his testicles. I didn't want to hurt them."

"No, you didn't. But you want to hurt me, don't you?"

His gaze grew feverish as she stalked toward him and he swallowed hard, struggling against his bonds. His feet were on the floor, but bound to the wall by ropes threaded through a pair of metal eyelets. His arms were upraised, wrists tied with more ropes above him.

"Tell me what you want, Nikhil," Belah said, regarding him from several feet away.

He bared his teeth at her and her pulse raced. Such a wild thing he was. He *hated* being tied up like this.

"I want to break you apart," he said. "I want to fuck every last measure of your arrogance out of you, to be *your* master and have you call my name while I'm buried inside you. I want to watch you fall to pieces beneath me, thanking me for my scant bit of mercy while I take my pleasure from you. I don't care if you're a goddess. Actually, I *do* care. That makes it better. You could probably destroy me with a touch, couldn't you? Or a *breath*… isn't that what you said to me before? So do it. Destroy me with a breath."

He grinned at her, and in spite of his foul words, she loved the game, but he couldn't ever hide his true desires from her. She sensed a mind that was on fire with all the possible scenarios that could result from his volatile outburst. One ending he wished for outshone the others—overpowering her and fucking her.

Oh, she wanted that, but she wouldn't let him win the game today.

Belah shed her clothes as she strode toward him. His gaze stalked her route, his chest heaving and his hard cock bobbing with each inhale. Her nipples hardened and she regretted having to draw this night out as long as she intended to, but Nikhil needed to see her power in effect. Not just a token show of strength.

When she reached him, she let her nipples brush against his hard chest and let out a hot breath against his ear. She tilted her head to meet his eyes.

"You will remember all of what I do tonight, but will have control over nothing other than your voice until I wish it, understand? If you ever wish me to stop, you only need say so and I will, but know that stopping sends you back to the army camp and out of my mind forever."

She exhaled slowly, making sure Nikhil saw the shimmering blue cloud of her breath. She rested her hands on his chest while the smoky tendrils made their way to his mouth. He tensed, and the sudden waft of fear surprised her, but he didn't flinch when her breath teased at his nostrils.

"Breathe, my love," she said. "You won't regret it."

Aside from asserting control over his body, the breath she gave him would also temporarily enhance his own perception. She wanted him to be her perfect lover. He was already dangerously close to that, anyway.

Nikhil closed his eyes, and for a moment, Belah enjoyed the helpless, sleeping version of him. His lashes were so dark, and he appeared so serene as her breath took over. A moment later he opened his eyes, raised his head, and said, "I am yours tonight. Do with me as you will."

"I drugged you because I don't want you to hurt yourself. You just have to tell me if you don't like what I do," she said.

"What is keeping you from doing it anyway? I have no way to react other than verbally."

Belah smiled and flashed her eyes at him. "Because I have power and you want power. I can give it to you. This isn't just a test, Nikhil. This is *how* I give it to you."

His aura pulsed, encompassing them both in a warm bubble of energy. Belah slid her hands down his ribcage, raking lightly with her fingernails. His breath hitched when she reached the tops of his hips and teased the arched rope of muscle that led in a vee toward his groin. Heat radiated from his cock, barely a hair's breadth from the skin of her belly. She cupped his balls and leaned closer, caressing the side of his neck with her lips and tongue.

His skin tasted sweet, his aura crackling against her as she gently stroked between his thighs. She slid her hand up his length, gathering the drip of moisture at the tip with her thumb and swirling it around and around the head of his cock.

The intensity of his desire enveloped her, increasing the aching hunger for his Nirvana. She had gone longer than usual between sessions with her harem and let herself become more depleted than she should have. The craving was so strong she nearly dropped to her knees to take him in her mouth and bring him off swiftly, sating that hunger. Now was not the time for her to fall to her knees, though. Not until Nikhil had a true understanding of the scope of her power.

Belah brushed her lips across his jaw as she stroked him, and her tongue darted out to drift along his lower lip. His lips parted and his own tongue snaked out, hot and wet, to slide against hers. She latched her mouth onto his, tongue sweeping deeper. Between them, her hand pumped his cock in swifter strokes.

With her free hand, she reached up and plucked at his nipple once, teasing it into a stiff nub, then pinched, squeezing harder and harder until a groan rumbled up from his throat.

She pulled away from the kiss and looked into his eyes. He stared back, his gaze intense and dark with desire. The jumbled emotions in his head pleased her. He was simultaneously desperate for release and resistant to giving her the satisfaction of making him come. The discomfort of his nipple seemed to be aiding that resistance more than giving him pleasure. So, pain was not pleasurable to him, but something he considered a trial that proved his worth. Belah bent and nipped at his other nipple, then grabbed it tightly between her teeth and pulled. At the same time, she squeezed his cock hard.

Nikhil hissed, tilting his hips into her hand.

She released him abruptly and walked away, leaving him panting and tugging at his bindings.

"This is just the start," she said. "By the end of the night you'll have a better idea how things will work with me. What my expectations are. I will give you the most immense pleasure you've ever experienced, but I expect you to reciprocate."

Nikhil grinned and licked his lips. "I can give."

"You don't understand," she said, stopping at a table near the doorway and opening a large, carved wooden box that rested there. From inside she pulled out two implements, along with small bottle of scented oil. "What you will be *giving* isn't what you think. My pleasure comes secondary to what I want from you."

She shivered at the thought of revealing more of her true power to him, but she couldn't impress him enough otherwise. He was too full of himself, too powerful in his own right already. If she wanted to ensure he believed dominating her was worth his trouble, she had to give him a more powerful creature to dominate than a mere woman, even a goddess. Still, she would have to restrict what she showed him to more benign displays of power, like her breath and the transfer of energy. Nothing that would show her true form to him. She had to maintain some secrets, after all, and knowing that the dragon her people viewed as her pet was really her true form would not serve her purposes.

She picked up the small leather circlet she'd set on the table, sliding the looped thong on one side to widen the opening. The first step would be ensuring he didn't accidentally spend himself before she wanted him to. She poured a bit of the oil in her palm, cupping it until she made her way back to him. She let it drizzle off her fingertips onto his hard cock for a second before slipping her oily hand over his swollen head and rubbing to distribute the fluid over his entire shaft and around his heavy sack.

Nikhil heaved a sigh and let his head fall back while she slid her palm up and down his length. His hips undulated in time to her stroking and she kept going, enjoying the accompanying pulse and swell of his aura with each slow pass of her hand. In a smooth motion, she slipped the leather ring over the head of his cock and tucked it around the base of his shaft, right behind his balls. With a sharp tug from beneath, she tightened it.

Nikhil let out a sharp cry, his head jerked up, and he stared first at her, then down at the binding that constricted the blood flow to his swollen member.

"What the fuck?"

Belah's eyebrow and the corner of her mouth twitched in amusement. "Just a little help to ensure you last through the night."

Though truthfully, she was growing more and more uncertain that she would be able to last. The familiar, empty ache that signaled she was dangerously low on energy had begun. It was akin to the lightheadedness she might feel if she hadn't eaten all day and wandered near the kitchens when supper was being prepared. Except instead of lightheaded, she craved the fullness of being fucked and soaking up the resulting energy from her sated partner, and her skin itched with the need to shift and fly. The only thing that came close to calming her the way sex did was feeling the night air rush over her scales and beneath her wings.

She would have to last. Tonight was too important to let her hunger get the better of her.

Nikhil gasped and panted, still staring down at his cock, incredulous.

"How does it feel? Be honest."

"Tight and … strange. I don't understand."

Belah chuckled. "You may be one of the most glorious and virile males I've ever met, Nikhil, but those *girls* who throw themselves at your feet and into your bed don't know the first thing about true pleasure." She reached down and allowed the tip of one sharp talon to extend from her fingertip. In plain view of his gaze, she raked it gently along the underside of his engorged penis. When she reached the crown, she scraped the gathered fluid that hung in a creamy droplet onto the dark hook of her claw and raised it to her mouth. She darted her true-shaped tongue out, the forked tip of it capturing his essence while he watched.

She closed her eyes, savoring his tangy flavor. Her eyes flickered again as her vision shifted to observe how his aura changed from witnessing the little revelations she gave him.

"What are you?" he asked, his throat tight with confused tension.

"I am your goddess. If you survive a night with me, then you will be truly worthy of dominating me when I wish it. Just as a cat can choose her master, I can choose mine."

Belah gripped his shaft again, giving it a slow, tight pull. She slid her palm along his oiled skin and he shuddered, but otherwise didn't respond. Only in the quiet dark of Nikhil's mind did she sense the pleas beginning, a silent but fervent prayer to show him mercy when she felt he had earned it. But he was too resolute to withstand what she had to give him to beg outright.

The thought was touching, but she wasn't quite finished torturing him yet.

She moved away again and reached for the bottle of oil and the other object she'd withdrawn from her toy box. She could feel his eyes on her, observing her actions, along with the vivid sense of his anticipation for what she might surprise him with next. When she held the object up in the lamplight, he struggled in earnest against his bindings.

"No," he said, eyeing the thick, oblong polished stone that she was liberally coating in oil. It was the same shape as the one she'd used with Nyla, Zeb, and Idrin the week before, only much larger.

"No? You don't want to watch me fuck myself with this? I know it's a poor substitute for your glorious cock, but I am feeling somewhat empty at the moment. What did you think I was going to do?"

He relaxed and gave her a sheepish smile. "Shove it up my ass."

"Oh, is that what I should do? Hmm…" She smirked at him as she settled onto the bed. "That never occurred to me. I might have to try it, now that you mention it."

Belah continued to muse on the idea while she reclined against her pillows and bent her knees, spreading her thighs for him to get a good view of her cunt. Gripping the dildo with one hand, she teased it through her folds, sliding it between the slick flesh the way she'd slid on his cock the week before. His gaze stayed fixed on the performance, his tongue darting out to lick his lips when she pushed the thick object deep inside herself.

It was one of her favorite toys, its bulbous, egg-like shape more versatile than the more uniformly proportioned dildos in her collection. She absolutely had other intentions with it besides fucking herself, but Nikhil seemed to be enjoying watching her. His eyes were hooded, his gaze fixed on the slow thrust of the dildo in and out of her slick channel. She cupped one breast and arched her back for effect. She could make herself come this way easily—she was primed for it already after the teasing tingle of his aura when she stood near him.

Tonight wasn't simply about pleasure. Its purpose was to establish parameters for any play going forward. If things went well, he would understand by the end what was acceptable when she agreed to take his place in the shackles, subjected to the kind of humiliation she intended to inflict on him tonight.

The simple thought of their roles being reversed nearly did her in. Belah's muscles clenched hard around the hot, slick object inside her and she pulled it out before she lost control.

She stood and walked on tingling legs back over to him. As she passed the table she picked up the bottle of oil and ducked under his bound arm to move behind him.

The dildo glistened with her own juices, which might have been enough lubrication for any of the men in her harem, but she suspected Nikhil was untried in the area she was about to explore. She wasn't cruel; she would make sure he was well prepared before she used it on him. His entire body clenched, but all Belah did was drizzle oil along the tops of his shoulders and let it trickle down his back. She set the dildo down on a nearby table and used both hands to work the oil into his bunched shoulders, massaging the muscles until they warmed and loosened under her touch.

She worked her way down his back, kneading the muscles as thoroughly as she'd stroked his cock. She needed him relaxed, which would be tricky, considering how hard his cock still was. As she reached the base of his spine, her ministrations slowed. She poured more oil into her hand and rubbed her palms together, coating them, then slicked them slowly over both his tight, round ass cheeks.

Nikhil's breath shot out in a gasp. "You're going to do it, aren't you?"

"Do what?" Belah asked, feigning confusion.

"You want to shove that huge thing into me. You are an evil goddess, aren't you?" He chuckled.

Belah smiled to herself. "You can tell me to stop, but I think you'll enjoy it if you give it a chance."

She popped her head beneath his armpit and looked up into his face inquiringly. Nikhil groaned.

"Fuck, do what you want with me. But you better believe I'm taking it out on you when I get the chance."

She grinned and sank her teeth into the fleshy side of his pectoral, savoring the tight hiss of air he expelled in response.

She stood behind him again and squeezed his ass in both hands, spreading the cheeks apart. Kneeling down, she could see the snug cuff of the ring that secured his balls and the tight, puckered opening that he held so dear. With one oil-coated fingertip, she traced a line from his spine down, slowly making her way to the center of that little rose. Once there, she swirled her finger around, spreading the oil until his opening glistened.

Nikhil's breath came rapidly and his ass cheeks kept threatening to clench tighter until she smacked him sharply.

"You need to relax, or this is going to be a lot more difficult for both of us."

She coated both palms again and grabbed his cheeks, holding them apart. With her thumbs, she teased, then let her forked tongue dart out and tickle the tender flesh.

He was a virgin in this way, she had to remind herself, so she should be gentle, but she would also be very, very thorough. She teased his ass with her tongue until she heard him release a frustrated groan. Then she pressed the tip of one thumb harder against his opening and was pleased that he let her beyond the barrier. She fucked him one knuckle deep before removing her thumb and replacing it with two fingers.

Those went deeper, fucking slowly in and out while his body quivered and his aura swelled. Belah sensed both how much he loved this, and at the same time, how much he hated that he did. To give him something new to think about, she bent her head and captured a mouthful of his ass in her teeth and bit hard.

Nikhil cried out. He didn't seem to notice when she added a third oiled finger to the mix and twisted her hand, hooking her fingers to find that well of magic potential that lived inside all men.

"No… *fuck*… Stop!" he cried.

Belah stilled and waited. Had he broken?

Nikhil swiftly backpedaled. "No, no, don't stop, don't stop. I didn't mean it." He panted out the words and pushed his ass back toward her. "Fuck me, please. Hurry up and fuck me, because I'm going to lose my mind if you don't."

Belah extracted her fingers from him and cleaned off in a nearby basin of water. Without a word, she untied his ankles, then reached up and undid his wrists.

She guided him to the bed and he went as docile as a lamb, still trembling. He climbed onto the bed and lay on his back at her instruction, letting her bind his wrists again without objection. She left his ankles undone, positioning him carefully so that his knees were pressed to his chest.

Nikhil's expression was full of awe when he looked at her, but there was still a calculated glint deep within. He still plotted how to give back to her the favors she was giving him tonight. She suppressed a shiver of arousal at the knowledge.

She retrieved the dildo and the oil and returned to the bed.

"You aren't getting out of this," she said, holding the shiny oiled object up for him to see. He swallowed hard and nodded. His face flushed red with shame and he closed his eyes and clenched his jaw.

When she pressed the rounded tip at his entrance, he winced.

"Remember, relax." She bent her head and pressed her lips on the underside of his cockhead, teasing her tongue out softly. His stomach muscles clenched, then relaxed as her tongue drifted lower. "Once this is in you, I'm going to climb on top of you and fuck you."

"You're good," he said. His muscles finally relaxed and she pressed the tapered tip of the polished stone dildo into him. While she pushed, she took him into her mouth and slowly sucked on the head of his cock, swirling her true-shaped tongue over his tip and tickling the underside. "You're inhumanly good," Nikhil said, laughing hoarsely. The laugh turned into a harsh groan when she pushed the dildo deeper.

His thighs tightened and he strained at his bindings, but he didn't tell her to stop. Belah kept pushing the dildo into him until the widest end of it was solidly entrenched, with only the narrow neck extending to the flared handle left outside.

She twisted it, enjoying his shuddering breath and the hard twitch of his cock.

"Tell me what you want right now."

"I want to come. *Fuck*, I want to come."

"How much do you want it?" She pulled the dildo slowly out of him, then pushed it back inside. His ass clenched for a second, then released, and he whimpered.

"Please."

She left the dildo inside him and moved up to look into his eyes.

"Please what?"

"Please fuck me, *Tilahatan.*"

The begging made her even wetter than she'd been before. Her entire body vibrated with need. As she hovered over him, she felt the magic that maintained the shape of her human body dissolving and barely held it together. She needed to make him come now or she'd change.

All teasing done, Belah spread her thighs over the head of Nikhil's bound cock. She brushed her wet folds over his tip just enough to make herself crazy and make him clench his teeth and curse at her.

"Fuck me. Fuck me, you fucking beautiful, manipulative bitch. I need my cock in you now."

She sank down slowly, savoring the friction of his thick cock as it filled her for the first time.

Belah's mind went blank once she fully encompassed him. Just having him inside her was the perfect end. She didn't want to move. She clenched tight around him, enjoying the way his Blessed aura shimmered and swelled around them both, his energy tickling her skin with the need to channel its way inside her when the floodgates were opened and that delicious exchange began. Though it made no sound, the sensation of his aura had a rhythm like music. His heavy heartbeat pounded like a drum and her muscles tightened and loosened around him in time to his pulse. She closed her eyes and savored every nuance of the experience tantalizing her senses.

She began to move, slowly at first, with simple, small undulations of her hips. Leaning forward, she rotated in tiny circles, letting her swollen clit rub against his pelvis as she let her breasts hover close to his face.

Raw hunger tinged with desperation and more than a little frustration made Nikhil's jaw clench and his eyes wild. He lifted his head, reaching for her flesh with his mouth, teeth snapping. Excitement surged through her at the knowledge that if he broke this tight leash she had him on tonight, he would ravage her. She didn't want him truly tame, though—what she wanted was to prove her power enough to make him docile while in her presence and to follow her commands.

"If you want to come, you will do what I say. Now lie back."

With a growl, Nikhil dropped his head back to the pillow, his hands struggling ineffectually at his bindings. He regarded her curiously, in spite of the feverish glint in his eyes. Between her thighs, his thick length pulsed and her need for his magic rushed back and forth like the currents crashing and retreating against the shores of the river. When it retreated she was acutely reminded of the necessity to refill her depleted well, but she couldn't rush this.

She reached past his head for the headboard of her bed, watching his face as her breasts moved closer to his mouth. But his eyes didn't fall on her chest as she expected. Instead, they widened and watched her hands move over his head, then shot back to her face and stared.

"Goddess, what are you?"

CHAPTER SIX

Belah looked at her hands. The tips of her fingers had all transformed into heavy talons, and her hands and forearms were now covered in luminescent blue scales. She let out a soft curse and closed her eyes to gather her last vestiges of control over her body. The heavy weight on her head betrayed the presence of her horns, too. This wasn't the end of the world, not if she hurried. Still, she cursed herself yet again for letting her hunger linger for so long without being sated by her harem. That's what they were there for, after all.

"I am hungry, is what I am," she said, letting her true voice resonate close to Nikhil's ear and her tongue flick out to caress the curve of his earlobe. He'd already seen this much, so there was no sense wasting the image that was likely already etched on his mind. She lifted her hips slowly, clenching around his cock as she slid up his length. "And you have what I need to fill me up."

She slammed back down hard; the glorious, thick ridge at his tip pressed against her inner walls, sending sparks of pleasure through her. Her pleasure wasn't what mattered now, though. He was so close already, and she thought she could maintain this half-transformation just long enough.

Hips rising up his length again, Belah gripped the headboard hard with claws digging into the wood while her breasts still hung over his face. Her nipples were tantalizingly within reach of his mouth and he gave in. He used his bindings to leverage himself, pulling his upper torso off the bed just enough to capture the tip of one full globe in his mouth and suck.

At the same time, his hips bucked up. His cock filled her and began fucking into her in earnest. The brutal strength of his pumping thrusts would have bruised a human woman, but Belah cried out with pleasure.

"Yes! Give me what I need! Fuck me like the animal you are! Ah!"

His body arched and sweated beneath her, mouth biting and sucking at her breasts like a man starved for the kind of nourishment only she could give. Over and over, Nikhil sank his teeth into Belah's flesh, and each bite and harsh suck of her nipples thrilled her more, her pussy already a flood of wet heat that rivaled the Nile in the rainy season. With slick, loud smacks, he kept going until Belah thought she would turn feral simply from the need to taste his magic again.

In the middle of it all, his bound hands struggled against the ropes. She sensed the pain seeping into his limbs from the burning cut of the cord into his skin. His Nirvana pushed so close, but the sharp sting delayed it in spite of the even more potent pleasure he gained from the dildo filling his ass.

Through her haze of pleasure and need, Belah narrowed her eyes. She grabbed both sides of Nikhil's head in her talons and pressed him back against her pillow.

"You *will* do my bidding tonight, and always, beast, if you want your rewards to continue." She pressed her lips tight against his, lashing her tongue deep into his mouth and consuming the rough groan that he emitted. With her mouth latched onto his, she released a slow breath to numb his pain and enhance his pleasure even more than the first breath she'd given him that night. Then she inhaled, stealing the air back from his lungs and drawing only his pain along with it.

The searing tightness of his bindings wrapped around her wrists like phantom shackles, and she cried out at the perfection of those rings of pain, a counterpoint to the pleasure of his cock swelling and pulsing inside her.

The pleasure took control of him wholesale. With a violent twist, Nikhil surged against her. He let out a guttural cry and his head flew back.

Belah was so absorbed with the combined sensations of his cock and the invisible ropes cutting her wrists that she was unprepared for the deluge of power he released into her, as sharp and hot as the flood of semen that erupted from his cock. She let out a sonorous cry that set the entire room vibrating. Every object that wasn't fixed to the floor or walls moved incrementally from the shaking roar that came from her own throat.

When she closed her mouth she saw the abject fear in his eyes and realized she'd shifted even more while fucking him. Her wings were extended and her scaled belly tensed above her pelvis. To him she must appear like some strange hybrid—half human, half dragon. She pulled back, trying to climb off, but clumsy in this state.

"No," he called. "Stay. You are beautiful."

Her vocal cords betrayed her, but she was too consumed by pleasure to object.

"This is what you need. My flesh inside you, isn't it?" Nikhil's gaze remained fascinated as he pumped up inside her, and she let out a gasp, still unsure about what he was seeing while she hovered over him covered in blue scales, wings outstretched and brushing the ceiling above them.

The sensations of his cock teasing deep into her didn't change a bit.

She cringed, hating her body's penchant for half-transformation when she was depleted. But he'd seen too much now. She couldn't take that back. Should she be the dragon, or the goddess? She didn't know now. She just wanted to be *his*.

"Stop!" he commanded, his hands struggling harder against his bonds, his eyes trained hard on her face. "Belah. My love. We are one now. All I am is yours." His pitch lowered. "And you are mine."

He pulled harder, muscles straining so hard at the ropes that the headboard creaked, and he didn't even seem to care about the broken skin and the blood beginning to trickle down to his elbows.

She came to her senses a second later and swiftly swiped a talon beneath the ropes that held him tied to her headboard, cutting the bindings off his wrists. Sweet Mother, she wasn't so cruel that she'd made him bleed, was she? It wasn't his pain that had encouraged her, but his wildness and his brutal displays of strength when he touched her. Not to mention his complete disregard for his discomfort and the way he'd used it to delay his own climax.

Now, he simply lowered his hands and brushed his fingertips over her sweat-coated scales so delicately she worried she'd broken him too thoroughly. She remained still, his thick cock still buried inside her, while he gazed in wonder and reverence.

His nostrils flared and his brows twitched together tightly. A strangled sound came from his throat and his eyes watered. She sensed a warring of emotion inside him. She waited, keeping her secrets visible while he absorbed what she was.

"You are she. The dragon who guards us?"

Belah closed her eyes and let out a sigh. There was no going back now. She should mark him, but to have this beautiful, strong-willed man so bound to her would destroy what she loved about him most. She wanted him to know her and love her absent of a mating bond that would tie them for eternity. The bond of the magic they'd shared during their coupling was enough. For an immortal like her to mark him would be to curse him by destroying his will entirely.

"I am she."

He raked his gaze over her and she looked down at her glowing body.

"I like you better like this, but you are magnificent when you come to us in battle." His cock swelled inside her again, the pressure hard enough to make her gasp.

Nikhil sat up, pulling Belah tight against him and kissing her. She regained some control over her shape finally, letting her wings fade back into her shoulders, but she left her skin covered in the glowing, sapphire-like scales and her swirling horns atop her head.

He flipped her and pinned her to the bed.

"You enjoyed having me be one of your pets for the night, didn't you? Tying me up and violating me." He reached behind and slowly extracted the dildo from his ass, setting it aside without a glance. Delicately, he tugged at the leather thong that kept the band tightened around his cock. It loosened and he slipped it off, tossing it aside too. His cock remained gloriously hard and ready.

"I don't *violate* my pets. I only do what I know will please them most. Were you displeased by anything I did?"

He pushed her legs wider and sat back on his heels, letting his large hands slide up her thighs. His touch was firm, yet gentle, and more curious than deliberate.

"You are my *Tilahatan*. You could never displease me. I need to understand what it is you expect of me, however. You bring me to your room, have me bound for your pleasure, and yet you take my pain away when that is what would let me last. I thought you wanted to torture me." He slipped his fingertips along the wetness coating the tops of her thighs and teased through her folds, sticky and flooded with his spend.

A more thoughtful expression crossed his face as he regarded her, pushing his fingers into her slick channel. Belah sighed at the tingling pressure and tilted her hips up into his hand. His thumb rested lightly on her clit, stroking slowly.

"You lie there as docile as a lamb now, letting me touch you. I've watched you for the past week and learned what I could from your other advisers. They warned me of my irreverent behavior toward you. They said never to touch you unless you invite a touch, and never talk to you unless asked to speak, never to even *look* at you unless addressed directly. I have broken all the rules from the start, yet it is I who made it to your bed. Why is that?"

A rush of delicious sensation flooded up Belah's body from his touch and she arched her back. She ached to have him fill her again, but he seemed intent on simply teasing her.

"Why?" he repeated. When she didn't answer, he said, "You are burdened by so much, aren't you? It all rests on your shoulders, the onus of being what you are. You wish to have the illusion of letting someone else bear it for you, even if it's all a fantasy. I bear the wounds of battle for your cause. So you believe I can bear the burden of releasing you from yours in the darkness."

Belah closed her eyes, panting from the pleasure he was giving her with just one hand and the sound of his voice. Before she realized it, he'd removed his fingers from her and flipped her onto her belly. Bruising fingertips dug into her hips, yanking them off the bed. His cock slammed into her, finding its mark like the arrow of an expert marksman.

He pumped into her hard, one thick forearm snaking around her chest and squeezing one breast. His hot breath gusted into her ear.

"This is what you want, isn't it? You want to be the beast that gets tamed, to be collared and whipped into submission. To have all control ripped from your hands so you can let go of your burdens."

As his voice rumbled rough in her ear, his cock steadily rammed into her. He had one hand braced on the bed beside her, and slid the other up from her breast to grip her around the throat. He squeezed just hard enough to emphasize how much control he believed he had over her. Belah reveled in it, pushing back against his hips with each punishing thrust.

"Yes," she whispered, smiling to herself. He understood.

He pulled back on her neck, forcing her head to twist around. Their cheeks brushed against each other's, the rough goatee on his chin abrasive to one of the few spots on her body she'd left with human skin. She felt his breath at the corner of her mouth and twisted enough to meet his kiss, letting him devour her.

Again his aura swelled along with his pleasure, but a wickedness tinged it that hadn't before. Just when she thought he would give her another delicious dose of his energy, he pulled out of her.

"Show me the truth," he said. "I need to see the beast if I am expected to tame her."

Belah almost objected, but the command in his voice sent a shiver running down her spine that nearly brought her to orgasm in spite of not being touched.

She bowed her head, swallowing thickly. To give Nikhil what he asked, she would be breaking the most important law that all dragons were bound by. Nothing good could come of him knowing her secret. Yet he was her most trusted army commander—now her general. He had been willing to die for her.

The thrill of having him know her completely, to love her in spite of being unmarked, was what decided the issue. He may be Blessed. He may even have a glimmer of a bond after the orgasms they'd shared, but neither of those things would influence his free will the way a dragon mark would.

Unmarked, he would know her completely and love her in spite of the truth.

Slowly, she turned to face him. "Not here," she said. "There isn't room."

She slipped off the bed, padding barefoot over to her private balcony. Silently, he followed. Her spine continued to tingle with the awareness of him following her, both of them naked and walking through the moonlit darkness, down the stone staircase from her balcony to her private courtyard.

In the center of her garden was a round, stone platform surrounded by lush vegetation and the scent of jasmine. Belah walked up the low, worn steps, into the center of the elaborate mosaic and turned to face him. He continued toward her and her heartbeat sped up with each step he took closer to her. His enormous silhouette blocked out the moonlight when he reached her, his heat radiating into her as potent as the crackling energy of his aura where it tangled with hers. The tip of his erection brushed against her belly, and her eyelids fluttered closed at the pulse that surged between her thighs in response.

She gasped when his fingertips slid between her thighs, parting her folds again and slipping deep into her.

"I want to feel you change around me. Will you do that?"

Silently, she nodded and let her will crumble away under his touch, releasing the powerful magic that held her in her human form. With a shimmering flow akin to mist sweeping through the delta, her body morphed and shifted. The pressure of his touch in her deepest place was a focal point for her shape to grow outward from. First her skin transformed entirely into the blue, velveteen scales, then her body began to grow, her joints and limbs reshaping. Her torso elongated, along with her head. Her wings stretched out wide again, spanning almost the entire width of the clearing once fully extended. Her tail reached just as far behind her.

She halfway expected him to recoil in disgust or to run in fear, but with each new revelation of her true form, his touch between her legs grew more urgent. That part of her didn't change as much as the rest. It grew slightly bigger, and even more engorged with pulsing blood, but Nikhil's deft touch adapted easily, his fingers plunging deeper into her hot wetness.

With his free hand, he began to stroke himself as his fingers fucked her. His eyes soon glazed and his hand fell away from her. The glowing pulse of his aura quickened and he aimed his cock at her opening, but to her alarm, he wasn't moving to pierce her flesh with it. He only stood back and stroked himself, leaving her untouched.

"No!" The loud, insistent cry sounded more like a bellow and he abruptly stopped, staring up at her.

One eyebrow raised, he said, "No? I'm your master tonight, am I not? And looking on such a magnificent beast as yourself, I am overcome with need to mark you."

She let out a hot gust of breath through her nostrils, one that ruffled his hair. "Please. You may mark me all you must, but please do it inside me. At least always touch me when you do it. It is too cruel to my kind to let us starve the way you were about to. It would be like me forcing you to ride into battle and forbidding you from killing any of our enemies."

He considered her words for a moment, then nodded. "Let me see my queen again."

She swiftly shifted back to her human form, the abrupt change resulting in a loud "pop" when air rushed in to fill the space where her larger body had been. Nikhil smiled in appreciation of her naked form.

"On your knees." The same commanding tone was music to her ears and she fell gracefully to her knees, gazing up at him.

Her entire body tingled as much as her cunt did, and she ached from the inside out to come, but was even more eager to fulfill whatever desires he had. His cock hovered in front of her mouth and she darted out her tongue to lick at the weeping tip. He angled himself closer and reached to grip the back of her head, fingers threading through her thick hair.

"You want me inside you? Then take me now, little beast, little goddess. Let's pretend I am your god tonight and that you worship my cock with that lovely mouth. Suck me until I spill my seed down your hungry throat."

Her body thrumming with eager hunger, she opened up and took him in, bit by bit, relaxing her throat as he slid past her lips and deeper. She rested her hands on his hips at first, sucking him in, then pulled back and licked around and around his swollen tip with her dragon tongue before taking him in again. She cupped his balls with one hand, kneading them gently until she heard him moan. His fingers tightened at the back of her neck and his grip urged her into a faster rhythm. Soon she was no longer in control and reveled in the loss of it. With a bruising grip he pushed her head down onto his cock, slamming deep into her throat over and over.

Tears streamed from her eyes and she could barely breathe, but holding her breath was something she could easily do. She lost herself to his need, no longer able to do anything but hold onto him with both hands while he fucked her mouth, his panting becoming rougher and more erratic. Suddenly he let out a yell and pushed her hard onto him, holding her there with his cock so deep he nearly strangled her with it. A hot, salty flood shot down her throat, his flesh pulsing with each violent ejaculation. The flavor of his spunk was every bit as delicious as the fresh flood of magic that flowed through her as he came.

His fingertips loosened at the back of her neck as slowly as his cock softened in her mouth and slipped out. Belah licked her lips and blinked drunkenly up at him. His thighs began to quiver in front of her and a second later he sank to his knees, head bowed and chest heaving.

"Good girl," he said, touching her chin lightly with his fingertips. "Would you like a reward for pleasing me so well?"

Belah smiled, her soul rejoicing over how well this man seemed to understand her, how willing he was to please her exactly as she wished to be pleased.

"Yes, master," she said, and let him push her back down onto the stone.

She stared up at the night sky, the bright disc of the moon reflecting the fullness of need between her thighs. The stars flickered with each lap of his tongue between her legs. The rush of the Nile to the east mirrored the current of pleasure through her body, and the sudden gusts of wind blowing through the trees masked her breathy cries into the night when he brought her to her climax, over and over, until nothing existed but the scent and feel of his body when he moved up beside her and held her in his arms.

CHAPTER SEVEN

The days that followed made her wonder if she were living in a dream. During her days, she behaved as always, being pampered by her servants, dressed in her finest tunics and gold and jewels to hold court. She would sit on her throne with Nikhil seated among her advisers. Always she could feel his eyes on her throughout the day, and it drove her mad with need. The wait to have him back in her chambers where their roles would reverse made her dizzy some days.

The nagging thought that she should mark him lingered, but she rejected it. She loved the idea that he wasn't really hers, and yet he stayed. Her siblings would probably castigate her for allowing a mortal—even if he was Blessed—to see her true form without marking him.

With Nikhil, she awoke with a pleasant thrill that the day ahead was filled with the unknown. She hadn't felt this way in countless years.

Every day he kept her guessing, and at the end of every day, he managed to satisfy her.

Each morning before he left her bed to return to his own quarters, he would whisper a command in her ear. Some secret thing he wished her to do for him, and only him that day.

The weeks he spent with his troops were the loneliest times, but he always returned, their reunions some of the most memorable moments.

One morning after such a reunion, he stayed with her for breakfast and allowed her servants to dress him while she was dressed for her day. After the servants left, he rifled through all her things, exuberant with some secret surprise. Finally, he pulled out a pair of large, bronze scarabs from her jewelry box and examined them. They were ear clips, joined by a long chain that was meant to hang down over her chest, linked to a matching golden breast-piece.

She thought he was going to clip them to her ears, but instead, he pushed the vee of her gown aside to bare her breasts and clipped each ornament to a nipple.

Belah gasped at the sudden, sharp sensation. She'd worn them on her earlobes many times without discomfort, but to have them attached to a part of her so much more sensitive made her instantly wet.

"Nik, I have to go out there and be the *queen*."

He grinned deviously. "Yes, and whatever you do they will love. You go bare-breasted all the time. In fact, that's one of the reasons your army is so loyal. Why I am so loyal."

A steady thrum of sensation ran from her nipples to her groin and she closed her eyes.

He left for a moment and returned with a heavy golden collar, that he secured around her shoulders. It draped coldly over her chest, curving just above her bare breasts and warmed quickly to her temperature. In the center of it was another scarab that matched the ornaments attached to the tips of her breasts.

"See?" he said. "You look resplendent."

He turned her toward the mirror she rarely ever looked into. Before her, she saw a beautiful woman who was every bit as regal as Nikhil believed. Her shoulders were squared beneath the arc of golden scales that shone on her chest. Fine, blue linen draped over her shoulders, hanging down to her hips where it was gathered beneath her navel with a gold belt slung low enough to display her flat, bronze belly. And the two scarab ornaments gleamed on the tips of her full breasts like a pair of tiny, suckling infants.

He stood behind her with his mischievous smirk and kissed her neck.

"Don't you agree?" he asked.

She smiled back at him in the mirror. "I do."

"Good," he said. He cupped her breasts and removed the clips, teased her nipples with delicate circles of his thumbs. The sensation made her gasp at how sensitive they'd become and an even heavier warmth flooded between her thighs.

As quickly as he removed them, he replaced the clips again and spoke low into her ear. "You will think of me every time they vex you today. You will think of what I plan to do to you when we're alone again tonight. I promise I will be good during the day, as long as I know I have a leash on you, so don't disappoint me."

* * *

By the end of the day, Belah's nipples were entirely numb, but the presence of those scarabs during had enhanced her awareness of her own body to the point every inch of her itched to return to her chambers and to whatever he might have in store for her.

When she walked through the door, she was ready to rip off her clothes and let him have his way with her, but something made her wait. She had already spent the entire day holding dominion over her kingdom. Alone in his presence, she was no longer the master, but the pet. She expected her pets to be ready to obey her commands, so shouldn't she behave for him as she would want one of her own to behave for her?

A pang of guilt shot through her at the thought of her pets who had been neglected ever since Nikhil had arrived. She should remedy that soon—perhaps share them with him on occasion—though she was loath to witness him with any other.

When she made her way out onto the sunset-gilded balcony, she let out a soft gasp. Before her was laid a sumptuous feast with Nikhil standing across the table from her, backlit by the setting orange globe of the sun over the rippling waters of the sea on the horizon and the lush foliage of the Nile Delta on the opposite side. He gestured to the seat across from him.

"Please eat, my little beast. You will need your strength for tonight."

Belah's insides quivered and she nearly groaned in frustration. "You are intent on tormenting me for as long as possible, aren't you? You must have figured out by now that it isn't *food* I gain my strength from. At least, not where my true power is concerned."

Nikhil came around the table and pulled her chair out for her to sit. She obeyed, but the closeness of his large body and spicy scent made her grip the sides of her chair hard to suppress the urge to overpower him. Tonight she would let him command every aspect of their coupling. She had a feeling that given free rein, he wouldn't disappoint her. At the back of her neck, the light brush of his fingertips startled her, until she realized he was unfastening the clasp of the heavy, gold collar that still weighed down her shoulders. It came away, leaving her suddenly weightless, and she let out a sigh of relief at the loss of that burden. He disappeared for a moment, then returned and bent his head to her ear.

"Did you think of me at all today?" he asked, brushing his warm palms down her shoulders and arms to her hands, where he twined his coarse fingers between her more delicate ones. He squeezed, lifting her hands and placing them flat on the surface of the table in front of her. "Your eyes kept moving to the side of the room all day. It could have been the sun casting a glare, I suppose... Yet you never quite looked at me."

Belah's nostrils flared at his closeness. She'd craved this for the entire day—craved his touch, his smell, and knew if she had dared to glance his way for very long, she would have called a halt to everything and ordered everyone out, then ordered him to fuck her on her throne. That wasn't how this was supposed to work. She wanted him to give the orders where it concerned her pleasure, not the other way around.

"I feared I would never look away again if I did," she said.

"Hmm, is that all you feared?" He ran his hands back up her arms and paused at the tops, letting his knuckles brush against the sides of her aching breasts with the scarab jewelry still tightly attached to each nipple.

Her breath came out in soft pants and she tilted her head back against his shoulder before answering him.

"I wanted to command them all to leave and order you to fuck me right there. I may have even ordered you to take me with the entire room still filled and let them all watch. They could all have seen what a magnificent man you are. Then all the men could have had a turn after you were done, just to understand what it's like to be so privileged that you get to fuck a goddess every night."

His fingers made slow circles around the ornaments attached to her breasts. With each circuit closer, the scarabs grew heavier and her nipples throbbed painfully.

"Every night?" he asked in a low voice. "Is that what you are offering? To be my toy every night? And what will I be to you?"

He cupped her breasts in both large palms and jiggled the scarabs. Belah let out an involuntary whimper at the painful tug that so exquisitely sent fresh jolts of agony through her body.

Catching her breath, she said, "By day, you will be my general, whose secret desires I fulfill by simply thinking of you. And by night—*every night*—you will be my master. A god for me to bow before until you have answered my prayers. You wished to die and become a god by my brother's side. I can make you one in my bed, and you never need fear death again."

The low rumble Nikhil emitted vibrated against her and he gently prised the scarabs off her breasts. Belah gasped as sensation rushed back into her abused nipples. She dug her fingernails into the table in an effort not to move—to only do what he commanded. She wanted to massage the soreness from them, but relished the feeling just the same. The pain pulsed as acutely in each hard nub as the pleasure pulsed between her thighs.

Nikhil's hands returned to her breasts, delicately touching. She turned just enough to see his face, mouth turned down in a slight frown. When she glanced down at her breasts, she understood why. Both nipples were bruised around her areolas, with an alarming purple pattern from the clips on her jewelry. Each soft brush of his thumbs over them made her hiss from the pain. He glanced at her, and she realized from his dark gaze that as concerned as he may be, he was intensely aroused.

"What are your prayers tonight, my little beast?" he said, pinching both nipples between thumb and forefinger. He squeezed gently, as though testing her, and a burning rush of fire shot through her.

She gritted her teeth, wishing for more. "I pray you take your pleasure from me however you wish."

"I'm no fool, *Tilahatan*, your pleasure is every bit as important to me as mine is to you. This kind of pain would be counterproductive, if I had to endure it. Don't lie to me."

Belah smiled and arched her chest into his touch. "Is my own pain counterproductive to your pleasure? Don't lie to *me*." She spread her legs wide enough for the slit in her skirt to fall open, baring her knees and a swath of bronze thigh visible almost to her groin. "Because my pain is half of my pleasure. They will heal by morning, trust me. The other ache won't subside so easily without your attention."

One large hand clutched harder at her breast, fingertips digging in with bruising ferocity. The other dipped down between her legs and spread her open, sliding between her hot folds. He thrust two fingers into her roughly and she let out a cry at the sudden, though welcome, invasion. Her hips involuntarily bucked. Still, she craned her head around just enough to meet his gaze. The devious glint in his eyes was even more thrilling than his rough handling of her body. His mouth crashed against hers, claiming her while his hands kept her pinned to her seat, squirming for more. One hand pressed against her chest, toying with her breast, the other tight against her hips with his fingers spearing her.

He seemed more inclined to torment her, pulling away a moment later leaving her breathless while he sauntered back to his seat. He sat with an insouciant slouch and dug into his food, only offering her a casual glance every now and again. Belah remained still and erect, both hands resting on either side of her plate where he'd placed them, waiting.

After a few minutes, he gestured with a piece of bread to her plate. "Eat, little beast. I meant it when I said you would need your energy."

She scooted forward in her chair to reach her food, only too conscious of the slick, swollen flesh between her thighs and the lingering sensation of his touch on her skin. None of the delicious dishes before her held any flavor when all she wanted was him. Every so often she glanced at him, increasingly irritated by his casual smirk. Beyond that cocksure attitude, she could easily see the very aroused pulse of his aura and sense the wicked glee that accompanied whatever he had planned for her after he ate.

After sating his apparently considerable appetite for food, he sat back and regarded her from over the lip of his wine glass. He took a sip and set it down, his gaze narrowing.

"Did you really wish to be fucked on your throne today?"

Belah frowned, wondering if she should be worried that she'd shared that little secret. The truth was that she knew better than to do such a thing, but the very idea of the helpless humiliation was what caused the image to pop into her head around mid-day. She simply wanted him inside her and had let her mind wander to how it might happen in that very moment.

Nikhil sat up straighter and grinned. "You truly did, didn't you? You are a naughty beast. I had no idea."

"No!" Belah blurted, sitting forward abruptly and wincing when her breasts brushed against the bowl that still sat in front of her.

A look of concern flashed across his face, but he sat back and listened. "Explain yourself, then."

"I don't gain power from fucking only you. My harem serves a greater purpose that you are only beginning to fulfill for me. I haven't visited my pets since you arrived, and it's taken its toll. That little fantasy I shared with you was merely how my mind wandered today. I pictured you taking me first, and since we were surrounded by all the others…" She trailed off, remembering looking into the faces of each of her other advisers and all the noblemen and petitioners arranged around the huge room, and wondering what their reactions might be if she actually *did* something like that. In another life, it wouldn't have been unthinkable. In this life, she had a bigger image to maintain.

"Ah," he said, tilting his head back and gazing up at the sky. "You gain sustenance from fucking, and you were hungry today. So you were fantasizing about a forbidden snack, is that it?"

She shrugged and smiled, pleased that he seemed to grasp her needs so easily. "More or less. I don't need to fuck to gain sustenance from it, either. You have seen as much."

A slow smile spread across his face and he shifted in his seat. His aura brightened, obviously responding to the memory of having his cock shoved down her throat the first night they'd been together. "But don't your… *pets*… miss you? Who is seeing to their needs while you're preoccupied? I would feel terrible if I knew I were depriving them of their queen without good cause. How long has it been?"

The earlier guilt returned and she frowned. "They are well-trained and do just fine when left to their own devices. But I should see them soon. What I've given you, they will need soon too. They become unruly when I'm gone so long."

His eyebrows raised. "What you've given me? Do you mean that rush of… *something*… that leaves me feeling like the most powerful man in the world? That I could conquer the world, if you ordered me to? The power that makes me feel exactly like the god you would have me be in your presence? Why do your lowly pets need something like that?"

"I don't offer it to them often. But just as small, infrequent doses of herbal remedies can improve their health, so does my gift. If I gave them too much of it, then they would expect to be the ones sharing my bed every night." She felt her cheeks warm after the confession and its implication. Nikhil's smug look would have been irritating if it weren't for the flash of eagerness that he quickly hid.

Instead he looked away, lips pursed and brow drawn together as he considered some deep thought. She couldn't read his precise thoughts without feeding him her breath, but she still sensed a deepening excitement over whatever new idea he'd come up with. He didn't seem inclined to share. Turning back to her, he gestured.

"Stand and remove the rest of your clothes." He spoke evenly, his deep voice enveloping her with a caress as soft yet as commanding as the wind urging her to stretch her wings and glide on its currents. Just as effortlessly, she stood and stripped.

"Go to the doorway and raise your arms and spread your legs."

Belah suppressed a smile at that command. He was going to bind her in the same spot as she'd bound him that first night. She went placidly and did as she was told.

He stood and came to her then, his body flexing with a cat's grace as he walked. His pale shirt fell open to reveal his strong, bronze chest. When he reached her, he stood so close she could feel the pulsing of his aura against her skin and his warm breath in her ear. He gazed into her eyes while he slid his hands up one arm and secured her wrist to the binding at the top. Each limb was bound the same way, with his hands a slow caress over her skin until the silken ropes were tightened just enough that she couldn't escape.

After tying her second ankle, he lingered in a crouch in front of her, his face aligned with her groin. He inhaled a long, slow breath through his nose.

"You smell like the Nile after a rainstorm," he said. "And I know you are just as wet. I find I'm thirsty just now." He pressed his mouth to her bare cleft and slipped his tongue between her folds, hooking the wet tip of it under the hood of her clit.

Belah shuddered at the sudden pleasure that warm stroke sent through her body. He pressed his mouth tighter against her, sucking her swollen bundle between his lips hard enough to make her cry out. His fingers gripped hard at her hips while he lapped at her, drinking her flood of arousal like he was, indeed, parched. But it wasn't until he reached up and pinched both her nipples suddenly that she lost herself, hips bucking against him with the most sudden, unexpected, and intense orgasm. He was relentless, licking and sucking while his fingers sent rhythmic jolts of pain through her in time with the undulating surges of pleasure that coursed through her.

Soon he pulled back and stood, his shadowed face glistening with her juices. He kissed her abruptly, tangy tongue sliding into her willing mouth as though he owned that part of her as much as the tender flesh between her thighs. In that moment he owned all of her and she would resist nothing he chose to do to her. She loved every second.

He alternated between drawing her to the peaks of pain by tormenting her nipples over and over and by teasing the rest of her body with tender caresses that drove her wild with the need to come again. For the first time in her considerably long life she craved to be given that pleasure more than she desired bringing her partner to their own Nirvana. Nikhil was every bit the master of her pleasure. Every sensation that passed through her body, he carefully orchestrated with his touch.

After her third or fourth orgasm, he disappeared behind her into her room for a moment. She could turn her head for a limited view, but he was beyond her field of vision. Still, she could hear him moving around, perhaps undressing, and she could easily sense his carefully reined-in excitement that was even more vivid than before. It made her squirm in her bonds and her skin tingle in anticipation of what he had planned for her. She almost regretted not slipping a tendril of her breath to him when they kissed, but somehow it felt right that she let him have his secrets in this.

Soon he approached her, the warmth of his body sliding against hers and his breath gusting into her ear.

"I have a surprise for you," he murmured.

Belah was too distracted by the feel of his thick, hard, and velvety length brushing against her backside to do more than nod. He hadn't fucked her yet and her muscles clenched tightly with the wish to be filled and fucked by him again, but on his terms this time.

But Nikhil didn't press between her thighs like she hoped he would. Instead, his warmth left her, with only the harsh stinging slap from his hand on her backside to keep her company. That burn thrummed through her and a fresh flood of slick heat dampened the tops of her thighs.

The sharp *crack* sounded suddenly, making her jump before she even registered the searing sting of the strike on her back.

"Ah!" she yelped, arching from the unexpected pain. It was even more intense than the little tugs and pulls he'd given her damaged nipples, so much so that tears came to her eyes. When the fire dimmed to a low, throbbing ember, she relaxed, savoring the aftereffect that made her body feel more alive than she had in centuries. "Again, please," she said, panting out the words.

Nikhil chuckled behind her. "This is how you become mine for good, little beast. The whip is how the beast learns who its true master is."

She closed her eyes and waited, and soon enough the whip cracked and the pain shot through her.

Again and again, he struck until her entire back was a field of fire as exquisite as the feel of the sun on her when she flew the highest. Tears streamed down her face and her chest heaved. Yet he wasn't quite finished.

With eerie precision, the next strike hit the top of the cleft in her ass, and the next few crisscrossed over her cheeks. The stinging stripes of each one seemed to bind her body tighter and tighter, as though he were a devious spider wrapping her in a cocoon of pain to turn her into a tender snack for later. Her entire body vibrated with the sensations and with her ever deepening need for him.

From the corner of her eye, something dark and thin whooshed by, hitting the wall beside the doorway with a loud thump. The handle of the whip hit the floor beside her. A second later, Nikhil's hot, sweat-covered body was pressed against hers, his panting breaths in her ear and his arms wrapping around her from behind, hands pawing at her breasts like an animal digging into its kill.

Fresh pain bloomed through her back, accompanied by new spikes from the sharp bites he gave her neck and shoulder. With both large hands he gripped her ass cheeks and spread her apart. The thick, hot tip of his cock pressed urgently into her, and in one hard thrust he buried himself in her hungry depths, the harsh stretch a welcome comfort and the perfect counterpoint to the exquisite field of sensation that covered her entire back.

He cupped her breasts as he fucked her, worrying her nipples yet again until her entire body was a tangle of warring sensations. Her arms ached from the pull of the ropes as he pushed into her and she pushed back, trying to torque her body so he could get deeper inside her.

He fucked her harder and harder, as though aching to reach deeper. Finally, he let out a frustrated roar and pulled out. He ducked down behind her and tugged her ankles free from the ropes that held them, then came around in front of her. Both hands gripped her roughly by the backs of her thighs and hauled her close. She immediately wrapped her legs around him and let out an incoherent cry of triumph when he slammed deep again to the hilt and pounded ever harder into her. He clutched tightly at her whip-striped ass and pain threaded through her again.

Nikhil's dark gaze never left her face, their eyes locked. With each squeeze of his hands on her ass or brush of his chest against her nipples she winced, and he smiled.

"You first, my love," he said, dipping his head to flick his tongue over her bruised nipple. The bite of the ropes into her wrists was a sweet reminder of how little control she had, and with a cry she surrendered completely.

Magic pulsed through her body, flooding her soul and mind with power as it rushed to find its home in Nikhil. His sweat shone from the glow of energy that filled him and his face contorted with the sudden eruption of his climax deep inside her.

His thrusts gradually slowed, and he let his forehead rest against her shoulder. When he stopped moving he continued to hold her against him and Belah relished the closeness and the fullness of his cock still buried inside her.

With one arm still wrapped around her tender backside, he reached the other up and swiftly released her wrists from their bindings. Without a word, he carried her to the bed and laid her down, letting her arrange herself on her side with a pillow tucked under her head.

He regarded her silently for a moment, then seeming to come to a decision, he donned his clothes and left the room. Belah lay there, perplexed by his contradictory behavior, and wondered whether he had some new wicked surprise in store for her. She pondered the possibility and was surprised to realize how much the mystery of it thrilled her.

Her shoulders ached from being held up for so long, but moving anything hurt. She reveled in the pain—something she so rarely experienced and that provided her with the long absent reminder that she was a living, feeling creature with needs beyond simply stretching her wings at night and soaking up magic from her pets each morning. Nikhil was more than she could have hoped for already. His magic was more potent, and he seemed attuned to her needs on a deeper level than she'd ever expected. None of her past mates had been as attuned as he was—she may have encouraged them to live longer, if they had been, but it would have been supremely selfish to force her burden onto a mate who had no wish to live longer than a normal human might.

Belah shifted on her bed, wincing as she tried to find a comfortable position that didn't irritate the tiny wounds he'd given her. Every inch of her skin seemed too sensitive, even the bits he hadn't abused. She finally settled on her side with a pillow under her head and her hips twisted so the angry welts on her sides didn't have too much contact with her bed.

He'd outdone himself. Her entire nether region throbbed and swelled in agreement. That heavy need would destroy her, but she wasn't about to deny it so soon. She closed her eyes, imagining what secret surprise he might bring back.

Her eyes sprang open again when her door creaked and Nikhil entered, closing the door quietly behind him. A moment later her bed dipped and his hand was at her shoulder, gentle but urgent.

"What hurts most?" he asked.

She stared at him. She hurt everywhere and loved all of it. She'd been prepared to endure the discomfort through the night… and enjoy the reminders when he fucked her again.

Yet here he was, with an ointment that she knew from the scent would heal her. Meri's ointments always worked. This wasn't what she wanted.

When she didn't answer, he dabbed a tiny oily blob onto one nipple and rubbed it in a slow circle. Her nipple tingled in spite of the rush of pain that shot through her from his contact.

In a gruff, low voice, he began to speak while he anointed her nipples with the medicinal ointment.

"I want to hurt you."

His small confession was contradicted by the gentle way he cupped her breasts. When she looked into his eyes, his eyebrows raised and he repeated the statement.

"I want to hurt you."

"Hurt me."

With fingers coated in the healing ointment, he squeezed her already bruised nipple hard. Every sensation of healing disappeared, replaced by Nikhil's need for pain. She watched his eyes grow dark.

He shook his head and released her nipple. "No. Tonight you are my pet. That's what you call the members of your harem, right? Pets? Tonight you performed well. You endured a ruthless battle the same as my favorite horse. I think I whipped you even more than I do him. You deserve tenderness for now. I can hurt you again tomorrow to drive you to fulfill my needs. But after you have done your duty well, I will always cherish you."

Belah closed her eyes, relaxing. An overwhelming urge to cry rose up in her and she suppressed it, unsure where it came from. Relief from the pain she wanted but that kept her so high she felt like she was flying when he gave it to her. His statement grounded her, but gave her hope. She could stay rooted here for him, as long as he promised he would send her flying with his penchant for pain and pleasure tomorrow.

It didn't matter that she could literally fly. She had never felt such a release as she had tonight when he'd whipped her and tortured her. She'd never flown so high.

His fingertips still swirled gently around her bruised areolas. When he ventured a soft brush across one tip, she gasped and opened her eyes.

Nikhil's face glowed in blue light, more beautiful than ever. He seemed enraptured by her and his hand gently squeezed her breast again.

"You do me such honor, *Tilahatan*, to share your bed, to allow me to touch you the way I most want to touch you. Please tell me you are not merely fulfilling my greatest wish. Tell me you want it too."

His eyes drifted down to her breasts where his hand was still steadily caressing her.

Belah's brow twitched. How could he not know she wanted him?

"I've let you have control of my body all day, Nikhil. It is still yours. You know the rules, though. I'm queen and empress, so by morning I need to be able to fulfill that role."

He smiled and dipped his finger into the pot of ointment. With a gentle sweep, he spread more of the creamy substance over her bruised nipples and Belah closed her eyes, enjoying the delicious sensations. She kept her eyes closed when his fingers drifted away from her nipples and trailed an oily path down her belly to her wet cleft. His body hugged hers while he teased her to the point of begging, then he covered her with his body and thrust deep, taking his pleasure simply while he whispered his love into her ear.

She fell asleep, content in his arms.

CHAPTER EIGHT

After that night, their nights together became wondrous explorations of his creativity and her capacity to endure pain and pleasure combined. He repeatedly requested that she wear the heavy scarabs on her nipples during the day, but included other secret tortures—things Belah had to commend him for. His sexual creativity seemed boundless, particularly where it concerned driving her to distraction while she sat upon her throne, conducting her kingdom's business.

It became a challenge to avoid showing any outward sign of how his games affected her. One day it would be the curved dildo he'd attached a leather strap to so it would remain buried inside her all day, rubbing just so against her tender inner flesh so perfectly she nearly orgasmed several times. Another day would be the pair of spiked bands he attached to her upper thighs that sent tiny barbs of pain every time she moved.

She was enjoying just such a day with those perfect bands of pain driving her wild enough to rush through her daily business, when an unexpected cloud passed over the sun, casting the entire brightly lit room into eerie shadows. Glancing outside,

Belah still saw the burning orb in a cloudless sky and her jaw set hard. Such a darkness on a clear day could only mean one thing.

Unconscious for the first time that day of the sharp spikes Nikhil's bands caused her, she stood. From outside the palace, she heard the cacophony of nearby wildlife rushing to escape in the wake of one of her kind approaching. The alarmed whinnies of horses echoed through the hall, along with the thrum of flapping wings as hundreds of birds suddenly took flight. Low chanting of the people of her kingdom reverberated through the air, echoing from all around.

When her brother's massive, dark shape filled the doorway, everyone in attendance dropped to their knees and pressed their foreheads to the floor, muttering incoherent prayers. The very visible cloud of darkness that accompanied him was likely the reason they cowered. Even Nikhil slipped out of his seat, face stricken with alarm as he prostrated himself on the ground.

"Welcome, brother," she called to him as he threw back his black hood and strode toward her, his dark, curly hair blowing wildly with some unseen Northern wind that seemed to follow him wherever he went. The darkness clung to him as well, blotting out the presence of every other aura in the room until her brother, Ked, stood before her, towering over her even where she stood on the raised dais where she held court.

He said nothing at first, his eyes narrowing as he took her in with measured scrutiny. Belah's skin grew chilly under that gaze and she pressed her lips together, preparing herself for the criticism she sensed he was preparing to unleash.

Rather than speak the words she knew were on the tip of his tongue, he said, "We must speak in private, sister."

Belah blinked at him, surprised. His powers cloaked them so fully he could have easily berated her right where they stood and no one would hear a word of the exchange. He could just as easily have spoken directly into her mind without even arriving here in person. They hadn't seen each other in so long, the telepathic communication between her and all her siblings tended to dwindle. The power it required was rarely worth it unless they had news that affected each other. For Ked to fly here must mean he had very grave news. Cold dread washed over her as she nodded and turned to lead him through the large door behind her throne.

When they reached her study, which had reverted back to its original purpose now that Nikhil spent every night in her bed, she turned to him.

"Are you going to tell me why you're here?" she asked, crossing her arms over her chest.

"Why do I need to speak of things you already know well enough?" His voice rumbled, deep and rough and filled with the darkness of an approaching thunderstorm. His closeness was as disconcerting as always, and the reason others of their kind gave him as wide a berth as the lower creatures did. He knew her secrets without having to be told. He knew all her darkest, guiltiest secrets.

He was the biggest one.

The spikes digging into her thighs suddenly felt like ridiculous, childish toys—an absurd indulgence compared to the stark wasteland of a life her brother had chosen for himself in the aftermath of their mistake. She didn't dare draw any more attention to the bands than he could already sense. To do so would be to admit the small spike of shame she felt at his very presence now.

Yet his eyes drifted down her body, to the level of the pain she felt coloring her aura where the bands pressed into her, slicing without actually breaking her impervious skin.

"Yes, I do it for him," she said, preempting his question.

Ked's mouth twitched for a second as though he were dismayed. Her brother was a void where emotion was concerned—excellent at uncovering it in others, but completely lacking any himself—except when he was in her company.

"You do it for yourself. This much I know because I know you too well, sister. If you had marked him by now, only then would I believe you did it for him. We are selfish creatures when we are unmated, no matter how often you lie to yourself about how generous you are with your pets."

Of course this was what his visit would be about, but how could he know?

Ked loomed close enough that his breath brushed the top of her head as he stared down at her. He gripped her shoulders in both large hands, firmly but gently. With her own powers, she sensed his barely contained urgency.

His voice vibrated between them, so low it was more of a deep disturbance in the air than an actual sound. "I know because of what we have shared, sister. Did you think our connection would fade the way a bonded human's connection will fade if you neglect to replenish it frequently enough? Every time he takes you, I taste a piece of what he gives. My blessing made him what he is, but the fact remains that he is Blessed, and so you must mate him or you are cursing him." With the last statement he squeezed harder and gave her a slight shake.

Belah closed her eyes and let out the tense breath she'd been holding, careful not to release her power, though she had the strongest urge to do just that to try to placate him. When she opened her eyes again, she tilted her head back to meet his gaze. The depth of emotion she saw—love, concern, even that same shared shame—made her want to comfort him rather than make excuses.

"Ked… don't."

"Did I make you this way?" he asked in a low voice tinged with worry.

Sweet Mother, that wasn't the question she needed to hear.

Belah expelled a breath. "Maybe we did this to each other. Maybe Fate had a hand in it. Does it matter now, though? We are what we are."

She reached up and brushed her hands through the sleek, black fur that covered the cloak he wore—something from another, colder land that stood out among the loose, pale clothing preferred in her kingdom. A garment that reflected the darkness and brutal elements of his own self-exile.

In truth, the pain of their past had faded and she relished the reminder that Nikhil gave her, each spike of pain reminding her of the agony she'd felt when her child had been taken away. But to mate him would irrevocably alter his character. It would destroy the mystery she loved so much, and would incite her need to breed again. The last time she'd loved this deeply, the product of that love had nearly destroyed her—or the loss of it had, anyway.

"You never loved the others, did you?" Ked said, pulling back and gazing down at her.

Belah's mind filled with the telltale darkness of her brother's power, digging into her deepest emotions. No matter how far beneath the surface she had buried it, he could find the truth. She shoved hard against his chest.

"Get out of my head! Who I love or don't love is none of your concern!" She spun away, striding toward the window to try to find some sunlight to clear away the shadows he still pushed into her mind. The intimacy of the contact was too much after so long apart.

The darkness retreated, but Ked followed, pausing behind her. Thankfully, he refrained from contact this time.

"That's the only way you could mate the others after me, wasn't it? Because you never actually loved them. Did you think your indifference was a favor to the children you bore? Do you even realize how detached your line has become? This craving you have isn't isolated. It seeps through the magic connection whether you want it to or not. Your descendants will probably always have similar cravings."

"Don't you think I know that? The only child unaffected by my craving was…" *Ours.* The word stuck in her throat, choking her. She hadn't been this way before. She'd been as normal and perfect as her mother had wished her and the rest of her siblings to be. The child she and Ked had made had been the product of a union that should never have happened among dragonkind, but their son's origins didn't diminish the love she had for the child, or the loss when their mother and Fate had taken him away.

She and Ked had both punished themselves ever since, in different ways. She'd been at it for so long that now she craved the pain of her attrition as much as the pleasure she required for sustenance.

"If you love him, mate him," her brother said. "Make a child with him and let yourself finally heal. At least one of us should be allowed to have a life."

"Did it occur to you that it may be too late? I *need* what he gives me. Mating him won't change me. But it will change him, and I need him the way he is now."

Ked's gaze dropped to the level of her thighs again, reminding her of the all too present painful pressure. She could sense the train of argument he refrained from speaking aloud. She'd had the same argument with herself countless times since realizing that Nikhil was the one man who truly satisfied her. She could train him again after she marked him, but she would always know he was merely a tamed beast, conditioned by the magic of her immortal mark to do her bidding.

The muscles in Ked's jaw flexed. Once upon a time, that tension might have meant something different, but now all she sensed was regret. He turned away and moved back into the shadows away from the window.

"I used to fill that need for you, when it wasn't complicated by... other desires. If he can fill it for you, you have my blessing, but take care with him. His aura is dark—dangerous."

Belah turned and leaned back against the window sill, regarding him with a perplexed smile. "More dangerous than you? Maybe that's why I love him."

Ked's expression grew more serious. "Keeping him bonded to you too long without marking him is a risk. No matter what he is to you, just know that I am still your protector. That will never change, sister."

Her protector. The word reminded her of how Nikhil had behaved the night after he'd first started their daily games of secret, sexual torture. In spite of the exhilarating abuses she'd endured at his hand—the bruises and welts she only wished could leave scars—he had been tender at the end, seeing to her care in the aftermath. Did that mean he would be her protector? Beyond being the general that defended her kingdom, would he defend her body, her honor?

If only Nikhil could mark *her* instead of the other way around—the way her brother's love had irrevocably marked her soul so long ago. With Nikhil she wished for a tangible reflection of the depth of her feelings for him, yet her nature meant she never scarred—nothing could pierce her skin the way Nikhil's every action had branded her heart and soul.

There may be a way, but she had to be sure—she had never attempted it herself.

"I do want him as a mate," she said. "This life is a burden to bear alone, you know this as well as the rest of us. But do you ever wish for a partner who can bear the burden for you? One who can take the control away? He lets me breathe. Were I to mark him, I would be shouldering the suffocating burden of his life as well as mine. I want him to mark me instead."

Ked's shoulders rose and fell with his heavy breath as he turned toward her. "My burdens are my own to bear. They will never be truly lifted, sister, and neither will yours. Any reprieve his actions give you are an illusion. But if a simple mark will help, for the sake of a memento, I will tell you how to do it. You must make me a promise, first."

Belah's heart raced. She ached to be able to predict her brother's words, but his thoughts were cloaked so well she likely couldn't even glean a hint if she used her breath to get inside his head.

"What is it?" she whispered.

"You may let him mark you, but if you still refuse to give him your mark, you must give him up. He is Blessed—too long unmated to their bonded dragon and they tend to go mad. He needs your mark as much as you believe you need him."

He stood silent, watching her and waiting. Give him up? How could she give him up? She wanted to keep him forever! No… she wanted to be *kept*. Which was a thought ill-befitting a dragon. Her brother was indulging her as much as possible already. She would have to decide soon which course to take.

Slowly, she nodded. "Yes. I will either mate him or find him another." Calmed by the thought, she nodded again. It could work well that way. The power of his Blessing may prevent a weaker dragon's mark from changing him so much that he lost what she loved about him. Whether or not he would agree to such an arrangement was an issue she would have to deal with later.

"How can he mark me?"

"With your own magic, sister. Your fire is the key."

With that, Ked grew cloudy and amorphous, and in the blink of an eye, the huge, dark shape that was her brother disappeared.

CHAPTER NINE

B elah stared at the empty space her brother had occupied, still processing what he'd told her. The confirmation that her fire would enable marks to be etched into her skin had her mind racing with possibilities. The escalation of Nikhil's games made her want to be marked by him in some way more and more. She wanted memories of his touch. Tangible evidence that he'd been in command of her body. As much as she would love to mark him to keep him with her forever, she wanted what he gave her now even more. She would rather carry memories of these times than mark him and have a shadow of the man she loved exist beside her day by day.

The small spikes digging into her upper thighs now made that desire achingly sharp. She could feel the pain, but it was no more than an acute pressure. How much more sensation would she receive were his toys to actually break skin? Her hands went involuntarily to her breasts and she closed her eyes, imagining a pair of scarabs attached by teeth piercing through her nipples. Even the imagined pain caused her body to shudder with need.

Ked's question remained in her mind. Had her brother done this to her? Perhaps, but so indirectly he should bear no blame now. She had lived with the pain of loss for so long, and the stigma of their shame, that she needed these small reminders to feel whole. The grief had filled her so thoroughly that when it faded, she was left empty. Nikhil had filled that emptiness with his brutal attention in a way that made sense to her for the first time in ages. Not even the pleasure provided by her pets or their eager gifts of magic had sated her so well.

The door to her study opened and shut softly behind her. Belah closed her eyes and breathed in Nikhil's familiar scent, her skin prickling in anticipation of his approach. Part of her ached to tell him all her secrets, even that ancient darkness that still lingered deep inside.

The truth was that her union with her brother had altered her forever, even after the child she'd carried of his blood had been born and taken. She never let herself think of the child anymore—where he might have gone or what kind of dragon he'd become. Was he even an immortal like his parents? Their mother had refused to share the truth, and Fate had made it clear Belah was never to know.

Nikhil's presence was unlike any other mate she'd taken in the past. He didn't seek to fill her with light and love, but pulled her into his darkness and held her there by every thread of pain he inflicted. And she reveled in it more with each passing day.

The closer he came, the more her body ached for his potent touch. The flesh between her legs swelled into a tight knot, hot with wet desire and throbbing to be parted by his body in any fashion he saw fit. Yet when he finally reached her he merely rested his large hands on her shoulders, warm and comforting.

His breath teased at the loose strands of hair at her nape, beneath the upswept waves of her locks. With silken caresses, his lips trailed over the bare curve at the side of her throat while his hands drifted lower. He said nothing, but as his touch continued down her body, his fingers dug in harder. He cupped her breasts, pulling the sides of her gown apart to reveal her creamy flesh, then pinched her nipples harshly, twisting and tugging at them until she cried out. The gown fell to her waist and with a rough tug, he forced it to the floor at her feet.

Again his hands dug into her curves, kneading and squeezing with all the strength she knew he had, marking her the only way he could with the force of his own desire. She loved the bruises he gave her, but they were too fleeting. Still, in the moment, they were precisely what she needed.

Belah sighed under Nikhil's touch, leaning back against him as his hands dipped lower to wrap around the bands at her thighs and squeeze. A harsh cry escaped her throat at the sudden rush of sensation. Her chest arched forward and she turned her head, giving her mouth to him and moaning into his kiss while he kneaded the bands harder into her legs, each new bit of pressure inciting fresh jolts of desire through her.

Her arousal flooded out of her, hot and wet, coating her thighs and the leather of the bands. The fertile scent wafted to her nostrils and she spread her legs. Nikhil responded with a groan, ending the kiss with a bite of her lower lip and gazing down her torso, eyes blazing.

"These must be your new favorites. Maybe we try something similar, but closer to your cunt next."

He released his hold and the pressure around her thighs subsided, leaving a dull throb behind. He traced the edges of the leather bands, drawing her slick juices along the top edges between her thighs, so close to her aching flesh she nearly begged for his touch. Nikhil seemed too enthralled by her reaction, and too fascinated with whatever new idea had popped into his head.

"Try whatever you wish, my love," Belah said, hoping that just now he would at least try to give her pleasure.

"Mmm, perhaps a bauble or two for the prettiest part of you," he said almost idly. His fingertips slipped further in and teased along the edge of her outer lips, drawing moisture back and forth over the sensitive skin. The heat between her legs grew unbearable and Belah moaned, nodding distractedly. She let out a sharp hiss when he gripped each fold of flesh between thumb and forefinger and pinched hard. A deep chuckle rumbled forth from him. "Yes, I think my little beast would enjoy that, wouldn't you?"

"Yes," she gasped, the affirmative as much in response to his question as to the sudden thrust of his fingers filling her cunt and twisting inside her.

Abruptly she found herself turned and bent over the window sill, breasts pressed against the far corner of the wide ledge. Behind her, cloth rustled, and a second later, Nikhil rammed his thick, hard flesh into her. He grabbed both her hands and twisted her arms behind her back, pinning her wrists together with one hand while the other gripped her upper thigh again, squeezing at the spiked leather in time with his relentless fucking.

Beyond the edge of the window she nearly hung out of, Belah had the most glorious view of moon rising full and bright over the river—*her* river—and her kingdom beyond. Everything outside this little bubble he kept her in belonged to her, as far as her eyes could see. Yet inside the span of his gaze, she belonged to him. He commanded both her pleasure and pain, and at his command, her body shuddered and fell apart with the power of her orgasm. Nikhil's heavy cock swelled and flooded her insides with his own climax at the same time.

In the haze of the aftermath, he sat her down on a nearby bench and cleaned her up. He made a conscientious master, which should not have surprised her. Men followed him into battle, after all. It was only natural for her to fall under his spell so easily. She loved the contradiction of his tenderness in the wake of the exquisite pain he could give her, and the pleasure that accompanied it.

He knelt before her and unbuckled the leather strips around her thighs. Belah gasped at the rush of sensation followed by relief from the pain. The absence of it was every bit as exhilarating. The frown that creased his brow worried her.

"What is it?" she asked.

Nikhil brushed his fingertips over the reddened indentations in her legs and shook his head. "I thought you only a fast healer the last time you wore these. I didn't see your skin after you took them off before. Why is there no blood?"

"My body can't be pierced by human implements. No sword or spear, or even needle, is capable of breaching my skin, even in this form."

Nikhil's gaze shot to her face, his dark eyes wider than she'd ever seen them, but his frown deepened in spite of his surprise. Slowly, he narrowed his eyes as he took in her own forlorn look. "You don't sound happy about that fact, *Tilahatan*. Yet it is fitting for a goddess to be so incorruptible. Why do you look so sad now?"

Belah's chest warmed at the sound of concern. "Of all the men I have ever bedded, you are the only one who I have ever wished *could* corrupt me. Your touch makes me forget the burdens of immortality. I want more than you can give through your own power."

"I would gladly give you everything you wish for, if you can tell me how."

Her confession to her brother rushed back, yet Belah hesitated to share it with Nikhil. The timing wasn't right. She still needed to give their relationship more time, explore how far he would really go in fulfilling her needs, before she shared her desire to have him mark her. It may have been a foolish wish, but she wanted the unconventional mating to happen on the same day, with a private ceremony, and only after she had told him everything. Because after he was marked—even if it was by a younger, weaker dragon—things may still change. She simply wanted more time to enjoy him before they did.

Still behaving as the tender, caring master, Nikhil helped her dress and walked with her back to her chambers. In spite of the short walk, the silence between them made her ache to tell him everything now.

His aura flickered with his undisguised disappointment. She didn't understand why this aspect of her nature should bother him so much until they reached the room and he sat in one of the wide leather chairs, looking even more dejected. He pulled a golden box from the folds of his robe and set it on the table beside him, giving her a wan smile.

"It was going to be a surprise for tonight," he explained in response to her raised eyebrows. "But now that I know your skin is so damn impenetrable, I suppose my cock piercing your pussy will have to suffice."

Curious, Belah walked to the table and touched the box, running her fingertips over the exquisite relief design that covered the lid—a wide pair of wings spanned the width, with the shape of a woman in between. He'd brought her a gift. One he couldn't give her because her own nature had interfered.

"My love, don't look so sad," he said, wrapping an arm around her and tugging her down onto his lap. "The little clips you use for your other jewelry make sense, now that I know. These were meant to be different... to pierce you... but I can have clips attached. Open it." He picked up the box and set it into her hand.

Shakily, Belah lifted the lid from the box. As she did, Nikhil's free hand began roaming over her torso again, caressing gently and undressing her bit by bit. His fingers circled distractedly around and around one nipple when she peered into the box. Three golden hoops lay within, each one boasting a tiny jeweled scarab with blue-black wings and pincers extending up and around, becoming the loop that would have pierced her flesh, if that were possible.

"Why are there three?" she asked, certain she knew what two of them were for, but confused about the third, smaller hoop.

"Mmm... for my three favorite parts of you," Nikhil rumbled, and dipped his head to capture her stiff nipple between his teeth while his fingers drifted to the other, plucking and squeezing it until Belah gasped when he hit just the right level of pain. Belah shifted on his lap, arching her chest closer to his mouth and enjoying the hard press of his erection into her backside.

"The third?" she asked breathlessly, though she knew from the tugging of his fingers at her waist where he was going. The closure of her belt came open finally and the panels of her gown parted across her hips, giving him access. He pressed his fingertips between her thighs, teasing lightly over the slick hood of her clit.

"I want to see you adorned with gold and jewels like the goddess you are. We'll have to improvise somehow."

"No, Nikhil. Show me what you were going to do before I ruined your surprise. Please." Her words came out as a plea that was contrary to her normal commanding tone, but he did this to her. He made her want to grovel at his feet for pleasure. To be used however he saw fit. "Just pretend I never told you."

"Very well, *Tilahatan*," he said and urged her off his lap. He brushed past her with a proprietary squeeze of her behind that sent a thrill through her. Whenever they were alone together, he was every bit her master.

"Come," he commanded, standing in the opening to her balcony with several lengths of rope draped over his palms. Reaching up, he threaded them through the steel loops embedded in the doorframe above him and let the lengths hang down. There was more length than was necessary to bind her arms above her head. Belah's mind whirled with curiosity about how elaborate his plan must have been. She hadn't intended to tell him the secret of piercing her skin tonight, but now she wasn't so certain she could keep it to herself.

She went to him and turned with her back to him. He raised her arms one by one and wrapped her wrists in the ropes. Instead of spreading her legs and tethering her ankles to the lower eyelets, he did something new. With a gentle touch, he lifted one leg and wrapped it several times in the rope just above her knee, tightening the wrap with an elaborate knot that was just snug enough to keep the ropes from shifting, but not so tight as to restrict her circulation. She watched in fascination as he looped the rope through another eyelet above her, raising her leg so it hung parallel to the floor with her knee bent and her toes pointed to the ground. He tugged gently at the end of the rope, pulling until her leg swung wide, then secured the end of the rope with a knot.

When he lifted her other leg, she found herself suspended in air and had the strangest urge to let her wings extend to maintain her balance. The itch subsided when Nikhil completed the binding and reached back around her, letting his hand slide from the ropes up the inside of her thigh to brush his fingertips over her spread folds.

He whispered in her ear while he stroked her clit. "I imagined how lovely your pretty cunt would be with a jewel permanently attached. You are already the picture of perfection, *Tilahatan*. You deserve to be adorned in gold. My most prized little beast, so pliant and eager to please. Would you have liked to have a jewel attached to you right here?" He squeezed her clit gently between thumb and forefinger, to emphasize exactly what part of her anatomy he referred to.

Belah loved jewelry of any kind, but it had never occurred to her to attach any to the parts of her Nikhil seemed so keen on decorating. That he prized these most sensitive parts of her so highly made it all the clearer to her how perfect a mate he was. If only marking him wouldn't destroy the things she loved so much about him, she would do it in a heartbeat.

"What do you think, Belah?" he asked again. Her name breathed against the back of her neck made her shiver. He rarely used her name, preferring to address her with any number of terms of endearment. She loved all of them, but the way he said her name made blood rush to her head swiftly enough that she grew lightheaded.

"That sounds… nice," she whispered, too aroused to speak any louder.

Nikhil moved back around her and dropped to his knees, hands cupping her bottom to pull her to his mouth like a ripe piece of melon. He tongued her cleft with abandon, occasionally drifting his mouth to her outer lips and nipping hard to add delicious spikes of pain to her pleasure. Belah was powerless against the onslaught and let her head fall back as he commanded her climax to rise from deep within. He coaxed her more and more urgently with his tongue until she wanted nothing more than to give in to him and let the pent-up magic rush through her like a torrent. Her cry echoed above them, his slow lapping between her thighs continuing for a moment until the quivering of her thighs subsided.

Nikhil stood and wiped her juices from his lips and chin, smiling at her. He stepped between her thighs as though preparing to spear her with his cock.

"Wait," she said. "I want you to do what you were going to do. There is a way. It is a secret you mustn't share with anyone. But I want it, so I will tell you. I want it so much."

Nikhil paused with his hands resting on her knees, his gaze already feverish with his need to fuck her again and his aura pulsing wildly. Yet he pulled back with a slow nod.

Very deliberately, he walked to where the box rested on the table and picked it up. From within, he pulled a small, thin, slightly curved object that glinted silvery in the light of her chamber.

"Tell me what to do."

"Hold it in front of my mouth," she said.

When he came close and held it up, she could see it was a hooked needle similar to the ones Meri used to stitch up wounds. Her stomach flipped with excitement over this new experience. Both her nipples and her cunt tingled in anticipation of what was about to happen.

Nikhil's eyebrows rose expectantly and Belah took a deep breath. She closed her eyes, summoning the magic to her lungs and conjuring the fire she so rarely used. With lips opened into a tight "O," she expelled her breath. Bright blue flame licked out in a liquid stream, curling around the needle and Nikhil's fingers where he held it. He bared his teeth and hissed from pain, but held on tight until the needle glowed with heat.

"Sorry," Belah said, drawing the fire back into her and immediately blowing a cooling blue breath onto his scorched fingertips.

"If this works, then there is no need for apologies, my love," he said as he bent to kiss her.

With his free hand he cupped one breast, kneading it roughly and pinching her nipple hard enough to drive her wild with need again. Just as he was about to press the needle to her flesh, she cried out.

"Wait. Make sure you're ready with the ring before you start. I heal quickly, remember?"

"Don't worry, I am ready." He swirled his tongue around his mouth and produced one of the pieces of jewelry held tightly between his teeth.

Pulling her nipple taut, he leaned close, pressed the sharp point of the needle to the pink flesh, and pushed. Belah watched, too hypnotized by the sight of the metal sliding through her skin to look away. When the harsh fire of agony flowed through her body, she cried out, throwing her head back and arching toward the source of the pain. It was every bit as acute and delicious as the pleasure of an orgasm, and it left her gasping for air.

Before she could recover from the first wave of intense fire, another one hit when he pierced her second nipple, and she bucked against her bindings.

With the flood of pain pulsing from both breasts through the ends of her limbs, her eyes flew open and met Nikhil's gaze. The wild creature she'd bound in this very spot their first night together looked back at her, crazed with hunger and his aura pulsing just as savagely as the pain that shot through her breasts. He wasn't finished yet.

Dropping to his knees again, he paused with a groan before her open pussy, already flooded again with her desire. Closing his eyes, he turned his head and sank his teeth into her inner thigh so hard he would have taken a bite out of her, if his teeth were capable of penetrating her skin. Gathering command of himself again, he turned back to her glistening folds and squeezed the hood of her clit tightly between thumb and forefinger. With careful precision, he shoved the needle through. More prepared for the hot flash of pain this time, Belah mustered the presence of mind to watch while he deftly followed the needle with the loop of gold and bent to squeeze the tiny ring closed with his teeth.

He let his mouth linger against her flesh for just a moment longer, his tongue testing the tiny ornament with maddening flicks. When Belah was ready to beg for more, he sat back on his heels, panting and staring up at her.

"*Tilahatan*, you are so beautiful. A creature worthy of worship. You did not even bleed." He rose slowly and stepped back from her, surveying his handiwork. One large hand drifted down to grip his hard cock, and he stood stroking himself while staring at her, eyes flitting between the sparkling jeweled scarabs on the tips of her breasts and the third one resting coolly over her clit.

Belah squirmed against her bindings, the ache of fresh need overwhelming her more than the pain of the piercings.

"Please, Nikhil," she begged, watching him continue pleasuring himself and aching for just a glimmer of the power that swelled in him.

His lips spread in a wicked smile and he slowed his strokes. "You are so wet for the things I do, such a hungry little beast. Knowing I command your pleasure, that it is mine to give or take, makes me hard for you. I like to see you squirm, to know how much hotter that sweet, tight quim of yours will be once I let you have my cock. Let me hear you beg some more, little beast."

He stepped close again, but paused just at arm's length and continued stroking himself with one hand. With his other, he reached out and tugged at one of the rings that now dangled from her nipples, and a pleasant buzz of pain burned into her again.

"Think of all the fun we can have with these. And with this." He lowered his hand between her thighs and flicked lightly at the scarab resting there. His touch made it vibrate straight through her clit, and the intensity of the competing sensations caused her to cry out once more.

"Please! Before I heal, fuck me. Fuck me while I can still feel everything!"

Nikhil's smile faded into a look of raw desire and he released himself. With both hands, he gripped her hips while he aimed his cock between her thighs. Her hot, sodden flesh parted when his thick tip pressed into her. As he slid deeper, the underside of her new bauble rubbed harder against her clit, pulling at its piercing just enough to remind her how fresh the pain was. Nothing but pleasure remained once he'd sunk to the hilt inside her.

"More," she whispered. "Please, I need more."

He bent his head to her breast as he pulled out, capturing one gold ring and the nipple it pierced, biting down on the damaged flesh until she yelped. Then he slammed back into her, swift and hard, his pelvis pressing and grinding until she gasped and begged again for *more, more, more.*

Soon, Belah lost herself in the pulsing cadence of sensations—the rising pleasure accompanied by staccato beats of pain until she had no sense of anything else. He seemed to know exactly how to drive her higher and higher, closer to the brink of madness. She was nearly lost when he slowed. He still fucked her, but with tortuous deliberation, staring down at her intently.

"No, please don't stop. I need more," she whimpered.

"Show me some of what you are. I want to see the beast in you, my love, to watch the creature I have broken come apart while I fuck her. Just a piece of the truth. Those glorious horns you couldn't help but release that first night. Or your wings. Show me, and I will let you fly."

"Yes," she said, and immediately gave up bits of the tenuous control she had over her shape. Her magic could hold her form indefinitely with little effort, but during sex with Nikhil, she often had the urge to let go of her true shape after he'd pleased her so well that night with just his fingers. Her horns came first, protruding slowly from her temples and coiling back over her head like thick, twisting vines. Then her wings erupted from her shoulder blades, stretching and flexing in the evening breeze.

Nikhil fucked her again in earnest, his eyes sparkling with excitement as she continued to let elements of her true shape emerge from beneath her skin. She maintained her human shape just enough to avoid interfering with her bindings, but let the texture of her skin become the blue scales and let her long tongue flick out to tease at the line of his jaw.

He groaned as he slammed into her over and over, his hips pounding out a rhythm that sank deep into her bones with each press against the jewelry attached to her clit.

"Yes, *Tilahatan*, you are my little beast. Mine. And I will fuck you until you scream my name, begging me for more, begging me to hurt you again. Someday, *Tilahatan*, I will make you bleed for me."

The very suggestion of shedding blood just for his pleasure sent Belah over the edge. Her voice rose up to the heavens, resonating enough to make the entire river valley grow silent in its wake.

CHAPTER TEN

"I have neglected my pets for far too long," Belah said. "You distract me from my duties. I've become a poor mistress to them." She ignored Nikhil's scowl from the bed behind her as she dressed before her mirror.

It had been months since her last visit to her harem. Ever since Nikhil had joined her, she'd needed only him to satisfy her need for magical sustenance. A recent visit from a very concerned Meri had spurred her into action. Her pets were restless, bored, and more prone to bickering and acting out with the rest of her staff lately. They needed a regular outlet for their pent-up energy and could only entertain each other for so long.

She shouldn't go in there feeling like it was a chore, though. Dropping one sandal to the floor, she sighed and looked up at Nikhil apologetically. Regarding him for a moment, she tilted her head.

"What is it, love?" he asked. "Tell me you changed your mind and decided to come back to bed with me." He patted the edge of the bed beside one naked, tan thigh.

"No. I can't avoid my duties, but maybe you can help."

His scowl deepened. "I have no use for your pets. They're too soft."

"I mean help *me* get in the mood to go to them, and be here afterward when I return." She frowned, realizing that she'd been away from her harem long enough that today she should avoid withholding her Nirvana from them. It meant she'd need to be even more in the mood than if she were just orchestrating their pleasure for her sustenance. But the idea of simple, mindless fucking didn't have the same allure as it used to.

She turned back to the mirror, irritated. Nikhil's large, naked form slipped up behind her, his hands sliding down her bare arms until his fingers clasped around her wrists. He tugged her arms behind her back, forcing her to arch her breasts toward the mirror. With one hand holding her wrists together, he used the other to unfasten the clasp of the robe over her sternum and pushed it open. The pair of scarabs at her breasts caught the sunlight and gleamed with deep blue light. Belah smiled, thrilled anew at the image and the memory it incited of that glorious night when he'd given them to her.

"What will your pets think when they see you like this, pierced with rings befitting a slave? A slave to a rich master, of course, but a slave nonetheless." His hand spanned her chest, thumb and forefinger teasing simultaneously at both sparkling scarabs.

"I… I admit I hadn't considered that," she said. It truly would be an awkward explanation if any of her pets asked why she was pierced as she was. They likely wouldn't ask outright, but she would sense their confusion and uncertainty, and it could very well add to their unrest.

Nikhil's dark eyes studied her in the mirror as his fingers continued to tease her breasts before sliding in a ticklish trail down her stomach and dipping between her thighs to find the third scarab. Belah inhaled sharply at the sudden burst of pleasure that shot through her when he slipped his finger deeper between her moist folds.

"How well can you disguise your identity?" he asked.

Belah gazed back at him, perplexed. "I can change my human appearance at will, but there are limits. I can't fake my gender, but everything else is superficial."

He moved away for a moment, and when he returned, he slipped a band of tooled leather around her neck. Belah recognized the pretty little collar he'd presented her with a few weeks earlier as an introduction to a new, private game of his.

Like all his games, she'd loved this one. Loved being ordered to kneel at his side while he ate his meals, letting him feed her small morsels from the palm of his hand. Loved when he'd bared his hard cock to her and ordered her to suck it, then left her naked and kneeling with her cheek to the floor and her bare ass in the air, waiting interminably for him to do as he wished with her.

All it took was the buckle sliding closed for her knees to bend and she was kneeling on the floor in front of him, still facing the mirror.

"Show me," he said. "Make yourself look like a slave."

His tone wasn't even commanding, but she didn't need to be ordered to carry out his request when she wore the collar.

With the power of a thought, Belah shifted her appearance, watching her reflection as she transformed. Her upswept black braids disappeared, leaving behind a bare, shorn scalp. Her skin darkened from the honey-bronze she preferred to a more sun-darkened shade, befitting one of the women who worked the barley fields. The fine trimmed nails at the ends of her fingers grew ragged, and she turned her eyes from their deep, vivid blue to a dark, earthy brown. The shape of her face grew more angular and just slightly gaunt and her body slimmed, her breasts becoming smaller, tipped with dark brown nipples.

She craned her neck and peered up at Nikhil behind her, eager for his approval. He cupped her cheek and smiled. "Good little beast. I think we can fulfill your obligations to your pets and entertain ourselves in the process."

"What are you going to do? I can't just wander down there looking like this. The guards would have me executed. Or they would try to, anyway."

Nikhil retrieved a length of rope and attached it to a ring at the back of her collar. "You won't be going alone. The empress has a new slave for her harem who needs to be broken in today. She's entrusted me to deliver this lovely Nubian beauty to the harem chamber and let her pets initiate her to their mistress's preferences. Of course, I will be there to oversee—and maybe even participate—so I can give the empress an accurate report of the slave's performance." He tugged gently at her collar. "Rise, little beast. It's time."

Belah stood and waited while Nikhil dressed himself in the outfit he regularly wore to court. She admired how very *official* he appeared, right down to the stern, businesslike expression on his face. The nobility in his bearing struck her for the first time and she wondered if the shift in mindset to that of a slave was affecting her on a deeper level. He had let his short-cropped hair grow over the months, so that now it draped in dark, silken waves over his shoulders. His garments were no different than she was used to, but looked even brighter in contrast to the drab skirt he wrapped around her hips after divesting her of her finer gown. He left her bare-breasted as a slave would be, and smudged charcoal over her scarabs to dull the shine. With the same blackened fingers, he lightly touched her cheek, rubbing more dark color in places until she truly appeared as though she'd been pulled out of the fields and brought to the palace.

He led her down a circuitous path through the palace, away from her chambers and down hallways that were rarely traveled and smelled musty with disuse. Exiting a small doorway, she found herself in the kitchen garden, only a stone's throw from the pregnant bank of the Nile, churning from the winter rains.

Finally, they made their way through the bustling courtyard where the servants worked, and Belah forced herself to bow her head and slouch to avoid raising any suspicion. She felt strange in this new shape, unused to the cool air flowing over her bare scalp.

Surreptitiously, she absorbed the mood around her. No one seemed the least bit interested in her, but she was pleased to witness how deferential all the servants were to Nikhil's presence. The respect they showed him was tinged with fearful awe, and she heard low murmurs of stories of his exploits on the battlefield as he led her past. Here and there, she also caught bits and pieces of rumors that he was favored by the empress and that she was so fond of him they wondered if he would become her consort soon. The idea gave her a rush of pleasure and pride at how much they seemed to revere him already. Perhaps it was time to move forward with her plan to have him marked.

They entered the palace again through the servant's entrance, and from there they bypassed her throne room and walked silently down the hallway toward her harem.

Belah kept her gaze cast to the floor while Nikhil explained his purpose to the guards outside her harem's doors. She remained as still and obedient as any slave, in spite of the growing heat between her thighs at what was to come.

"She looks too skinny for one of the empress's pets," one guard said.

"That's easily remedied," Nikhil said. "She has good bones and a nice, firm backside." He emphasized his point by grabbing one cheek through her skirt and squeezing hard enough that Belah yelped in surprise and glared up at him. Putting on a show for the guards wasn't part of what she'd envisioned for the day. Her guards were expressly forbidden from laying a hand on her pets.

Glancing between the two guards, she sensed their avid interest, but they kept themselves tightly restrained. When they opened the doors to the harem, she could feel their eyes on her as sharply as their envy of Nikhil for being permitted entry into a place they considered sacred.

The doors thumped shut behind them, and Belah's senses awakened as they always did whenever she entered this room. The aromas evoked a sense of hunger—part spicy incense and part raw sex. Usually the energy in the room rose to a crescendo at her very presence. Today, the mood was more subdued, the residents listless and uninspired compared to past visits. They seemed uninterested in her, which left her aching with guilt over how long she'd been away. She suddenly wished she could shed her false persona and rouse them with her usual greeting.

Good morning, sweet pets. Tell me your dreams so that I may make them come true.

Slowly, her pets' attention redirected to the entrance where she stood just behind Nikhil, partly blocked from their view. His own aura pulsed with curious interest as he scanned the room, but it wasn't until he glanced back at her with a sly smile that his aura swelled with fresh arousal reflected by the bulge beneath his clothing.

Turning back to the room, Nikhil took a breath and said, "Your mistress has sent me with a gift today. This lovely little slave was bestowed on her by a southern king, and she wishes for you, her pets, to welcome the girl and introduce her to all the ways in which to provide for the mistress's pleasure."

The first member of her harem to venture forward was Zeb, their de-facto leader, followed closely by Nyla, whose hand was gripped lightly in his.

Belah kept her eyes downcast while Zeb inspected her. Her skin thrummed with excitement at simply being regarded so intently and so openly by the most prominent and virile male in her collection. Still, in spite of Zeb's stature, he was softer around the edges than Nikhil. All the members of her harem were soft, gentle, yet thorough lovers. How would they behave under Nikhil's command?

"You have your mistress's permission to break her in completely," Nikhil said. "Anything you think the empress would like the girl to experience. We both know quite well what she likes, after all." Nikhil's voice pitched low at the end, as though he was sharing a secret with Zeb.

From under her lowered lashes, she saw Zeb smile. "Well, then… the first thing we need to do is see how much endurance she has. When the mistress is hungry, she requires us to last quite a long time." He glanced back at Nyla. "My love, why don't you pretend to be our mistress for today? She always preferred you among the females."

Nyla nodded and came forward, squared her shoulders and tossed back her hair, then reached up and touched Belah gently beneath her chin. "Hmm, you are a pretty little slave, but we don't wear collars once we're admitted to the harem."

Belah barely heard what she said. When Nyla came close, all she was aware of was the full, rounded bulge of Nyla's pregnant belly and let out a sharp, involuntary gasp. Had she been away so long that she missed her two favorite pets breeding? Tears pricked at her eyes and she blinked rapidly to avoid letting them loose.

"Oh, honey, no," Nyla said, caressing her cheek and completely misinterpreting Belah's distress. "It isn't anything to be afraid of. The mistress is very good to us, you will see. But first, I think we need to bathe you, get some of this dirt off before we show you how things are done here. Let's get this collar off and I can show you around."

Nyla's fertile fragrance was intoxicating to Belah, and she let the young woman unbuckle her collar and let it fall to the floor. "What's your name?" Nyla whispered.

"B-Bekha," she said, almost wincing at her near-mistake.

"I'm Nyla. And that is Zeb. We will take good care of you until you're comfortable with us."

Belah smiled shyly and let Nyla lead her into the room. She was already halfway down the steps into the large room, being led toward the doors out into their private courtyard where the bathing pool lay, when she thought to look back to Nikhil. He was whispering something to Zeb, who nodded and glanced in her direction with a wide grin. The flesh between her thighs tightened and warmed with arousal. Nikhil was always full of surprises and she couldn't wait to find out what he had in store for her today.

She didn't often participate when her pets were initiating a new member to their numbers. Zeb was in charge of the initiation and she preferred to give the new additions time to acclimate to their surroundings and their harem-mates without her scrutiny. She believed it would be easier for them to become comfortable with their peers if she weren't hanging around watching. Zeb was always honest with her about his opinions afterward. The day after she'd brought Nyla to them, she'd seen right through his admiration for the young woman and had hoped the pair would find love together.

"Come," Nyla said, eyeing her with a smile. "You can take off your clothes now. I promise not to bite." She shed her own loose-fitting robe and stepped down the stairs into the clear water of the pool, beckoning to Belah to follow.

Belah paused and smiled shyly before letting her skirt fall to the ground. Nyla's appraising look made her blush. She'd never been under such scrutiny by one of her pets before. They were always deferential and ready to do her bidding, but she decided she liked seeing this more direct, critical side of Nyla. She would make a good mother.

In fact, Belah decided that if the day went well and she had the right opportunity, she would love to secretly bless Nyla's unborn child. This would be the perfect opportunity for such a thing. It might be her last chance to do it, too, if Nyla and Zeb decided to leave the harem before the child was born.

Her expression must have turned sad, because Nyla approached her again with a concerned look and tugged at her hand. "Come in… the men won't bother us if we don't want them to, but part of the initiation requires you to be with all of them at least once."

Belah nodded silently and tentatively descended one step into the cool water, then another while Nyla watched.

Nyla led her farther into the pool and urged her to sit on one of the raised wooden benches that lay just beneath the surface in the shallower end. She swam to the edge of the pool and came back with a floating tray shaped like a little boat, laden with clay pots and a soft cloth.

The young woman eyed her jewelry with interest.

"You must have been a treasure for your former master," Nyla said. "Those are very pretty jewels. Did it hurt to have them attached?" She reached out one finger and gently touched the scarab that dangled from the tip of one of Belah's nipples.

"I like that it hurt," Belah said, deciding honesty might keep things interesting.

Nyla's eyes widened. "Really?" She scrunched up her nose cutely. "I don't think I would like that. Especially not down there." She gestured to the gleaming jewel that caught the sunlight from between Belah's legs. "I mean, I look forward to the pain of childbirth, but that's an honorable pain. I don't know if I could endure it for any other reason."

"It doesn't hurt now," Belah said. "It actually feels nice, especially when I'm with a man. Or if you touch me like that."

Nyla's gaze shot to Belah's. A soft pink blush rose up her cheeks, but the pretty young pet didn't stop touching. Instead, she reached for a round aromatic bar of soap, lathered it between her hands, and spread the suds over Belah's breasts, then cupped both small mounds in her hands and worked the soap in slowly. She stared in fascination at the tips of Belah's breasts and toyed idly with the small rings. Each little touch sent fresh zings of pleasure straight to Belah's core.

"This doesn't hurt?" Nyla asked.

Belah shook her head. "Not a bit," she said and moved to reach for a cloth. Nyla stopped her with a hand on her wrist.

"No, no. If I were the mistress, I would do all the washing, from top to bottom. So just be still and let me, okay?"

Nyla wasn't lying. Belah relished pampering her pets in just this way—drawing their pleasure out slowly made it all the sweeter when they released their Nirvana for her to consume. Belah dropped her hand back to her side and let Nyla continue soaping up her body. After a moment, Nyla urged her to stand on top of the submerged bench and turn so that the young slave could gently wash her backside and the backs of her thighs. Nyla was gentle and thorough, and took her time rubbing the lathered soap up and down her legs. She moved around to Belah's front, sliding her hands back up her inner thighs and taking care to gently spread apart Belah's folds to soap between. Belah let out a soft sigh when Nyla's fingers stroked over her swollen clit.

When Nyla urged her to turn again, Belah saw they had a small audience standing at the edge of the pool. Zeb and Nikhil stood side by side, watching avidly. Nikhil had removed his shirt and was as bare-chested as any of the other male pets, though he stood out among them with his height and powerful build. The other men were fit and attractive, but not one of them watched her with such raw hunger as she saw in Nikhil's eyes.

Nyla urged her back down into the water and helped her lie back and submerge herself to clean her face and head. She let the young woman support her while she floated on the surface, looking up at Nyla's pretty face.

"They're excited to try you out. Such a pretty new slave is a treat for us, you know. You're the first one who's come since I joined the harem."

"What was it like for you?" Belah asked, genuinely curious about the process.

Nyla's eyes sparkled as she glanced at the crowd at the edge of the pool. Her gaze landed on Zeb and Belah saw another flush tinge her cheeks.

"When I was initiated, they started by rubbing sweet oils into my skin from head to toe. All those hands on me was nice. They rubbed it into every part of me to make sure I was ready to take each one of the men. The women kept rubbing me all over while the men took turns filling me and taking their pleasure. I had to endure it for hours, to hold back my own release until Zeb told me I could. You see, the mistress likes it best when we are needier—when we hold back so long that it's like a… a storm cloud finally letting loose the rain."

As she spoke, her hand traveled up and down Belah's torso, scooping water and rinsing the last bit of soap off her skin. She dipped her hand between Belah's thighs again and spread her open letting the water lap at her hot flesh.

"I think you're ready," Nyla said when her fingertips found Belah's slick core and slid inside and back out. "You're excited about this, aren't you? Is it the big warrior who brought you that you like the most, or one of the other men? You can tell me if it's Zeb. If he is the one you like most, I can tell him to get you started."

Belah let her feet find purchase on the ground again and surveyed the group of her pets as though trying to choose, though she already knew the answer.

"No, Zeb is yours. I want him," she said, pointing at Nikhil. "Do you think he'll want me?"

"I have no doubt," Nyla said in a low voice. "All the men look ready for you, but him especially so."

Nyla twined her fingers with Belah's as they made their way out of the pool. The entire way, Belah's eyes remained locked with Nikhil's. His dark depths were filled with a stronger lust than she had ever seen there before and she let her mind reach out. What she found hidden behind that gaze was an almost terrifying primal craving—a need that burned deep within him to finally fully conquer her, body and soul, and she was ready to give him everything.

CHAPTER ELEVEN

The small crowd of Belah's pets parted, allowing Nyla to lead her back into the harem's quarters where she was pleased to see the sunken central seating area had been arranged with more pillows and soft, colorful blankets.

Nyla directed her to kneel atop one low cushion and Belah obliged, her skin tingling with anticipation as all her other pets came in and arranged themselves against the cushions around her. Some of the women reclined against the men who began idly caressing their breasts. She wanted to look around to find Nikhil, but forced herself to face forward and wait. After a moment, Zeb entered her field of vision, carrying with him the ornate wooden box that held her favorite toys and oils. He set the box down and opened it ceremoniously for Nyla, who extracted one of the small bottles and handed it to one of the waiting men by her side. She passed around a couple other bottles of scented oil, then turned to Belah with a smile.

They began with warm, slow caresses, slick with the fragrant oil sliding over her shoulders and back. Several pairs of hands roamed over her body, front and back. She had no idea which of them were attending to her backside, but Nyla and Zeb diligently massaged the oil into her breasts and belly. They moved in tandem, one on either side, each murmuring the words of a familiar song in harmony with each other.

The rhythmic touches and the sound of the song lulled her and she found herself relaxing more and more. Even when a pair of hands behind her cupped her backside and spread her apart, she only sighed with the pleasure. Another hand slid down between her cheeks, rubbing the oil in little circles around the tight opening. In front of her, Zeb pressed both large hands to the insides of her thighs, urging her to spread them wider, so she did. Nyla slipped a hand between her legs as well, helping Zeb spread her folds apart and rubbing more oil between to mingle with her already copious juices.

"Remember," Nyla whispered, "you must hold back for as long as you can."

Belah sighed and nodded, her mouth open and slack from the pleasure all her pets were giving her at once.

A rougher, harder pair of hands gripped her shoulders suddenly, and pair of lips brushed against her ear. "Bend over, little beast. I want to watch them fuck you now."

Nikhil, yes.

She wanted to speak, but dared not give away how she knew him. Simply knowing his eyes were on her while this happened made her already swollen flesh ache with need to be filled. She hoped *he* would fill her soon, too.

Nyla took her hands and guided her down so that her elbows rested on another pillow before her, then the young woman lay on her back in front of Belah and spread her bronze thighs wide, displaying her sweet cunt for Belah to see.

"You will bring us all to our peaks before you reach your own today," Nyla said while she drizzled a thin stream of golden oil onto her bare mound. The oil trickled slowly between her pink folds, and Belah accepted the invitation to touch her finally. She bent close, moving forward just enough to brace her elbows between Nyla's thighs and stroke her fingertips from the top of Nyla's mound down to the bottom of her open slit, spreading the oil as she went. Resting on one arm, she used her other hand to slowly rub the oil in, though she became distracted when someone else's hand began the same treatment with her own backside.

More oil hit the rosebud of her ass at the same time she bent to press her mouth against Nyla's waiting cunt. She lost herself to the flavor of the woman in front of her and the sensation of a pair of rough, familiar hands kneading and toying with her ass. Of course Nikhil would eagerly take the opportunity to torment her this way, and she would happily accept whatever he chose to do to her now.

His fingers slicked up and down between her thighs, rubbing her juices and the oil over her ass repeatedly until she wanted to beg him to finally fuck her—to do something—*anything* besides torture her. She let out a soft moan against Nyla's clit when the cool, smooth sensation of one of her favorite plugs met the brief resistance of her opening then slid in, stretching her and stretching her until she gasped in surprise. He'd chosen the biggest toy in the box—so big she had no doubt he must intend to replace it with his cock later. At least she hoped he would.

Once the plug was seated snugly in her ass, his hands slid up her spine slowly and his fingers squeezed at the back of her neck, pressing her harder into Nyla's pussy.

"You ready to get fucked now, little beast?" he said gruffly into her ear. "Make this pretty one come first, and then you can have your first cock."

Belah murmured her assent into Nyla's tangy opening and began tonguing her in earnest. She couldn't bear that heavy pressure in her ass, teasing her with the desire to have her cunt filled, too. Nyla's hips rose up to meet her sucking mouth and swirling tongue, the woman's hands gripping the sides of Belah's head. Soon, she was crying out her ecstasy and Belah's tongue was flooded with her delicious juices and the fresh flood of power from Nyla's climax.

She licked Nyla's pussy once more and pulled back to see Zeb at his lover's side. He gave Nyla a slow kiss and moved around to position himself at Belah's rear. Nyla moved away and a shadow took her place. Nikhil's knees came into view before he lowered himself to a kneeling position, his engorged cock proud and stiff before her.

"My turn," he said. "And Zeb's."

In one swift motion that he had to have planned, he pushed his cock between her lips at the same time as Zeb's thick, hard length rammed deep into her waiting pussy. Belah moaned around Nikhil and let him control the speed with which he thrust into her mouth. She closed her eyes, opening her mouth wide and greedily sucking, wondering if she could get away with a subtle shift of her tongue to tease the underside of his cock in the way she knew he loved.

Her body was nothing more than a vessel meant to accommodate the pair of cocks filling her now. Zeb fucked her harder than he ever had, which surprised and excited her. The harder he pounded into her, the closer he brought her to the edge of pain, which nearly sent her spinning into oblivion. It was a struggle to hold onto her sanity, being filled so completely by the two men along with the thick plug filling her ass and shifting slightly with each fresh push of Zeb's cock.

"That's right, little beast," Nikhil said, cupping the side of her face with one hand while his other still gripped hard at the back of her neck, fingers digging in almost painfully. "Take my cock deep. Suck it harder. Yes, sweet thing, use your tongue like that. Fuck!"

His steady thrusts grew more and more erratic when she finally let her tongue shift just enough that the twin forks at the tip could tickle at the underside and tease repeated at the sensitive membrane below the opening. Nikhil groaned and pulled out of her abruptly, but he left the very tip of his thick head pressed against her lips and his hand still cupped the back of her head while his hot seed shot into her open mouth. Belah closed her eyes and savored his delicious flavor, so hot and sweet and permeated with the power that surged into her where their skin came in contact. It was all she could do to suppress the need to let go when Zeb's climax hit and his energy surged into her like a blast.

Nikhil moved away and another of her pets took his place. This time it was another of the females who smiled as she reclined before Belah, her legs spread wide and her pussy well-oiled and glistening. Another cock sheathed deep in Belah's hot cunt, and she recognized the familiar, thick curve of Idrin's ebony appendage, no doubt curved that way specifically to torture her with pleasure.

In his thickly accented voice, he said, "The warrior tells us you enjoy rough play. That your pleasure comes from pain. Is this true?" As he said it, he bent over her, covering her back with his chest and reaching around to tug at the rings that pierced her nipples. Belah gasped at the sudden jolts of pain that shot through her, making her cunt clench hard around his cock.

"Yes! Please, oh, I love that most, but you're going to make me come."

Idrin let out a low, honey-sweet chuckle but refused to stop tugging at the scarabs that adorned her breasts. "You will have to hold on, little one," he said. "This is a new thing for me and I think I like it too much to stop just yet. Perhaps my cock in your pretty bottom will hurt as nice as your little buds?"

He squeezed her nipples once more before leaning back again. The heavy thickness of the plug slid out of her, the friction so tantalizing when coupled with the slow thrusts of Idrin's cock. She forced herself to bury her face in her female pet's pussy, hoping for a distraction. Idrin had one of the most magnificent cocks of all her male pets—she had chosen him for that reason in particular. Only Nikhil's cock was a more amazing piece of male anatomy, in her eyes.

When the glorious weight of Idrin's head pressed against her already tender rear opening, she braced herself for an even greater stretch. Even though she was adept at accommodating something that large, it was still a shock the first time he pushed into her. The plug had only gone a little way in preparing her, and while she was still slick from the oil, the pain of his girth made her gasp and cry out.

Nikhil was beside her then, reclining on a large pillow and resting his cheek against the thigh of the woman Belah had her tongue buried inside until the moment of Idrin's invasion. He reached a hand toward her and cupped her cheek.

His eyes searched hers, almost wild in their inspection. He pulled her face close and kissed her hard, then whispered in her ear, "Your pain drives me wild, *Tilahatan*. I can't wait to fuck you properly myself, but I won't until every part of you is dripping with your pets' juices. This is your lesson not to neglect them."

Belah let out a whimper of assent, which was all she could manage with Idrin's cock pushing deep into her ass.

The female pet in front of her made an impatient noise and Nikhil's hand went to the back of Belah's head, pushing her down again. She lapped eagerly at the sweet, slick flesh that throbbed under her tongue. Her own clit ached, the weight of the little jeweled scarab teasing at it with every thrust of Idrin's cock. She needed more. Already flush with energy, the only thing remaining was her own need to be sated, but she couldn't let herself climax until all her pets had first.

When the woman's cries grew loud and her hips bucked against Belah's mouth, she pulled back, giving Nikhil a look of triumph as she licked her lips. His eyes narrowed and he surged toward her, hungrily pressing his lips onto hers and licking the other woman's juices off before plunging his tongue deep inside her mouth.

His urgency nearly threw Idrin off balance, but the big man behind her adjusted easily. He shifted positions with his cock still inside her and pulled her down with him. She groaned at the change in position and the friction of his cock in her ass. Idrin's hands went to her thighs, cupping her behind the knees and pulling her legs up wide while his hips slowly pushed up into her.

Sweet Mother, he was good. He was opening up her pussy, giving access to whoever else chose to take her. Belah let her head fall back on his shoulder and nuzzled at his neck.

"Do you want her now, master?" Idrin asked, and Belah only idly realized that he was speaking to Nikhil.

"Not yet."

Belah opened her eyes just enough to see Nikhil hovering over her. His eyes were half-lidded and glazed with the same hunger she recognized from their evenings alone—the look he got when he was holding back until he was sure she'd had her fill of the pain he bestowed on her. One of his hands slid down her torso and between her thighs. Idrin still held her tightly behind the knees, pulling her legs wide and displaying her wet pussy to the entire room.

Nikhil barely touched her, though. His fingers slipped down her folds, teasing past her clit to the place where Idrin's body joined with hers. The sensation, even as light as it was, made Belah moan.

But instead of moving to fuck her himself, Nikhil stood and motioned to Belah's remaining pets.

One by one, the men fell to their knees between her thighs and fucked her while Idrin held her hard against his chest, his cock idly pushing in and out of her ass like he had nowhere better to be. Belah had trained them to her standards, after all, and they could hold back their orgasms for as long as she desired them to.

Nikhil stood watching, his cock as huge and erect as the trunk of a palm tree, yet he seemed content to watch her get fucked by all her own pets. While she looked at him, with yet another cock shooting into her, he smiled.

The lazy spread of his lips made her entire body quiver and it was all she could do not to come. The wicked glint in his eyes was what gave her the biggest thrill. That look meant he had something even bigger than this planned. It was almost frightening how devious his mind could be, yet every time she used her powers to understand him, all she felt was his deep hunger to dominate her, which was exactly what she wanted.

She surrendered to that hunger yet again, abandoning herself to the pleasure and pain being inflicted on her now. Idrin's cock in her ass was simultaneously the best sensation and the worst. With every stroke, she came close to orgasm, and with every stroke, she felt such exquisite agony she nearly made him stop. Soon the spend of the other men fell down between her legs and coated Idrin's cock, making her ass slick enough for him to push into her with little resistance. She let her head fall back against his shoulder as her pets took their turns.

Multiple fingers toyed at her jeweled breasts, and even at the ring that adorned her clit, while numerous cocks fucked her, one by one. She needed to come soon and struggled to hold back. She wanted Nikhil in her when she did. And she wanted Nyla within easy reach. Yet she didn't know how she could articulate the need.

Idrin's lips pressed against her ear and his arm twined around her shoulders, pulling her closer to him.

"I know who you are, Mistress. I like your games. This one was unexpected, but I'm glad to be buried inside you now, to be able to witness you helpless in the face of pleasure for once. I want you to come with my cock inside you, Mistress, just once." He slid one large hand from the back of her knee down until his long fingers pressed between her thighs. Her cunt was empty now and his fingertips teased at her raw, slick flesh, toying with her piercing with deliberate little tugs that sent the perfect combination of sensations through her clit until she thought she'd go mad from the effort to restrain her climax.

"No!" she cried. "Not yet, please." Her gaze shot wildly to Nikhil, imploring him to finally take her. "Please," she whimpered.

But Nikhil only gestured for one of her slaves to move into position. "Clean her with your tongue," he said. Belah let out a low groan when the obedient male pet settled between her thighs and his tongue went to work licking and sucking all the collected juices from her aching folds. By the time he was finished and Nikhil gestured for him to leave, her entire body vibrated with the pent-up energy of her orgasm.

Nikhil moved with slow, deliberate motions as he positioned himself between her thighs. Belah couldn't keep her eyes off him as he studied her parted folds, as though inspecting the previous pet's diligence in cleaning her up for him. Fresh wetness flooded from her, coating her inner thighs and no doubt covering Idrin's balls as well. His cock continued to push in and out of her, each movement adding to her already addled state, but she needed to hold off longer. She needed Nikhil's cock filling her, too, and she wanted to somehow have Nyla close so she could bless the woman's unborn child with her power when she came.

Seeming to approve of the state of her pussy, Nikhil finally pressed the head of his cock to her tender flesh, beginning with a teasing swipe from the piercing down the length of her slit. He pushed into her so slowly she wanted to curse, but knew it would ruin the ruse for the rest of her pets if she spoke out. As it was, her lower body was trapped by Idrin's solid grip, his breathless whispers hot in her ear reminding her how excited he was for her to finally come with him inside her.

She turned her head, looking for Nyla, and spied the woman reclining against Zeb, who was gently stroking between her spread thighs while the pair of them watched the scene together. Nyla's eyes met hers and she smiled encouragingly. Throwing caution to the wind, Belah swept her tongue out to lick her lower lip, making sure Nyla saw the bluish tinge and forked tip of her true tongue. With what little power she could focus through the barrage of distracting sensations, she reached for the woman's mind and subtly urged her to come to her.

Nyla crawled across the blanketed floor, her pregnant belly full and round beneath her. When she reached Belah, she kissed her with the languid pleasure of someone who knew they had the upper hand.

"I knew, you were special," Nyla whispered. "None of us have ever lasted as long as you have. You have the endurance of the Mistress, so why am I not surprised? You are her, aren't you? Don't worry, I will keep your secret."

Belah could only nod. Her eyes fluttered shut as Nikhil pulled his cock out and shoved back in hard, the tight friction and fullness from both men pushing her closer to the point of no return.

Nyla watched, entranced, as Nikhil's cock slid in and out of Belah's pussy, until Belah whispered her name again and reached a hand out to grip Nyla's hip, urging her closer. The female's luscious scent hit Belah's nostrils at the same moment Nyla's aura surged with the arousal of awareness of what Belah wished. Belah shifted her upper torso just enough so Nyla could carefully position herself with her glistening cunt parted over Belah's mouth, one knee wedged between Belah and Idrin's shoulders.

Belah reached up with both hands, bracing them on the backs of Nyla's spread thighs, and slid her tongue against her pet's delicious, juicy folds. Nyla let out a sweet little cry of pleasure when Belah's twin forks swirled over and over her clit, her aura pulsing wildly.

Belah was only half aware of her tongue's actions. The pounding thrusts between her thighs made it difficult to concentrate on much else. Idrin had stopped moving much beneath her, but his breaths came hot and fast against her neck and his chest heaved beneath her. The hot press and friction of Nikhil's huge cock had conquered them both, it seemed.

Beyond the swell of Nyla's thighs, Belah heard Nikhil's voice repeating rough and commanding, "Come now, little beast. Come on these cocks that fuck you. We are ready."

His rough hands slid down her thighs, beneath where Idrin gripped her, and with one thumb he rubbed at her clit. Nyla's hips ground back and forth above her mouth, sharp little cries coming from the woman as Belah fucked into her with her elongated tongue. Her pet reached down and squeezed Belah's breasts, toying and pinching at her nipples almost distractedly as her aura swelled, filling with more power with every stroke of Belah's tongue.

The three auras blended together in a delicious mixture of energy that Belah craved to absorb. She let herself be enveloped in them, closing her eyes and relishing the sensory overload. Nikhil's voice repeated his command again and again and she let the moment stretch for just a little longer. That split second between needing release and giving herself over to it was like the space between a thought and an action. Time stood still and the universe opened up for her.

She plunged into the abyss with a cry, barely able to reach up and focus the flood of her energy where she wished it to go. It still flowed out of every pore, but with her palms pressed against Nyla's rounded belly, she directed the bulk of it to the child within.

Children, she hastily amended. *Twins*. She laughed delightedly against Nyla's spread pussy at the realization. Such a good omen, and to have them both be dragon blessed. She had given back more today than she'd kept by neglecting her pets.

Only a breath of a moment later, the other three echoed her cry. Nyla's hands went to her belly, covering Belah's and clutching them tight as her hips bucked with her orgasm.

Beneath her, Idrin thrust hard, holding her down against his pulsing cock as it shot deep inside. And between her thighs, Nikhil let out a loud curse and sank once more to the hilt until the flood of his semen filled her. The entire time their energy coursed through her, her orgasm persisted and she became a conduit for the magic. It flowed from her lovers, into her body, and with the force of a thought she aimed it back through the palms of her hands into the pair of unborn babies inside Nyla's womb.

Blessed children, you will be loved and treasured by dragons. We will be your protectors for as long as you live.

With a sated sigh, Nyla moved to the side and collapsed into Zeb's arms, letting him nuzzle and whisper into her ear.

Idrin slipped out of her and released her legs. Belah was too weak and giddy from the exchange to move, but Nikhil was there, his strong arms scooping her up and pulling her back down as he reclined onto his back, carrying her with him. Around her, her pets sank into the pillows, relaxed and satisfied, their earlier agitation completely gone.

Nikhil's heart thudded beneath her ear, his arms squeezing her to him tightly enough to alarm her. She glanced up to his face and was greeted with an unreadable mask, his dark eyes fixed somewhere above him.

"Thank you," she whispered.

His gaze shifted to meet hers, the muscles of his jaw twitching with tension. Within his eyes she caught a glimmer of that wild beast, as though it were caged and pacing, eager to be set free. Reaching out with her mind, she risked a deeper look, but before her powers could sink into his mind, he spoke.

"Never again, *Tilahatan*. This was my gift to you, but *never* again will another male lay hands on you, whether he be slave or king, or even a god. You are mine."

CHAPTER TWELVE

Nikhil led her back the way they came without giving her the opportunity to bathe again.

"It is time for the mistress to judge her worth," he'd said shortly to Belah's pets, who gaped at his abrupt manner in the aftermath of their orgy.

Nyla tried to object, but Belah shot her a warning look as Nikhil fastened the collar around her neck again and yanked her toward the door while she was still hurriedly wrapping the skirt back around her waist.

A cool evening breeze blew through the palace's public courtyard as he led her back through. The slick remnants of pleasure her pets had left all over her skin dried into tight patches, no doubt visible to anyone who glanced at her. The people did more than glance this time. They openly stared and pointed. Belah could hear the thread of rumors beginning like a pebble tossed in a pond—had she displeased the empress? What would happen to her?

In spite of their derision, Belah's senses went wild. Her nipples hardened more with every utterance of the word "whore" and her pussy grew hot with the tittered suggestions that she might be forced to spread her legs for all of them, if the empress wished. Belah would have never tortured anyone that way, but knew she wasn't immune to rumors. None of her subjects seemed to live in fear of such a threat, at any rate, as their auras all pulsed with avid interest.

A harsh yank of her collar brought her up short.

Nikhil stepped around her in the center of the courtyard and all the curious citizens shrank back. His eyes flashed wildly beneath his brows as he stared at them all.

"You are all ungrateful peons!" he yelled. "Your empress expects more respect from you for her other subjects. This young woman just endured a harrowing test. Which she passed. Her reward is a night with her goddess. You should all be so lucky."

Grumbling, he moved on and Belah followed, dazed by his outburst. When they reached her room he pushed her to her knees and let her leash fall to the ground before disappearing back out the door.

Belah remained there, dazed and staring at the floor for a few moments, until Nikhil returned with a bustling column of her servants, each one toting a bucket of steaming water, which they carried into her bathing chamber and dumped into her tub. She watched as though outside herself for the first time that day, too confused by her experience, followed by Nikhil's shift in mood, to be able to properly process how she should react. He was fully in control now, and seemed to understand as much. When the last servant exited her room, Nikhil stripped naked, then returned to her.

"Look at me, *Tilahatan*," he said softly, kneeling down to her level and nudging her chin up with one gentle finger.

She raised her head and met his gaze. Deep weariness filled in his gaze, reminding her of the day she'd found him on his death bed. If she didn't know better, she might think he'd just returned from a protracted battle, and one hard-won. She ached to tell him that he *had* won, in the end. He had her heart.

His rough fingertips grazed her bare scalp and moved lower, unclasping her collar and throwing it across the room. Then he abruptly scooped her into his arms and carried her into her bath chamber, lowering them both into the steaming water.

The tub was large enough for them both to stretch out comfortably, but he kept her cradled in his arms, holding her on his lap while he gently cleaned her with a soft cloth. His hand moved over her with swift efficiency, rubbing the sweet soap into her skin over and over until every remnant of the day had been removed. He dipped the cloth between her thighs and she opened up for him obediently, though she expected the same rough, quick, utilitarian movements he'd used on the rest of her body.

He slowed when he pressed the cloth against her folds, and for the first time, Belah realized how ragged his breathing was and how tightly his shoulders were bunched beneath the arm she had draped over them.

She reached down and guided his hand against her, the strokes meant to clean more than arouse, but his fist clenched and stilled, refusing to be budged.

She took a deep breath, letting herself absorb the emotions flowing out of him. Nothing but want reached her. Desire for her to be his alone, to share with no other, but his underlying need to satisfy her overrode that desire. He defined himself by her satisfaction. Yet he still presented himself like her master.

"I do not like you like this." His voice grated coarsely against her ear. "You are not a slave and I would not make you one, ever. I don't wish to own you the way you own your pets. Whatever you give to me, I need to know you give it freely and not because I torture it from you. Please… bring my little beast back. Show me I have not broken your spirit today." Nikhil's words cracked with emotion, the hitch in his voice finally giving Belah the jolt she needed to understand what he feared. He didn't want her docile any more than she did him. Without that flame of rebellion and wildness inside him, she would never have been drawn to him. Seeing her submit to a roomful of slaves had been too much for him to witness.

Belah slipped off his lap, letting herself sink beneath the water. She held her breath, remaining beneath the surface with her eyes closed. In the hot cocoon of her bath, all her senses dulled except the awareness of her magic. She ached to calm his worry and could have easily with her breath, but knew he needed so much more than a temporary remedy today. If only she could offer him a permanent remedy instead. Beneath the water she let the illusion of the slave girl dissolve. As she rose from beneath, her preferred human shape returned as though being born fresh.

Nikhil's gaze slipped down her wet body, the weariness disappearing to be replaced by that desire that he'd left banked. When she let her horns and a glimmer of her scales appear, his need blazed hotter. If she had requested, she sensed he would surrender to her now, and let himself be commanded. He would kneel before his goddess.

Instead, she simply slid back into his lap, smiling at his surprise.

"Nikhil. I am yours."

His hands squeezed, holding her closer as he pulled back slightly to look at her. "Are you really? Can you tell me with certainty that there isn't some piece of you that you hold in check? If you are *mine*, truly, I want more. I don't want to hide behind some glamour to be with you in public."

"You wish to be my consort? That would be a public declaration of your service to me. It could never be the other way around."

He regarded her silently, his gaze flitting from the tips of her horns down over her sapphire-colored scales. Even her nipples were blue when she shifted to this degree, letting just enough of her true nature show. Nikhil raised one wet hand and hooked the tip of his pinky through one shining golden ring, tugging just to the point of pain.

Belah's power surged, resulting in a flash from her eyes that was reflected as blue light in his pupils.

In a gruff voice he asked, "What does your kind do? Surely, you take mates? Or do you only breed with your own brothers?"

The question made her stiffen in his arms. "The legends are often fabricated for effect, I hope you realize," she said, avoiding his gaze.

"I am not blind, little beast. Your brother was careful, but I could see plainly how his visit affected you. The two of you share too much. But I am not concerned with what gods and goddesses do together. My entire life I have heard the stories of how close you and Osiris are—what you once shared. What I want is to give you the thing you wish for. Let me give you a child."

"What makes you think this is the thing I want?" Belah's mind whirled, trying to remember where Nikhil had been during her conversation with Ked. Normally she would have been aware of his every movement through her palace, but her brother's magic had the confounding ability to distract her and dull her own power when he was near. Ked would have known if Nikhil was listening. So if Nikhil eavesdropped somehow, it had to have been her brother's doing.

"Isn't it?" Nikhil asked. Beneath Belah's backside, his cock stiffened.

He reached a hand up to turn her head back so their eyes met, and she let him, unable to control her own reaction because she wanted it. Her nature made her crave it. Normally her mark on a man would be enough to incite her desire to breed with him. She'd always viewed that tactic as an artificial incentive. With Nikhil she knew that love, and perhaps his Blessing, were enough to make her want a child with him. The problem was that the mark was still required to make it happen.

"I can't want it with you," she said, tears welling in her eyes. Her lip began to quiver and she bit it viciously.

"Why not? I would become your consort in public. We could have our own vows in private—with Meri and your brother, and whoever else knows who you truly are. I'd hoped after all this time with me you would already carry my child, but now I believe it isn't so simple with you. What do we need to do, Belah?"

Belah stared at him, confounded by his use of her name. She was always either elevated by his words of grandeur or diminished by his sweet pet names. He'd called her Belah again for the second time in as many weeks. Not "little beast," or his favorite version of "goddess." He'd used her name. Right now, they weren't adversaries in any way. They weren't a master and his beast. They weren't a goddess and her subject. They were two people in love, and he wanted to know how to make her his bride.

Tears trickled over her cheeks, unbidden, and her eyelids burned.

"Nikhil, I'm immortal. You are not. If I mated you, my power would overwhelm you to the point that you would be my slave. I will never make you a slave."

He nodded gravely, his jaw set. After a moment, his brows rose again. "I would become like you if I could. Is there not a magic spell that can transform me? I want to be your equal, Belah."

His need pressed into her mind and she clenched her eyes shut tightly. He wanted it so badly, but what he wanted was simply impossible.

"No, my love."

"Never?" he asked.

"I cannot turn you into a dragon, and the only way to make a child with you is to mark you, which I won't do. Not unless you wish to lose your free will. If you only wished to be another of my pets, then I would do it. But even my pets have the power to do as they wish. They are treasured and pampered, but can choose to leave if they wish. You would not have that choice. Sharing my bed means you will live longer than most already. Let us enjoy this time. Perhaps you will tire of me in the future, and then we will part."

A low growl rumbled from his chest and his hands squeezed her hip.

"Never, *Tilahatan*. Now that I have you, why would I ever desert you? I am yours, mark or not." He rose up out of the water, still gripping her hips, and set her on the edge of her bath. "And you are mine," he said, pushing her knees to her chest, letting her thighs fall wide, and looking down at her spread pussy.

Belah's flesh heated and grew thick and full under her lover's gaze. His fingers parted her slowly as he licked his lips, his soft caresses familiar, yet incendiary.

With one finger, he idly flicked the little scarab jewel that was attached to her clit. A jolt of pleasure shot through her.

"Nikhil!"

He chuckled. "I take what's mine."

Slowly, he bent and captured first her scarab between his lips, letting it pull at her flesh, then swiped his tongue lower, tickling up between her cleft and lingering in a slow swirl at her clit. Belah leaned back onto her elbows and then lay back entirely, enjoying the languid way he devoured her, as though she were a special treat prepared just for him to savor. He seemed content to simply taste her, without pushing her higher. He preferred to make her come while giving her pain, which was her preference, too. Every nerve in her body was under his control during those moments—every sensation hers to feel under his touch, and she wanted them all. He would work up to it, and she would relish each slow stretch of pleasure tiered one atop the other.

"I want to be mates in the eyes of the gods. Husband and wife, the two of us." His dark gaze met her from between her thighs, but Belah only wanted him to keep doing what he was doing.

She grabbed his thick hair and pressed his face back to her core.

He licked her once and raised up over her, pulling her hands away from his head and holding them above her head with one hand.

"Little beast, remember who your master is." As if to emphasize his point, one thick finger swirled in the well of her pussy, gathered moisture, then slid deep into her ass. Belah squirmed, elated by the pleasure of that invasion. She alternated between wanting to expel him and keep him tight inside her.

"You had that Nubian in your ass today. He was big, and you didn't complain. I want what he had. And I promise I'll do more justice to your ass than he could ever think of."

Before she could process his comment further, Nikhil flipped her body and pulled her toward him until she was forced to step back into the bath with her hips bent over the edge. Out of the corner of her eye, she saw him reach for the cloth again and the bar of sweet-smelling soap.

Again, he parted her folds, this time with soapy fingers, working his way up and down along her slit and over her spread ass cheeks. Each slick sweep of his fingers made her hotter. Suddenly, he smacked her hard on the ass with one wet hand, the moisture making the contact sting in a way it wouldn't have had they both been dry.

Wet heat flooded between her thighs and she tilted her hips against the rounded edge of her bathtub, needing the sharp pleasure of her scarab to rub harder at her clit.

Again, he smacked her, harder this time. "No moving, little beast. I need to wash the spunk of all those other men off you before I take my fill tonight. The dark one came deep in you, didn't he?"

Belah's mind was already wild with pleasure, and she had trouble processing his words at first. "The dark one" was another term used for her brother, and the suggestion brought back an ancient memory that made her almost cry in protest. Of all the illicit things she had done in her long life, her relationship with Ked was still sacred. They were long past that phase of their lives, and the loss they'd shared was something neither of them spoke of anymore.

Nikhil's avid attention to her tender ass reminded her what he really meant by that comment and his earlier reference to the Nubian. Belah had all but forgotten about the day, but now the events returned in vivid detail. Idrin, with his black-as-night skin and his cock buried deep in her backside. She'd been a different person then, one who would be willing to take whatever they chose to give.

Nikhil swirled his soapy fingertips around her slick, tight opening before she could reply. He plunged a thumb into her and fucked in and out with the most delicious roughness that was all the more exciting for how straightforward he was about it, twisting it like he needed to scrub her from the inside out. The invasion was rough enough to cause pain and make her push back toward him, her cunt throbbing. From beside the bath, he grabbed an empty ewer and filled it from the bathwater, pouring it over her while he spread her open with the fingers of his other hand.

Steaming hot water sluiced over her tender flesh, searing her with pleasure. It didn't hurt, but the extreme temperature change shocked her in the best way. She'd never felt such heat beyond a strike or the pain of the piercings he'd given her. Every bit of pain Nikhil bestowed on her was sacred to her, and this heat in particular thrilled her for its newness. She loved the tender, escalating burn of it that aroused all sensation, coming close to pain and almost surpassing it. What would it feel like if the pain escalated gradually?

"You like the heat, beast? Maybe I could better cleanse you with my own seed."

With another smack on her ass, he urged her to stand. Belah followed him out of the tub, hypersensitive to his touch when he dried her off and led her to her bed, wondering how he would replicate that sensation. She was at his mercy, but could still direct his attention in some ways.

He treated her so delicately in these in-between moments, as though he reverted to the worshiper rather than the master when he wasn't giving her pleasure. These were the moments when his love showed the most.

Now he gripped her hand in his and led her through her chamber, looking back with adoration every few seconds, enraptured with her every step.

When her horns hooked one of the sheer draperies that hung across a doorway he led her through, she remembered she'd been slightly shifted the entire time. In the confused tangle, he laughed and pulled the cloth off, smiling down at her and smoothing his hand up over the length of her horn.

Her nostrils flared at the sudden sensation and she let out a moan. She'd forgotten how sensitive her horns could be in the right hands. Specifically, in the hands of someone who truly loved her. Sweet Mother, he loved her, didn't he?

She shouldn't have doubted it, and didn't when he positioned her on the bed on hands and knees with both her wrists and ankles bound.

Subdued, she let herself relax, waiting for his touch again, aching with her face against her soft pillow while her ass and cunt felt the cool breeze from her courtyard. She could only hear him moving around in her room.

The room illuminated around her gradually, the change increasing her anticipation of whatever he had planned tonight. He hadn't disappointed her yet. The scent of beeswax was unmistakable when he finally came into her field of vision a little later, his large hand caressing a hot line over the curve of her back.

"Close your eyes," he said.

When she did, every one of her remaining senses came alive. He continued to rub his hand gently up and down her back, the warm caress comforting, but not what she really hoped for. The aroma of the candles he'd lit surrounded her almost as potently as his own spicy musk, and his aura crackled with unspent need as though the entire afternoon had only been a diversion for him.

Suddenly the idle caress of his fingertips along her back was punctuated with a sharp burn of extreme heat that made her cry out in surprise. The scent of candlewax grew even stronger as the searing line made its way along the length of her spine in a molten path.

"You like this, don't you?" Nikhil rumbled, the gravelly sound of his voice betraying his arousal.

"Yes." Belah could only whisper, unwilling to disturb the exquisite pleasure she experienced. The hot wax lit up more than the nerves it came into contact with. The heat seared her in the line it made down her spine, but spread out in slow tingles over her entire body.

Nikhil shifted beside her and her pussy clenched with need and anticipation of whatever he would do to her next. Another hot line made its way down her back, and then another, but each time he let the line stop just above the swell of her ass.

Nothing he'd done to her before had ever incited such deep need for more. This little game of his was the ultimate tease— inflicting just the right amount of heat that lingered on the edge of pain without going over, but that made her skin ultra-sensitive to the point that even the lightest touch made her shiver with deeper desire.

A warm breeze blew through her room, carrying the scent of jasmine from her garden and making the wax that coated her back harden and tighten on her skin. She let out a little sigh at the new sensation, but it turned into a fresh cry of pleasure when hot wax suddenly dripped right on top of the swell of one ass cheeks and rivulets of the molten fluid began to trickle down the slope, tickling closer and closer to the center.

Her muscles were already clenching in anticipation of that hot line making its way further, but it must have hardened before reaching all the way.

"More, please!" she cried, already panting breathlessly, her cunt a hot bundle and her clit swollen so full that her little scarab rubbed tightly against the sensitive flesh beneath her hood.

"Shhh," Nikhil said, his breath hot in her ear. "I have a mind to keep at it until all the candles are spent. Tell me, little beast, what did you enjoy best about today? Being the toy for a roomful of your horny pets?"

"This," she said, knowing it was true. "Everything you do to me is my favorite thing. Everything you have yet to do."

"Mmm. I do enjoy surprising you."

Belah heard the soft pop of a cork and the scent of her sweet oil hit her nostrils, followed by a sudden, hot drizzle directly at the peak of the cleft between her ass cheeks. She cried out, surprised. That he'd had the foresight to heat the oil up should not have surprised her—the man always knew what would please her the most. As the oil's heat moved, she let out a low moan, again savoring how perfectly the heat of it hit that perfect knife edge of pain of every nerve ending it passed over without actually leaving them deadened in the wake.

When his fingertip teased around her puckered opening afterward, every part of her came alive. He dipped his fingertip in, coating her with oil, but instead of tease her more with his hands or his cock, instead she felt something a little cooler and slightly textured press at her opening. It was an unfamiliar sensation—not like any of the dildos she kept in her collection, but still rounded at the end and cylindrical in shape. He pushed it in slowly and then stopped, giving her a little tap at the center of her lower back.

"Hold tight to the candle, or else you'll set the bed on fire."

Belah groaned with understanding and subtle elation at this new game. When the first drip of hot wax made its way down the column of the candle and pooled at its base, she almost couldn't differentiate it from the hot wetness flooding her pussy. Nikhil spread her open with his fingers, and the even hotter flood of oil covered every swollen inch of her aching folds. He followed up with the cool, smooth weight of the largest dildo in her collection, pushing it slowly into her clenching depths. It was a struggle, then, to keep her ass clenched tightly around the candle while he fucked into her with the thick, round shaft, a toy she'd had carved and polished from jade to mimic the length, heft, and shape of one of her own kind. She rarely used it because it was meant for play when she had another dragon in her bed, which had been rare enough before, and likely would never occur again if she figured out how best to keep the man who currently fucked her with that exquisite toy.

The dragon dildo spread her pussy wider than she'd ever been stretched in her human form, hitting every single nerve ending inside her with its varied ridges and carved veins. He continued fucking it in and out of her, driving her to distraction when she sensed him move and his hands brushed against her nipples where their scarabs barely brushed the bedclothes beneath her. He teased her only briefly and when his hand moved away to rest on her shoulder, heavy weights stretched suddenly at her breasts, pulling her nipples taught and sending fresh pain through her.

She let out a sharp cry, confused by the new sensation until she opened her eyes to glance beneath her. Hanging from each little loop of her scarabs on golden hooks were two heavy globes, deceptively weighty for their small size.

"You can endure the pain, or give yourself relief. Your choice, little beast."

The pain, for all its newness, was likely to send her over the edge, and she wasn't quite ready for that. Not until he told her he was ready for her to climax. Belah pressed her cheek and shoulders into the bed to give her breasts enough relief. The heat accumulating around her ass was slowing, the more the wax built up and cooled, protecting her heated skin from more direct contact—at least until Nikhil discovered it and peeled the warm layer away. The removal of the wax from her skin was a sensation all its own, particularly from the sensitive flesh of her ass, and nearly set off a chain reaction. Her vaginal walls clenched tightly around the dildo, the bulbous end of it meant to represent testicles rubbed against her clit when it sank deep, and Belah almost lost it completely.

"Not yet, my love," Nikhil whispered in response to her desperate whimper. "Not until this candle is spent."

CHAPTER THIRTEEN

Belah lost track of time, engrossed as she was in the effort to stave off the orgasm that loomed. She was only aware of the increasing frequency of the hot wax around her anus accumulating, and then being removed by Nikhil, as well as every unbearably delicious sensation that accompanied that process. He fucked her so thoroughly with the dildo she could almost imagine the huge thing was a part of him, and her pussy milked it hard with every slick plunge inside.

Her juices flowed down her thighs and her entire body shook with the need to come. Finally, the weight of the candle dwindled and just as the heat of the flame grew so warm it must be close to the end, Nikhil blew with a sharp gust of breath to extinguish the flame. Instantly, he tugged the candle stub out of her and poured cool oil around her heated opening, shocking her with the sudden shift in temperature. Before she could acclimate to the change, the tip of his cock pressed into her and he shoved in so slowly, every nerve in her body came alight again from the exquisite friction of his entire length sheathing in her tight, stretched opening.

The huge dildo remained buried in her pussy, her muscles clasped so tight around it that there was no way it would slide out without help, and now his balls must be pressed against the end of it. He covered her back, bowing over her as he thrust deep into her ass. He cupped her breasts, making her nipples scream from the sudden renewed pain of the weights that dangled from their tips.

The weights disappeared, thumping down to the bed with little swipes of his thumbs to release them. Above her head, she saw him reach around to untie her wrists, and then his hands were cupping her breasts again and pulling her back up so that her back was flush against his chest and her ass sinking down onto his cock. He slipped one of his hands back down to resume control of the massive jade cock that was held captive inside her tight channel, and with one fresh thrust, she feared she'd fly over the edge yet again.

"Nikhil, please," she whimpered, so inundated with hot, slippery need she thought she'd lose her mind if he didn't command her to find her release soon.

"No words, beast," he growled, and the hand at her breast slid up to clasp around her throat. "If you want to come, you must tell me the truth, do you understand?" The juncture of his thumb and forefinger pressed harder against her windpipe, her airway closing bit by bit. Nikhil's hand was so large he nearly reached entirely around her neck and the power he displayed now made her believe he could snap her neck with just a squeeze, if he chose to.

She had no idea what "truth" he wished for, but the illusion of a mortal threat he held over her now thrilled her so completely it made her begin to tremble from the pent up desire to finally let go. Still, she only wished to please him and she let out a harshly whispered "yes."

He pulled the huge dildo out of her and plunged it back in, sending a fresh ripple of pleasure through her.

"Is this what your brother's cock feels like when he fucks you with it, *Tilahatan*? Is that what you so love about him? How many times did he make you his whore before you found me?"

Nikhil squeezed her throat tighter, his hips bucking hard against her ass as he plunged his cock over and over into her abused backside. He continued fucking her with the dildo with slow, hard thrusts that kept tempo with the throb of her pulse in her ears as her vision dimmed from lack of air to her lungs.

The blackness threatened to overtake her, but as she hovered at the edge of it, she found herself staring into the brightest light, the culmination of every ounce of pleasure he'd given her and the promise of peace if she let herself go. But he hadn't given her leave to let go just yet. She stayed there, unable to speak or move or even think for all the confounding convergence of sensations—pain and pleasure both, and the promise of a tumble into an abyss she had only ever wished for but never come so perfectly close to reaching in her life—her tragically unending life of having to endure loss and shame along with all her power and responsibility for thousands of years.

She found herself losing grip, not on her orgasm but on consciousness entirely, and reveled in that moment, willing him to tell her to come, but succumbing to darkness instead.

"Belah!"

Consciousness came rushing back to her and she gasped loudly. All movements had stopped and Nikhil's arms wrapped around her in a tight hug. His rough apologies filtered through the haze of need that still blanketed her so thickly she wasn't quite sure where she was.

Finally, a glimmer of his words seeped back into her half-conscious mind and she said, "Let me come and I will tell you everything."

She grabbed his hand in hers, nearly crushing it with the power of her need and pressed it back to her throat.

"No, *Tilahatan*, I can't…" He gasped out the words as though filled with fear, and his aura shimmered around him reflecting as much.

"Nikhil, I need this. Please don't hold back. Tighter, *please*. Take me to the end like this."

He let out a surprised grunt into her ear. "Did he never please you this way… the way I do?"

Belah shook her head. "No man has ever pleased me the way you do. I need you more than you know. Love you more than life. You master me as no other could. Please." Tears streaked her cheeks and he raised his hand from her throat to brush at the wetness.

With a rough, desperate groan, he resumed fucking her. First came the delicious slide of his cock from her ass and the sudden, violent thrust as he pounded back into her. He pulled the dildo out of her and tossed it aside, replacing it with his fingers, first cupping her soaked cunt and rubbing his palm against her clit before dipping four of his fingers into her clenching channel.

"Need to feel you around me when you come, little beast," he rasped in her ear and his aura flared wildly when her muscles tightened around his hand. The blazing red-black of it enveloped her, cocooning her in his need while her own aura surged again to the point of bursting, her energy twining with his.

His hand went back to her throat and squeezed, and at the same moment he sank his teeth into the flesh of her shoulder while he fucked her with renewed vigor, his cock and fingers inside both stretched openings while his hand slowly constricted her breathing again.

"Come for me, my *Tilahatan*. My beast. Mine," he whispered in her ear, pressing warm, strong fingers harder and harder into her throat until the edge loomed again and the comforting blackness lay beyond, waiting for her to fall into it.

With his body filling hers, claiming her, encompassing her, Belah let herself go. The release was so exquisite, so utterly *complete*, she wasn't sure where her orgasm ended and the plunge into that abyss began, but in that moment they were one and the same, and Nikhil had been the only one to ever take her there.

CHAPTER FOURTEEN

B elah found herself blessed with weightlessness more effortless than being carried on the winds. Nothing but light surrounded her, light of every color, as though she'd fallen into a well filled with the magic of generations of her kind. In this place, this wonder of a sanctuary she never believed she'd see, she knew peace for the first time in her centuries-long life. She basked in the absolute lack of burden.

Gravity gradually sank back into her, at first with a tickle, then an itch. The reminder of her one truth made her want to cry out in frustration. She could not die. As often as she wished for it, it could never be. Yet now she knew she could find a respite from the onus of her life, and Nikhil would be there to give it to her.

Except he wouldn't... not forever. Not unless she marked him and made him her slave. What could she do? Lose him to death eventually, or extinguish the spark of sheer dominant will in him that made her love him so much? Give him up to be mated to a lesser beast than she?

Even with the daily infusions of her energy that bonded him to her, he would eventually grow old. Even with the doses of her breath, his Blessing would eventually cause him to lose his mind in other ways. Her race was thousands of years old, yet no one in their history had ever approached her or her siblings with a problem as complicated as this.

But then most dragons were not like her. Most—if not all—preferred being dominant over their human mates or pets.

She still refused to mark him. With a silent, tearful sigh she resolved to never mark him, nor let another have that privilege. She would simply have him for as long as she could, and once the Blessing's power began to overcome his sanity, she would be there to put him down. It would be a gamble which demise he found first—death from old age, or death by her hand.

Slowly she became cognizant of her name being repeated over and over in an urgent whisper close to her ear. Two voices spoke to her now, one was Nikhil's unmistakably male voice, deep and raspy with anguish. The other was her physician, Meri, in a concerned, maternal tone.

Belah forced herself to full consciousness and inhaled sharply at the same instant she opened her eyes.

" *Tilahatan*! Oh, by all the gods, I thought I'd killed you. Please, please forgive me for everything—the things I said before—the things I did."

Belah turned her head to look up into his worried face, so beautiful with its strong angles and long, dark hair. His face, however, was not the same face she'd gone to bed with— the face she looked at now was unshaven, with deep lines of worry and dark circles under his eyes.

"How long was I unconscious?" she asked, dimly aware that her voice came out as barely a whisper.

"Mistress, you were more than unconscious," Meri said gravely from her other side. "Your heartbeat ceased for almost a full day." She glanced over Belah's prone form to Nikhil, whose relief was almost palpable. "It was all I could do to calm the man—he was sure he'd murdered you, as if that were even possible."

Belah lifted a hand to Nikhil's scruffy cheek and caressed him gently. "My love, I have too many things to tell you." To Meri, she said, "Please leave us. I will be fine soon enough."

When her physician closed the door behind her, she tugged at Nikhil's tunic, urgent to see to the first order of business before talking.

"Make love to me. Now."

His reverent stare immediately disappeared, replaced by the rough, primal urgency of the man she knew he truly was. He may have been the most devout man in existence, considering how he worshiped her wholeheartedly as a goddess in the moments when that was called for, but easily became the powerful creature she required who could subdue her own inner beast with a simple touch.

When he covered her with his body, he was too careful, however. Belah needed his energy too much to object. She was only just wet enough for him when he buried himself inside her, and it wasn't until he whispered in her ear, "My fingers itch to wrap around your throat again, *Tilahatan*," that the urgent lust surged through her and her muscles clenched hard around him. The memory of that moment just before she'd descended into the darkness would forever be etched into her mind and his whispered words brought it all back in sharp detail.

"Do it," she pleaded.

Nikhil shook his head, his brow furrowed and a twinge of the fear she'd sensed in him earlier bleeding through his aura.

"Not until you're well, my love."

"I'm well enough now! Just be more careful this time. I need it, and you want it. Please, Nikhil."

When his palm rested hot against her throat again, she almost came in that instant. Not a single ounce of pain was delivered—only his thick cock driving into her and his touch on her skin, his massive form hovering over her smaller body while he fucked her. He wasn't even pressing hard against her throat yet, only resting with the warm pad of his palm against the base of her throat and his fingers and thumb spanning either side.

Nikhil groaned and looked down between them, obviously aware of the change in friction due to the flow of her juices coating his thrusting cock.

When he pressed his hand tighter against her throat, she bucked harder, wanting him deep enough to hurt. He gave her his cock with ever deepening thrusts.

She could sense the boundaries of his self-control being challenged, but he held off, testing her limits bit by bit. He pressed his palm harder and her world went a little darker, her body wanting to struggle against him now. With a smile and an adoring look from her, he began thrusting more frantically into her until her body began its delicious ascent toward climax. At the same time, he squeezed hard against her throat, his eyes wide and wild with need.

"Yes," she mouthed to him, lacking actual breath to speak.

"I love you, Belah," he said, just before his mouth crashed against hers, his tongue plunging deep. He kept his hand against her throat while he kissed her, and she soaked in his climax while her own barreled over her.

Her world went abruptly dark with one more slight press of his palm against her throat—all her worries disappeared again, her overworked brain ceasing to exist, and there was nothing left but sheer sensation. Then his body pressed hot and hard over hers, his large hands on her throat and his glorious cock filling her. Her heart pounded harder than it ever had and her body thrummed from the magic flowing through her. His own energy crashed into hers, flooding her senses enough to make the darkness explode into a wild cacophony of light.

Just when she thought she'd smother completely, he released his hold on her and she felt him *breathe*, straight into her mouth, the hot gust of his life filling her aching, empty lungs.

Belah gasped and opened her eyes. Nikhil's dark, expectant gaze met hers and immediately turned triumphant. She grinned up at him with giddy excitement. His expression shifted toward cocky self-congratulation and he kissed her again.

"Was that the right way to do it, then?" he asked, pulling out of her and moving to her side. He pulled her back against his chest and let his fingers slide over her throat.

Her own fingers drifted up to tangle with his where they rested against her skin. She swallowed once, testing the soreness that lingered. When she spoke again, she sounded husky.

"That was perfect."

He said nothing more, only nuzzling at the back of her neck and letting his hand fall to cup her breast.

Her own hand remained at her throat, marveling at how she had never understood what power a single breath could have—or lack of it, in her case. She knew the power of her own breath, but only as an external influence. How the air inside her lungs could control her pleasure so perfectly, she could never have imagined. Yet he had shown her this part of her, had awakened in her a new need that only he could fulfill.

Soon, his breathing grew steady and even, his aura waning into the comforting, contented glow he normally had during the sleep that followed their lovemaking.

Belah remained awake and thoughtful.

Sometime during the night when the candles were growing low, he roused again, his aura flickering to life with his consciousness an instant before his body. Nikhil was an anomaly of a human in this sense—most took several moments to fully waken to the point of action after their auras signaled consciousness. His alertness was another reminder of the role he had filled for her for so long before she'd taken him to her bed. He was a warrior, and would fight and die for her. He would kill for her, too, but would her particular need for death be too much for him?

She could never die, truly, but now she knew he could give her a semblance of death with the squeeze of his hand around her throat. The same way he could drive her to the brink of insanity with pleasure, he could send her over into a much deeper abyss—one she had craved for centuries.

Beside her, he raised a hand and brushed a dark strand of hair off her cheek, letting his hand trail down her neck and over her breast. He left his hand resting over the full mound. The warmth of it comforted her, but the curious crackle of his aura signaled that he had something complicated to say to her.

"Belah, tell me what he did to you to make you so sad."

She closed her eyes, wishing she didn't have to have this conversation, but he was hers. He owned her heart, knew all her secrets, and was still strong enough to stay. This man would never betray her. So he deserved the truth. All of it.

"We were both complicit, Nikhil. My brother and I have always been close, from birth. When we were born, humanity wasn't as complex and plentiful as it is now, yet we were expected to procreate with this lower race. We were too young then… too young to understand our own powers and the hold they had over us. It's our nature to crave the contact of someone like us. Our brothers and sisters were more forgiving of human foibles, I suppose. Ked and I… we always ached for something deeper."

When she trailed off, he didn't move a muscle and she forced herself to avoid eavesdropping on his emotions. She'd become adept at it after loving him for so long now… she preferred his new games to be a surprise. She might have laughed at the irony—that she knew all the secrets of every one of her subjects, none of whom mattered much to her beyond her overarching protection of them. But he was too sacred to her to delve that deep into.

She still couldn't mistake his clenching jaw and his very apparent restraint when he said, "You found comfort together."

Belah took a deep breath, closed her eyes, and continued. "The humans we'd mated were so primitive then. All we could gain from them was pleasure and offspring. I did my part, as did my brothers and sisters. My soul hurt every time I mated a man who couldn't really know me. He could only worship me and let me fuck him into rapture. Two of them actually died. The others didn't survive long after. Humans were supposed to be our chosen mates. How could they be so perfect if they expired in spite of me mating them?"

Nikhil relaxed and pulled her close against his side. "Did you want these men? These… mates?"

Belah could remember each one in vivid detail. They were all ideal specimens of human male virility. "I wanted every single one. They were all perfect, but as soon as I marked them, they changed. They became tools to breed with—no more present than the toys in my box. Two of them expired mere moments after impregnating me. I have no idea why, either… They just… died. The other four I mated over the next few centuries lasted longer, but were little more than slaves. I didn't want them after they lost their minds to me. This is why I won't mark you, Nikhil. I could have a lower dragon mark you—one with less power than I have—and you might keep your mind, but I won't share you with another, either."

He said nothing, and that lack of response made her skin prickle. She held her breath and closed her eyes, simply soaking in his warmth and wishing the chasm she felt drifting wider between them didn't really exist. When he finally spoke again, she heaved a sigh of relief.

"You could enslave me… a willing subject. Yet you don't. To preserve my sanity?" He pulled her tighter and lifted her chin with one finger, forcing her to look at him. "I am yours, *Tilahatan*. You have marked me already. My soul is permanently seared by my love for you. My only wish is to become your mate in the eyes of the gods and our people… I am already yours in my own heart."

Belah closed her eyes and struggled to hold back tears. Craving closer contact, she shifted to straddle his lap and pressed her lips against his. With a low moan he opened for her and she pushed a breath into him, hoping yet again that her magic was all he needed to remain sane. She would breathe for him for an eternity, if she had to. Or at least as long as he lived… he might have an extended life span as her lover, but without being marked by her, he would eventually die. But her mark carried a much more volatile threat… if it didn't kill him outright, it would definitely leave him a broken man.

She would give him what he wished for, though. In the eyes of the gods and their people, all they needed was a wedding. And this wedding would be the most spectacular event in several centuries.

"Marry me," she said when she finally pulled away from their kiss.

He studied her for a second, his brows drawing together while her eyes darted back and forth, anxiously hoping to glean some hint of his mood from his eyes or his aura. Slowly, a smile spread across his face and his aura brightened. "Absolutely."

CHAPTER FIFTEEN

W hen Belah awoke the next morning, it was to the familiar tingling of Nikhil's aura when he was fully aroused, yet she didn't feel his physical contact otherwise. She slowly turned to face his side of the bed and found him lying naked with his head propped on one hand, the other slowly sliding up and down along his thick, engorged cock.

"Mmm, my plan worked," he rumbled.

"Plan?" Belah inquired, quirking her lips at him.

"You have this uncanny ability to sense when I'm at the edge. As if your instincts require that you never miss an ounce of my pleasure when I come for you."

"Hmm, looks to me like you were coming for yourself just now. It's a good thing I woke up."

She stretched a hand out to him and brushed the back of a finger along the underside of his cock, gathering the droplet of his juices that trickled down the smooth, hot skin. The musky scent of him intoxicated her and her own arousal grew when she delicately licked his essence off her finger. The salty-sweet tang hit her tongue with an explosion of essence and she closed her eyes to savor his flavor.

He let out a harsh growl when she slid her finger into her mouth. His aura brightened, as she expected it would, but the quality of its power shifted on the spectrum, a dark sheen surrounding it.

Nikhil's eyes flashed with the wildness she had come to love in him, but the accompanying shift in his aura troubled her. Leaning close, she pressed her lips against his and prepared to send a breath of her magic into his lungs, but abruptly found herself thrown back and pinned to the bed, Nikhil hovering over her with an angry look.

"What is that, little beast? When you breathe into me. Whatever you do leaves my mind numb. If we are to be married, you must not keep secrets."

Belah knew her confession from the night before would only go so far to satisfy his curiosity about her and her race. With just as sudden a movement, she wrested herself from his grip and flipped him off her as easily as if he weighed no more than her pillow. Straddling his hips, she let her talons and horns manifest while she held him down.

"Remember this secret, my love? There are aspects of being that are … complicated. Remember what I told you last night about my former mates?"

Nikhil glared up at her, but didn't fight her powerful hold on him. In fact, he grew distinctly more aroused in spite of his very obvious irritation at being overpowered. "I remember," he growled. "You are sparing my free will, which honors me."

"There is more than that. You have always been a particularly blessed man. No doubt your mother has spun the tales of your conception with you. You are a legend among the armies of the delta and your reputation extends beyond into the far kingdoms, even outside my own rule." She studied him, waiting to gauge his response to her statement.

His brows drew together in confusion. "My mother's stories were just fantasy—encouraging for a fatherless young man like me, but I stopped believing I had any kind of divine status the first time I took an injury in battle. You see my scars—if my mother's tales that I was begotten of a god were true, would I have such things? Before you came to me, death hovered over me, itching to snatch me into the underworld. I hoped that her stories at least meant I would be honored after my death and allowed to sit by the side of Osiris. If I owe any deity for my life, it is you, *Tilahatan.*" His gaze softened and grew heated with lust again as he tilted his hips up, his shaft sliding against her naked flesh between them.

Nikhil's warmth and hardness distracted her, but she owed him this truth as much as he'd deserved to understand her reasons for not marking him.

"She was partly right," she said, pressing her hips down harder onto his to halt his movements. "You are not the son of a god. Your father was the commander who was wed to your mother. You were conceived mere days before your father died. To honor his memory, one of my kind graced your mother with his presence in the night and gave you the Blessing you bear to this day, since before you were even born. Your mother simply believed that the dragon who made love to her that night was who put you in her belly, but you weren't his get. He only blessed you with his magic. The blessing itself is an infusion of the dragon's essence that ensures you are protected by my kind. It means you were always intended as a dragon's mate. My mate." She closed her eyes, tamping down the guilt over not revealing that the dragon in question had been her own brother, and steeling herself for the additional bad news she had to deliver.

"This is a good thing, is it not?" He had relaxed beneath her and she released her grip on his wrists.

"It is, normally. But our magic requires balance. A Blessing must be offset by a mark. Any dragon magic, in enough concentration needs a mark to balance it eventually."

"Or... what?"

The question she hated most to answer. "Or you lose your mind. This is why I rarely share my Nirvana with my pets. I have no intention of ever marking them."

Nikhil stared at her placidly for a moment before his eyes narrowed. In a completely reasonable tone, he said, "So, to be with you, my choices are either losing my free will or losing my mind entirely. Did you ever consider asking me to choose?"

Belah's stomach chilled at the distance present in his question.

"Nikhil, you not being marked by me is one of the worst offenses of a dragon. You know what I am. You know all my secrets. Our marks are the way we tie our mates to us. I am trusting you by not marking you. You could still tell all my secrets to an enemy."

His fingers twitched distractedly against her thighs and she noticed that his cock had softened.

He pushed her off and rolled away, coming to rest on his side, facing her. "I've always been loyal to you, why do you think I would betray you, even if my mind failed somehow?"

Belah closed her eyes and breathed in deeply. She hated his question because she hated her answer to it.

"It isn't about loyalty. It's about caution. You see us as gods. That is accidental, by the way, but we seek to maintain order through whatever means we can. You are not like the others. Not even my pets." She reached out and brushed at his overgrown scruff. He'd already seen her through death and still needed rest.

"I won't betray you," he said, and her heart broke at the plea in his tone.

"I know. My breath is the only way I have to keep that threat at bay. My power affects your mind. I could use it to control you if I chose to, but I only use it in its most benign state—to try to lend some balance to the inundation of magic you get from my body when we make love, and the magic you already carry from your Blessing."

"Is there no other way?" he asked, looking agitated.

"There is nothing more I can do, my love," she said, stroking his cheek. "I would gladly marry you today, but..."

But the wedding of someone as important as an empress required far too much planning and preparation. The public declaration—in front of the gods and her people—was the thing Nikhil wanted most. So she needed to make sure both the gods and the people were in attendance.

"You are a goddess. I want the entire world and all the gods to see how much I love you."

Belah gave him a rueful smile. His priority was making their love public. Hers was so much more. Belah needed to do everything she could to ensure he lived as long as possible, sane and happy by her side. Her breath may well keep him sane for the rest of his natural life, and so prolonging his life even more should be her focus. Unless she marked him, her own life-giving magic would be transient—what she gave him each day faded, the energy of their lovemaking losing effectiveness over the erosion of time.

"There is more at stake with this, Nikhil," she said, trying to ignore the light nips of his teeth on her skin—his renewed attention distracted her from the truth she needed to share.

"I'm not a fool, Belah," he said. "You're hiding something." He gave the side of her breast a hard bite that made her gasp and her juices flow hotly between her thighs. Sweet Mother, he knew how to get her going.

"I have an idea," she said, trying to decide how much of her idea she should share. It wasn't as if she hadn't spent wakeful nights considering every possibility.

She'd considered making a request of her siblings to combine their energy and bestow him with a gift of their power. It would be akin to the blessing he was given inside his mother's womb, only more powerful, yet would not carry the shackling magic of a mark that would irrevocably bind him to her like a slave. Again, she wished she were not immortal—that her mark didn't carry that curse with it. Any dragon but she and her siblings could mark him without that risk to his free will. And when the time came to die, they would have been able to leave this life together.

Nikhil would never agree to the type of ritual required to accept the magic of her and all five of her siblings, regardless of whether he viewed them all as gods. It required a level of physical intimacy she hadn't had with any of her siblings in centuries, and would require Nikhil himself to be the focus of their energy.

The more palatable option would take her much longer to achieve, however. There were only a handful of other individuals as powerful as she and her siblings, but whose magic required less physical contact than a dragon's did. The other races owed her some favors, and she would be calling them in.

His fingers between her thighs made her thoughts falter. His teeth on her nipple distracted her to the point of pushing his head back.

Nikhil laughed. "You were thinking too hard. Time for talking, little beast," he said, his fingers still toying with the scarab between her thighs.

Belah groaned. "Fine, just stop touching me for five minutes so I can think?"

With a grin, he raised his hands above his head, exaggerating his submission. Belah took advantage by climbing astride him again, gazing down into his dark eyes.

"It will take time," she said, hesitating to share the existence of her contemporaries. As far as her people knew, the dragons were their gods and their only gods. Telling him didn't mean telling everyone, though.

"There are others like me… races who are divinely blessed and powerful. Other… gods. You wanted all the gods in attendance, so they will be invited. And they will bring gifts. But delivering their invitations will be cumbersome and time consuming. Many are not easy to reach. It will mean an extended wait before the wedding can take place."

Nikhil frowned at that revelation. After a breath, he asked, "And their gifts will make me strong enough to take your magic without losing my mind?"

"Their magic will prolong your life, among other things. You still need to accept my breath to keep your mind healthy. I'm afraid without my mark, that will never change."

"My sanity is waning already, little beast," he said. "I need to be inside you now. Whatever plans you need to make for our wedding I agree to, as long as you stop teasing me." He lowered his hands to grip her hips and raised her up just enough to reposition her so that the furrow between her thighs spread over the head of his cock.

With a single, hard thrust of his hips, he buried himself inside her, then grabbed her hands and pulled them up above his head again. Belah looked down at him quizzically. Seeing the mischievous glint in his eyes, she twined her fingers through his and pressed his hands into the pillows above his head. As much as she preferred being overpowered by him, she still treasured the rare moments when he chose to have her remind him of her power. She leaned over him now, letting her bejeweled nipples brush against his cheeks while she pivoted her hips on his cock.

Nikhil growled low in his chest, his gaze growing more fevered the more she moved. He latched onto one nipple with his teeth, biting hard into her flesh. The glorious pain shot straight to her core, fanning the growing heat and making her channel flood with fresh arousal around his pumping shaft. Even pinned down by her, he commanded her pleasure, and clearly knew that he still had control of her in spite of her physical display of strength.

"Nikhil," she whimpered. The intensity of pleasure he gave her with his cock and his mouth made her lose her will to keep holding him down.

He took full control, flipping them and pushing one of Belah's knees up as he skewered her again and again, each thrust carrying more urgency. With a moan of desperation, he lowered his head and bared his teeth, biting into her breasts as though he were starved and only her flesh could sate his hunger. All she could sense from him was the pent-up agony of the hours before she'd regained consciousness and his need for her to return to him. The emotion channeled into a near-helpless rage within him that spilled out into his aura so vividly it nearly brought Belah to tears.

Forcing herself to push the pleasure his wildness gave her aside, she grabbed his head and pulled him to her mouth, focusing her energy on her breath. *"Ease your mind, my love, but let your heart stay wild."* She expelled a breath past his open lips and followed it with her tongue, kissing deeply.

After a moment, his movements became less erratic and more deliberate, his aura finally regaining the healthy red glow. He pulled away from her with a gasp for breath and stared down. His eyes had lost the desperation, and were now only filled with the intense hunger for her. He reached down and pushed her other knee to her chest, pulling back to gaze at the place where they were joined. Roughly, he gripped her ass and held her hips even higher so his cock rammed straight into her with ever-growing ferocity.

His cock battered her insides, each bruising thrust pushing her higher and closer to her peak. She hovered at the edge for an eternity, her body betraying her desire to finish. Nikhil snarled in frustration, at the edge himself, but unwilling to cross over without her.

Suddenly he pulled out of her and flipped her over, entering her from behind with a fresh push that hit home as though drawn in by the force of her need for him. Pushing her legs wider to span his thighs, he reached around her and drew her back against his chest. His hand went around her throat while his other found her clit and rubbed it mercilessly.

With only the slightest squeeze against her airway, the euphoria crept in like a warm breeze. On that breeze she flew, higher and faster than before, her orgasm coursing through her body as though on wings. Nikhil rode out his own, keeping up his punishing thrusts through the hot pulsing of his seed into her.

"That's my little beast, you need my collar tight around your throat to find your pleasure, don't you? Good girl." He let his hand fall away and she grabbed it and put it back to her throat. The soft pressure of his palm against her windpipe kept the fluttering pulses of her climax going until she shuddered and fell limp in his arms. He pulled her back down to the bed with him, wrapping her in his arms.

"I have no wish to kill you again," he said. "Death has been my instrument too many times. I will gladly kill for you, *Tila-hatan*, but your death is something I could not bear."

Belah curled into him, relishing the way he cuddled her like a kitten in the aftermath of their lovemaking. He stroked her cheek so gently she let out a soft sigh. Still, his reluctance to test her limits disappointed her. He had never once hesitated before, why would he hesitate in this?

Looking up into his eyes, she drew his hand back to her throat and held it there. "I can tell it pleases you to do it. It pleases me more than I can express when you do. I am immortal, Nikhil. Death is one experience I will never truly have, one I crave for all its remoteness from me. That you don't fear to push me into that abyss is one of the reasons I love you, and I trust you to push me all the way to the edge and beyond. But trust *me* to tell you that I will always return to you."

His gaze clouded and he grimaced as though she'd hurt him. "Do you really wish for death? Is my love, my manner of loving you, not enough? You desired a true master, and I am that man for you, yet you would prefer the darkness of the realm your brother rules over the sensations I can give you?"

She wanted to argue that in this scenario she and her brother were not the god and goddess siblings Nikhil had worshiped his entire life. Ked may embody darkness, but he had no significance where her fascination with death was concerned.

"I can never truly reach that realm, Nikhil. The place you take me is not the darkness my brother rules. It is a darkness *you* rule, that is only created during our union. When you took me there last night—that was the first time I have ever experienced it with such depth. Today was only like opening the door and refusing to let me walk through. As my true master, I trust only you to send me there, and to give me the reason to return again."

Nikhil relaxed, letting out an audible exhalation. His hands resumed their soft petting of her skin. He had often commented on the unusual texture and how he loved it. His fingers trailed down her stomach and began tracing patterns over her lower abdomen. The touch was enticing enough to arouse, but mostly it lulled her and she found herself dozing against him, her head nestled against his strong, scarred chest.

His voice roused her some time later, and she woke to find his hand cupping her cheek and urging her gaze to meet his.

In a decisive tone, he said, "I will fulfill this desire of yours to the extreme you wish, but only once more and according to my own plan. On our wedding night, I will give you the gift of that darkness one more time. Until then, and after that day, what we shared today is all I will give you. It's all I *can* give you, *Tilahatan*. You may ask me to kill a hundred thousand men in battle and I will enjoy every cut of my blade. I will come to your bed covered in the blood of your enemies and let your own cries of pain finally slake my bloodthirst. You may ask me to hurt you in any way you wish, because it makes you feel as alive as your cries make me feel alive. But after our wedding night, never again ask me to kill you. I cannot bear the silence of you in death, even knowing you will return."

Belah's skin prickled with excitement at his promise. "How will you do it?" she asked.

"Exactly the way you wish the most, my love," he said. He pushed her down to the bed and hovered over her, tracing a single fingertip in small stripes over the most sensitive areas of her skin. "I'm as skilled with a blade as I am with my cock."

The hard cock in question grazed against her opening.

"I can pierce you to the quick if I choose. Kill you quickly." He shoved himself into her once, hard enough for her to cry out. "Or I can tease you until all your juices flow before you even realize I've opened the floodgates." His fingertip made soft lines over different parts of her body, each touch making her shiver, while his cock teased around and around her swollen cunt, teasing at the opening.

The agony of his restraint drove her mad. She lay panting and begging after only a few moments.

"Do you wish for a quick death or a slow one, little beast? When I slaughter you, how bloody do you want it?"

Belah's mind was already gone from his teasing. Her thighs were flooded with her juices and growing wetter with every teasing swipe of his fingers, every promise of a blade cutting her. She could imagine him vividly with a blade, torturing a prisoner tied down to a stone slab. She'd seen him in his element many times and marveled at his precision and cold enjoyment of the process. The thought of herself tied down while he cut her with his blade made her muscles clench and ache for just that.

His soft touches made her wet from her pussy crying out to be penetrated. Her entire body craved that promise of bloodletting, of having his blade cut her.

"Make me bloody."

With a wicked glint in his eye, he shoved his cock into her again and fucked her even harder than before.

"It would be my pleasure, *Tilahatan*."

Sweet Mother, what had she become?

CHAPTER SIXTEEN

Belah lived in a dream for days on end, sometimes floating on the elation of her impending marriage, and other times in a dark cloud of loneliness. She fulfilled her responsibilities as empress. Nikhil returned to his duties as general of her armies. Threats to her borders were ever present and his expertise was sorely needed after his latest absence. Every night she ached for him to return to her bed, and spent too many evenings alone.

She still visited her harem, but with less enthusiasm. When she did, she took her fill of her pets' pleasure without taking her own, then gravitated to Nyla and Zeb and spent the hours talking to them and marveling over Nyla's progressing pregnancy, wishing she could share the same experience with Nikhil.

When the children were born several months later, their parents elected to stay in Belah's temple because their home villages were in a contested area of her kingdom Nikhil was intent on taking back. Belah gave them private quarters, but still visited them and their children regularly. The twins, Neela and Naaz, were a delight to her, and helped distract her from her despair over Nikhil's absence.

Her Blessed children.

Nikhil's promise of one last gift of oblivion on their wedding night never left her mind, but it seemed less important with the weight of her empire on her shoulders. She continued planning the wedding, which became more elaborate every day she waited for word that the guests she'd invited would attend.

Once the dragon messengers were sent with the formal invitations, she began her work with palace staff to plan the event itself, which would not take place for two more years, to allow time for all the attendees to arrive, and for her messengers to reach the most honored guests and return with them.

Those guests were her oldest friends, and Belah had no doubt they would come. She'd been long without a mate, to begin with, and requesting her friends' favors would be enough to signal the significance of this marriage. It was particularly significant because her own race traditionally never settled down with a single mate. Of course, Belah had her harem, but she didn't breed with them. Her own kind were encouraged to take several mates—and by and large they did. She and her siblings were the exceptions, but their descendants frequently had many husbands or wives. Collected them like the most treasured spoils of war.

Belah had no need to bear more children now, after the ones she'd already born. She had no wish to witness the death of them anymore, either. Unlike her, her offspring were mortal. They may be long-lived, but they eventually died after about a thousand years. She often wondered if that were the same for the first child. Would a son born from two immortals also be immortal? She didn't know. He'd been taken away upon birth—before even suckling at her breast—and her mother and Fate hadn't seen fit to tell her where they'd taken him. She'd spent thousands of years searching without any prospects and had all but given up hope she would find him. Reports of brother's fruitless searches proved painful reminders of the loss. Even now, Ked still had a small network of Shadows covertly looking for any sign of where their child had been hidden.

She spent too many days in Nikhil's absence wondering about that loss and alternately wishing she could bear a child with Nikhil. One last child. But perhaps it wasn't her place to bear a child out of true love. Besides her first, all the rest had been conceived by necessity, and while she loved them dearly as her blood, she had no lasting connection to them. Their fathers had been too weak to last with a dragon as powerful as she was.

Nikhil might last, but only if she destroyed his will.

Some nights she fell asleep fantasizing about marking him in the hope that he might miraculously withstand her magic. The subsequent dreams always twisted her wish into the worst outcome. Nikhil a drooling waste of a man begging at her feet and bound to her for eternity.

She always retreated to her harem the day after those dreams. Her pets had become more accommodating to this new Belah, who simply needed company more often than sexual sustenance, and strove to entertain her in other ways. She learned they had many varied talents and grew to know and love them even more than she had before.

Zeb and Nyla were doting parents, who never begrudged their mistress a chance to spoil their son and daughter.

Idrin was a protective uncle to the children, believing somehow that he had some part in their conception.

The truth was more complicated. During that one day when Nikhil had led the disguised Belah to her harem to be a toy for her pets, pieces of all of their essences had been transferred to the twins through Belah's Blessing. They may never manifest—the dragon magic itself would always take precedence—but the children would always feel an innate kinship with the members of the harem, or any of their offspring.

Belah ached to see the pair grow. They may not be the last children whose lives she had a direct influence in shaping, but it had been centuries since she'd been a mother, and she was so far removed from her own line that new generations of dragons barely gave her a thought, aside from the understanding that she was one of the few who made the rules that governed her kind.

Rules she herself was currently breaking.

As far as her siblings knew, she intended to mark Nikhil on their wedding night. That would never happen.

If everything went how Belah planned, something more amazing would come from the night, and she could prove to her siblings that they could have love with a mate without destroying their wills.

She hoped she wasn't wrong.

CHAPTER SEVENTEEN

In the midst of the chaos of her wedding day, Belah realized that she'd never actually had a wedding before. Not a true wedding, at any rate. Most of her former mates had been prizes or religious sacrifices to her. No wonder they'd expected to die. The prospect of death had shrouded them from the start, and her power had done nothing to counteract their fears or preconceptions. She hadn't endeared herself to them in any fashion—only marked them and used them.

Their pleasure had been apparent. They wanted her the way a zealot wants to be blessed by their god or a martyr wants death for their cause. Their desires had been so all-consuming, and after losing their wills thanks to her mark, they succumbed to the power of her apparent divinity. In their eyes, she was a goddess, and the purest way to please a goddess was to die in her name.

Nikhil had nearly done so himself, before even coming into direct contact with her. His touch on that first day they'd met was enough for her to know he was nothing like the others. He had made his sacrifice for her, no doubt, but he had his own craving for glory, too. He'd said as much when he believed he was near death—he wanted to be revered as the gods were.

Belah remembered that day as her attendants were dressing her in her bridal finery. She smiled at the thought that now Nikhil would find his glory in full view of the entire kingdom and all the gods, but his chief reason now wasn't for glory. She knew without a doubt that he wanted this day to prove that she was *his* and for no other reason.

In another room somewhere in the palace, he was being similarly outfitted in finery. Within the next few hours, they would meet together on the grand promenade outside the palace, be paraded through the capitol together on separate gilded litters for all to see. Behind them, wagons full of celebratory prizes would be thrown to the crowds in their wake.

Once in the gardens of the Temple of Ra, the ceremony would begin, with all the gods looking on.

Belah held back a laugh, picturing how that particular scene would play out and had to endure a scowl from one of her maids who was arduously attempting to secure her elaborate headdress.

All the supposed "gods" in attendance were close, personal friends. Her oldest friends. All immortal like her. Five of them were her own siblings. One was the ursa's summer queen, Sathmika, one the turul summer wind, Zephyrus, and the last two were the twin dionarchs, Neph and Nyx, the brother and sister leaders of the nymphaea.

The idea of kneeling before the nine of them seemed silly to her, but the significance of their presence still wasn't lost on her.

A wedding like this one was unprecedented among their kind. That they had agreed to be present honored her. Even more, that they had agreed to bless her soon-to-be-husband with their magic was the highest honor that she would be indebted to for a long time.

Before she knew it, her maids urged her to move and she went. Her headdress tilted off center when she walked and the woman who had been fixing it let out an alarmed squeak, making Belah stop. She turned back to the mirror to examine the contraption that rested on her head. It was a high, tapered cylinder painted in gold and stripes that secured to the top of her head and flared out wider as it went up. All her hair had been braided and piled inside it, but it wasn't nearly as secure to her head as it needed to be.

Seeing the quickest solution, she brushed off the panicked maid and manifested her horns inside the headdress. Once she was certain it was securely in place, she made a show of pressing the whole thing down harder, and then tilting her head side-to-side. The maid sighed in relief and they made their way out the door.

With each step down the corridor to her private exit to the palace, her thighs were jabbed with the delicious little spikes of Nikhils pre-wedding gift to her: a brand new set of barbed bands to remind her that she was his.

And on one of those bands she'd secured a sheath for her gift to him—but he wouldn't receive it until much later, after they were alone together as husband and wife.

The blade itself had taken some time and thought for her to come up with. The perfect gift for him would align, she hoped, with what his true gift for her would be.

Every day since their last discussion, she'd played his words over and over in her mind. He would give her the gift she wished for, but by his rules. Nikhil had a reputation as a torturer among his soldiers, and strangulation was not part of his repertoire. It had become clear to her that he only did that because it was what pleased *her*, not because it pleased him. After several inquiries of her guards, she learned that his methods were designed to cause much pain and bloodletting, but little permanent damage other than scars if a prisoner turned pliant quickly. He's a master, they said. His blades were his most treasured tools.

She wondered why he'd never approached her about using those blades during their games, but then their games had never crossed the line into true torture before. He'd been testing her with greater and greater pain all along, but when he learned her skin couldn't be pierced, he scaled back and redirected his efforts into other areas. That was when he'd tried humiliation at the hands of her pets, followed by strangulation by his own hand.

She raised a shaky hand to her throat, her body heating at the memory of that first squeeze and how focused every other sensation became when her power of true thought broke down as she ceased to breathe. How would it feel to reach the abyss through Nikhil's chosen path? If he indeed led her there tonight, would it be as glorious a journey as every other one he had taken her on so far?

Her eyelids fluttered closed with the fantasy just as her maids all let out simultaneous exclamations. When she opened her eyes, a huge shadow filled the entire corridor and a wall of black leather and fur stood before her.

She scowled up at her brother, peripherally aware of all her maids kneeling around them.

"You're scaring them," she spat in her native tongue to keep her maids from catching on to the conflict.

Ked glowered at her and responded in the same language. "This marriage is a farce. You have to mark him, Belah, and you know it."

"He's sane enough with my breath. I won't destroy his will by marking him. I don't care if we never have a child together. He is the one I want."

"And what do you think he wants? Is it only you or the glory you represent? He won't just be elevated to the status of a king after today. He'll be the consort of a goddess."

"No," Belah said, narrowing her eyes at her brother. "He'll be my equal in the eyes of my subjects. But he's even more than that in my bed. Is that what bothers you, brother? That another man commands my respect besides you?"

Ked closed his eyes with a grimace. After a harsh, defeated sigh, he said, "I love you, sister. I only wish for your happiness, but any dragon marriage not meant to produce offspring can be nothing but destructive. I fear this misplaced devotion for him will destroy you somehow, and the rest of us as a result. We can't live without you."

"He's only a man, Ked," she said softly, peering up at him. "I am still fully in control of my powers. I promise if I ever thought he would hurt anyone besides me, I would destroy him in a heartbeat."

Ked's eyes darkened, and along with them the entire corridor grew pitch black. Around them her maids whimpered in fear.

"He does hurt you, doesn't he? Did you lie to me before?"

"I have never lied to you," she said. She eyed the dark corridor beyond, wishing for a way out. She wanted nothing more of this conversation. Not on her wedding day.

Ked grabbed her wrist when she tried to move past. His unwelcome touch incited fury deep inside her. Her other hand shot up and gripped his throat. She shoved hard, her native strength surging forward enough to lift him off his feet and slam him against the wall.

Dark black eyes met brilliant blue—her own rage reflected in his deepest depths. His throat worked against her palm and she wondered briefly if being strangled would turn her brother on the way it did to her. Their games were ancient history, though. Child's play, compared to what she enjoyed now.

Through gritted teeth, she said, "You didn't make me this way, brother. I was this way before you ever touched me. That day when we did unspeakable things to each other—I will remind you, that was *my* idea. The pain you gave me, I begged for. Every moment of agony that resulted is *mine* to bear. Not yours. Nikhil gives me succor from my hatred of myself for that day and the aftermath, but never forget… IT. WAS. MY. CHOICE."

Ked's eyes only widened and he let out a strangled sound and a nod. Belah blinked and shook her head, coming back to her senses. She released him as tears began to stream down her face.

When her strength gave out, Ked caught her and held her. In a rough, tight voice, he said, "Hush, sister. I never blamed you. I always loved you." He let out a small chuckle, followed by an agonized cough that signaled she'd done some damage to him after all. Clearing his throat, he said, "I forget sometimes how strong you are. You always were the strongest of the six of us. It's no wonder I couldn't resist you then."

Belah exhaled slowly, finally regaining her bearings. "We didn't have many options at the time. We were too young and humanity was too primitive." She pulled back and looked up into the black eyes of one of the few people in the world who made her long life bearable.

She rested her hand against his cheek. "Nikhil makes me happy. Do you truly begrudge me happiness? I know it's not ideal, but this is how it has to be for us."

Ked gave her an affectionate squeeze. "My only wish is for you to be happy, sister. Whatever that means, I will be here for you, but I will be on my guard where your lover is concerned." He lifted a hand and swiped a thumb across her wet cheek, his brow furrowed. "I fear I've ruined your makeup."

She sniffled and laughed. Glancing around at her maids to ensure they were still prostrated on the floor, she simply let out a breath of her magic and let her will set her appearance how she wished it to be.

"Go, brother. If you are willing to sanction this wedding after all, you need to be in the hall with the rest of them."

He righted himself and turned to go.

As Belah was rousing her frightened maids, she heard him call her name once more.

"Belah. If he ever hurts you, you can trust that I will destroy him."

CHAPTER EIGHTEEN

B elah and Nikhil stared at each other, breathing so deeply that their chests rose and fell in unison.

The day was already hot, the scent of jasmine strong around them. Yet Belah's skin blazed even hotter with the need for his touch

They couldn't touch each other yet. They had to pledge their love and make it true in the eyes of the gods before they could have each other. From the second their eyes met before the line of gods who stood as their witnesses, she'd been as giddy as any village girl anticipating her wedding. It humbled her to realize—that this moment must be what every woman in love experienced, and it mattered little what her status was.

Nothing else mattered today but their love for each other. That she was immortal and he was only a man seemed immaterial in the face of what they were about to embark on together.

Beyond the raised dais they stood upon, her subjects watched with rapt wonder. The pair of them made quite a vision, bedecked in pure white robes edged in gold and jeweled embroidery, with golden headdresses and jewelry. Nikhil's bronze, muscular chest was bare, but had been painted with gold that gleamed in the afternoon sun, enhancing every hard line and rippling muscle of his physique. His long hair that had grown out over the time since his injury was bound up in a braided queue at the back of his head and an elaborate crown rested on top. Over one shoulder was draped pure white linen that cascaded down his back and was secured with jeweled scarabs that matched the ones at her throat and hips.

Belah smiled secretly, thinking that they matched her private ornaments, too. His dark eyes were lined with kohl, as were her own, and lent him a slightly sinister appearance, but the heat in his gaze when he looked at her betrayed his raw desire and his love.

The nine gods and goddesses she called her friends and family stood nearby. The twelfth figure on the dais was the temple priestess who directed them all into position with a soft murmur. Belah and Nikhil moved to face each other and kneel while the others encircled them.

The ceremony itself was no more than a blur around her. Belah followed each prompt as though some external entity had control of her reactions, but through it all, she found she couldn't keep her eyes off his. Nikhil's gaze never once left hers, and her need grew with each passing moment and each phase of the hours-long ceremony.

This was true torture, she decided. The endless pledges of their love, for which each of the gods requested a different promise and bestowed their own unique blessing in kind. The blessings meant little to Belah herself, but meant everything to her lover. Each one, ceremonially bestowed, would add years to his life and ensure a longer bond between them. In the eyes of her people, their bond would be eternal, and even though Belah knew that eternity wasn't in the stars for Nikhil, she wouldn't begrudge these few moments to allow him as much time with her as possible.

Each of her siblings' blessings were granted innocuously, with an exchange of breath that to all outward appearances looked like a kiss. For the sake of theatrics, they each went one better, using their powers to create the illusion of a bright glow around the entire ceremony that matched the color of their magic.

The others coupled their own blessings with similar visual effects that were secondary to the true magic. The turul seeress bestowed her gift with a song, the lilting tune so beautiful Belah couldn't help but feel tears prick at the corners of her eyes. She sensed the other immortals lending their magic to the effects to enhance the awe of the crowd that looked on. By and large their truest magic was invisible, but the show of power benefited them all.

The ursa queen's magic was the most visible of all of them. When she raised her hands to the heavens, clouds coalesced above them, and warm rains came down, drenching Belah and Nikhil both. Between them, a seedling sprouted straight through the stone and grew with surprising speed, up through the circle created by their clasped hands. It grew into a tall tree, branching out into a bright green canopy above them and flowering brilliantly in a burst of color that caused all the onlookers to gasp with amazement.

In the background, the turul's voice added a new song to the event, and beside her the nymphaea's magic rose as the brother-sister pair stood and began moving their lithe, tall bodies around the circle in a dance. They leapt and bent and swayed with the music, as beautiful in their flowing robes as the birds that graced the river's edges. She didn't see the entire dance, but every so often as they circled around her and Nikhil, she would catch glimpses and was sure they became those long-legged birds, with blue-edged feathers and long, curved necks. Above them the tree bloomed and the flowers fell in brilliant red waves around them until the entire surface of the sand-colored polished stone they knelt on was carpeted in brilliant red petals.

The heft of the dagger attached to Belah's thigh weighed heavy, pressing the spikes of the band harder into her flesh. In her mind's eye she saw the red petals turn to blood. The image probably should have troubled her, but it excited her. She had never once even *seen* her own blood. Her life's essence was protected beneath her impervious skin. Tonight, would he be willing to use her gift? He had told her that he would take her to that place one more time, in his own way, and had suggested that meant drawing her blood, yet he hadn't mentioned it again since.

She loved the way he took her to the edge of pure pain. How he'd learned to improvise when he'd learned she had such limits. He didn't go for outright violence beyond the whippings he'd given her, and his hesitance to push her to that final precipice too often betrayed his deep love for her. Death might not be permanent for her, but he had seen it often enough to know the impact of it. He had administered it himself.

He was a killer, and knew both how to kill and the repercussions of doing so.

Belah swallowed harshly. They had been apart for months, but she still remembered the last time he'd wrapped his large hands around her slender throat and squeezed just enough.

The dancers swayed into her line of sight, their actions mimicking the images in her mind. The male bent over the female, hands at her throat, his body arced so gracefully he could have been a tree bending in the wind. But he didn't clasp his hands as Belah anticipated. He pushed them higher, through his sisters' hair and pulled her up against him to dance entwined.

They were immortal like she was, did they wish to find the same kind of peace she did? Even if she could just sleep for a few centuries…

She bit the inside of her mouth. No. This was her wedding day. Nikhil was here now, and it was bad form to already be thinking about how she would exist after he was gone. After the blessings were bestowed, she would have a few centuries with him, she hoped.

More red petals fell around them, inundating her with their spicy scent. The nymphaea twins kept dancing, their movements generating strange magic that she'd never felt. The magic made her want to use her limbs, to move with them. But more than that, it made her want to lay Nikhil down and fuck him in the most acrobatic way.

She caught his gaze and his mouth spread into a wide smile. He felt it, too. She didn't have to look down to know that his gilded cock was hard beneath his wedding garb.

The nymphaea magic filtered over them like a mist settling. Most of it was directed at Nikhil, and each time they twirled and bowed close to him, they touched him. Each touch bestowed him with more of their magic, which held the essence of vibrant life coupled with stillness. That of a placid lake, as clear as a mirror on the surface, but teaming with life beneath.

Around her, the ceremony faded out, becoming secondary to the connection between her and Nikhil. She responded almost unconsciously to the instructions of the priestess as she made her vows. Her body thrummed with excitement when Nikhil's deep voice reverberated in her ears with the promises of his own wedding vows. Soon, the pair of them were urged to rise again and present themselves to the throng of onlookers who cheered so loudly the air moved from the force of their congratulations.

After their parade around through the streets and back to the palace, a celebration would take place throughout the city, while all the honored guests would join the happy couple in the great hall to celebrate. Belah itched for it all to be done so she could be alone with him again in their chamber.

Passing through the crowd on their shared litter, they were showered in piles of red petals. Her hand lay on her thigh, grasped tightly within Nikhil's larger one. He released her, but left his hand resting on her thigh and leaned close.

"Must we show our faces at the party? I have a mind to skip it and take you to bed now." His fingertips teased their way into the slit in her gown until his hot touch grazed the bare skin of her thigh.

Belah sucked in a breath at the charge of energy that shot through her from his touch. He was filled with magic now, more potent than anything she'd experienced. His very aura swirled with all the blessings he carried from the immortal races who had given their gifts to him. All Belah wished to do was taste a sample of this new power he held, but she would rather wait for them to experience each other wholesale as man and wife, rather than sneak tiny pieces.

Before she could push his adventuring fingers away, he stopped abruptly and stared down, tugging the fabric of her gown aside. Following his gaze, she saw the wide band that encircled her thigh had been exposed. That was not what caught his gaze, however. He knew she wore the bands he'd given her today, but he didn't know about the item she had attached to it.

He stared down at the small dagger that rested in its sheath at the top of her thigh. Bright blue stones had been set in the hilt in a perfect representation of a winged serpent, and the leather sheath had a similar pattern embossed in it.

"It is my gift to you, my love," she said softly. "I planned to give it to you when we were alone. It… it has my magic in its blade."

Nikhil's mouth fell open slightly and he licked his lips. His gaze rose to meet hers, heat and hunger flashing deep within. He swallowed hard.

"It will cut you?"

The eagerness in his voice made Belah's piercings tingle and a fresh wave of heat flooded between her thighs.

"Yes."

With a shaky hand he touched the hilt and pulled it partway out of the small scabbard. The marbled metal gleamed in the sunlight, but also seemed to glow with an inner light. Belah had overseen the painstaking process of crafting the fine little blade, but the final step she had done alone. Her own dragon fire was what made the metal glow, making it the only thing that could pierce her skin. A more personalized gift could not exist.

Slowly, he returned the knife to its home. His hand moved to the back of her neck and with eyes blazing with fierce lust, he took her mouth. His kiss was hard and hungry. Belah made a soft sound of reproach—they were in public, in full view of all her people, being paraded around so her subjects could see their empress and her new consort together for the first time. But when Nikhil's hand pressed down against the band that encircled her thigh, the spikes dug in and all other thoughts left her mind but the exquisite and sorely missed pain only he could inflict on her. While he pressed with the heel of his hand, his long fingers stroked higher and Belah spread her thighs for him, moaning into his kiss.

Tingling heat almost seared her throbbing clit when his fingers grazed it. He pushed two fingers deep into her flooded channel and growled low in his chest.

"Fuck, I need you now, *Tilahatan*." He pulled back, panting heavily. He pulled his hand away from her and gazed down at his dripping fingers.

In a daze, Belah could only nod, too elated by his long-needed touch to care that they were currently the biggest spectacle in the city even if they just sat quietly side-by-side. She let him pull her into his lap and with a frustrated untangling of their robes, she managed to straddle his hips.

Only raw, hungry need gripped her now, as she reached between them to find his cock. His shaft was buried beneath his own robes and the belt he wore wouldn't easily come loose. Finally, she extended a sharp talon and sliced cleanly through the front of his robe and reached inside, tugging him free. Gold paint still coated every inch of his glorious length, except for the underside where his juices had begun to weep from the tip and flow down, washing the tiny metallic flecks along with it.

Nikhil gripped both her thighs and squeezed around the bands, his grip urging her closer, the pain making her even hotter. She positioned him at her entrance and then gripped his face between her hands, gazing down into his blazing eyes.

The thick head of his cock pressed into her the tiniest amount and they both gasped. The sensation was both familiar and brand new. Something about the magic he exuded now made every bit of skin-to-skin contact between them even more exquisite than it had been the last time they'd made love months ago. The little pulses of pain she received whenever he squeezed her thighs just served to punctuate the pleasure when he began to thrust up into her.

There were so many things going through her mind that she wished to say—to tell him how happy he made her, how excited she was for the long life they would share. Instead of words, she pressed her mouth to his again and kissed him. He devoured her in turn while his hands roamed higher. He pulled savagely at the sides of her gown. The fabric tore, baring her breasts to him. The gown slid down her arms, leaving her back bare to the onlookers who now cheered even louder than before when Nikhil bent his head to take the tip of one breast into his mouth.

Belah undulated atop him, reveling in the thick, hot weight of his rigid cock that she had missed so much as it thrust up into her. When they broke away for breath, she glanced behind her, for the first time aware of the magnitude of their public display, then past Nikhil's head to where the throngs of people extended down the street their litter was traveling along.

The four men carrying the supports of the rear of the litter grinned up at her, not even fazed by the extra effort it must take them to carry a litter rocking from the couple fucking atop it. She arched her back and thrust her chest out, moaning when Nikhil responded by switching to her other breast. Around them, the crowds cheered louder. Their excitement saturated the air, amplifying her arousal and encouraging her to fuck even harder.

With each thrust, the jeweled scarab between Belah's thighs rubbed harder against Nikhil, sending fresh thrills through her in a rhythm that matched perfectly with his thrusts and the steady, painful throb of the spikes that dug into the flesh of her thighs.

Though the frenzied excitement of the crowd became a blanket around them, she was still more than acutely aware of Nikhil's wild, pent-up need for her. He fucked her as savagely as he could in this position, yet she could sense the restraint. This was merely foreplay for him, but would be enough to tide him over until they could finally be alone much later. He squeezed her thighs ever tighter, escalating her pain and pleasure for a moment before relaxing his hold and slowing his thrusts.

"They're enjoying the show, aren't they, little beast? And it looks like you enjoy giving it to them, too. Let's make it last until we get to the end, shall we?"

Panting, Belah nodded. She ached to come, but could hold back if he could. The look in his eyes told her that what he truly desired was to use his gift on her, and that only then would he truly be satisfied when he finally found his release. His body was close to climax now, though, so she relaxed onto his lap and kissed him, simply enjoying the way he filled her for a few moments and catching her breath.

After a few more blocks down the street, passing more wild, excited citizens, Nikhil gave her thigh another little squeeze and they began again. They fucked like that for what seemed like hours, and may well have been. When the richness of their surroundings signaled their close proximity to the palace, she began fucking him in earnest, and he responded in kind. No longer did he lave her breasts with teasing attention of lips and tongue—now he used his teeth, biting the supple flesh over and over until once again the world fell away and Belah knew nothing but the delicious mix of pain and pleasure that sent her flying every time he gave it to her.

Nikhil's grunts of pleasure and harder thrusts signaled how near he was to his own climax, and Belah clutched him, her thighs gripping tightly. The glow of his aura surrounded them both in a bubble so bright and vibrant, nothing outside registered. Her world became a pinpoint of focus on the sound of his cry when he finally came with a violent thrust inside her. A split second afterward, the magical energy that accompanied his orgasm flooded into her and pushed her past her own point of no return. She arched back and sang up to the skies, her exaltation strong enough to drown out the sounds of cheering that still came from outside the palace walls.

It wasn't until their tremors had subsided that she realized they had arrived. The litter had stopped and now rested on the ground at the top of the palace steps.

Nikhil's face and body were coated in sweat, dark tendrils of his hair escaped its binding and was plastered to his neck. The gold paint had rubbed off his chest and shoulders in places, and Belah looked down at herself to see it had been transferred onto her breasts, hands, and arms.

Sudden cheers erupted around them both when Belah rose to stand on shaky legs, Nikhil's hand gripped in hers to steady her. He rose easily beside her, his cock now stowed beneath the folds of his skirt. They looked around at the litter bearers and the palace staff who had come to greet them for the banquet.

Everyone beamed brightly at them, not the least bit scandalized to see that their empress had consummated her marriage to her consort before even reaching their bed.

CHAPTER NINETEEN

Belah and Nikhil departed the wedding banquet late in the evening to raucous cheers from the crowd. Many of the guests hadn't witnessed the spectacle of their lovemaking all the way through the streets of the city, and the attendees could talk of little else.

The hours at the party had dragged, in spite of Nikhil's occasional teasing touches. Belah still wore the spiked bands around her thighs, which he took advantage of beneath the table, but neither of them were inclined to put on another show. They would have to wait.

Every so often one of the guards had come to their table to whisper in Nikhil's ear. Nikhil smiled and nodded then gave Belah a sly, hungry glance. It was apparent he had some surprise planned and her body tingled in anticipation.

Now they were finally free of the party, walking hand-in-hand down the corridor to their chamber.

When they reached the doorway to her study—the room that had once been Nikhil's recovery room—he pulled her back.

"Take off your clothes," he said softly, rounding her to stand and face her.

"We're almost at the room…" she began, but he cut her off with a kiss that left her breathless when he finally pulled away.

Dark eyes stared down at her, his expression intense and determined, yet filled with love. He eyed her from head to toe before lifting his hands to the clasp at her shoulder that held the gown together.

As he undressed her, the burdens of the day fell away. With each item of her wedding finery that fell to the floor, another piece of Belah the Empress disappeared. Bit by bit, he took away that persona that she had worn in public, reminding her that when they were alone together, she was only his precious little beast.

Once naked, he urged her to her knees and she went willingly, bowing her head. From above, he gripped the top of her headdress and lifted it off.

He stood silent and unmoving for a moment after dropping the headdress to the floor among the pile of her clothing. With the lightest touch, one bold hand brushed over the length of one of her horns. Belah shivered and let out a ragged sigh at the pleasure that simple touch incited.

"You had these beneath your headdress all along?" he asked. "So you were my beast today, too, weren't you?"

"Yes."

His other hand came up and he gripped both of her horns in warm, gentle fists. He pushed her head back, forcing her to look up at him.

"It is and will always be my honor to be your master, little beast. Now stand."

She did as she was told, shaking slightly now with anticipation of the night ahead. To her surprise, Nikhil knelt before her. With deft fingers, he unbuckled the bands about her thighs. From one, he retrieved his gift, attaching the small dagger to his own belt before rising again to take her hand and pull her behind him down the corridor again, naked save for the indentations his gifts had left on her thighs.

The scent of fresh-cut wood hit her nostrils several yards before they reached the door to their chamber. Belah's curiosity overwhelmed her. What had he done in the few hours since they'd arrived? He had never left her side, but all those surreptitious whispers with the guards must have something to do with what she would find inside when he opened the door. All she could sense from him was the power of his excitement to use her gift. That excitement amplified her own ten-fold.

Outside the door, he paused and turned to her, regarding her silently for a moment.

"Stay," he said, and moved to stand behind her. A second later, a cloth covered her eyes and he secured it at the back of her head. All her other senses heightened with that simple change, to the point she could easily hear his heart beating heavy in his chest. The scent of his male musk grew stronger, and the very brush of his fingertip down her spine made the rest of her body ache for his touch.

Before her, the door opened and the scent of cut wood surrounded her along with the other familiar scents from the room. Nikhil didn't lead her toward where the scent originated, however. Instead, he took her into the bathroom and made her stand at the edge of where she knew her wide, sunken tub to be. He left her standing alone and even though she itched to take off the blindfold and look around to see what waited in the other room, she knew better. More than anything, she wanted to experience his gift to her exactly the way he intended to bestow it.

She could hear the sounds of him undressing and a few moments later he returned and led her slowly down the steps into the warm water of her bath. The tub itself was deep enough for the water to reach her waist while standing, and Nikhil whispered for her to "stay" again once he stopped them in the middle of the tub. He moved away again and returned, bearing the scent of her soap.

Slowly he began to wash her, beginning by tilting her back in his arms and submerging her for a moment before standing her up again. He washed her hair with gentle massaging motions, making sure to give her horns more attention too, which caused the already prominent ache between her thighs to grow. Working his way down, he lathered her breasts with both large hands, cupping and kneading them. He tugged at her jeweled rings for a second, toying almost idly. Without a word, he moved both hands to one breast and Belah could feel him worrying at the ring that pierced that nipple. Suddenly the ring itself slid out of her flesh and the weight of the scarab disappeared. She let out a little sound of startlement.

"Shh. I want you completely bare before we start."

"But the piercing will heal."

"Then I shall pierce you again after. It isn't something I would ever tire of."

His fingers tugged at her other nipple's ornament until that, too disappeared. He massaged her now bare nipples between soapy fingers, squeezing and tugging enough to cause her clit to throb and her core to grow even hotter than the bathwater. She was panting and whimpering with need when he slid his hands down her torso and urged her thighs wider beneath the water. He didn't immediately remove the piercing there, though, instead choosing to torment her further by teasing the fingers of both hands between her folds, parting her and sliding back and forth under the pretense of washing her.

When he finally removed the scarab, Belah was close to begging him to fuck her. His fingers returned to her clit, now so bare the sensation was wholly new and foreign when he stroked. With one hand at her throat he pulled her back against him.

"This is only a small taste of what I have in store for you tonight, little beast," he said. His hand squeezed her throat while his fingers rubbed between her thighs. He knew exactly how much pressure to exert in both places to drive her mad, and before she knew it, she was plummeting semi-conscious into that glorious abyss.

She came back to herself only a moment later, cradled in Nikhil's lap at the edge of the tub, the blindfold gone. He had her wrapped in soft linens to dry her off, his large hands gently rubbing the cloth over her skin.

Belah gazed up at him with a sleepy smile and noticed that his skin now had a strange bluish glow to it that she had never seen before. Sitting up, she looked more closely, wondering if it was a hallucination or some strange manifestation of the power he had absorbed from her.

"How do you feel?" she asked, brushing her fingers over his cheek.

"More alive than I have ever felt. Like I never need to sleep again. If you were to ask me to conquer the entire world today, I believe I could do it. Do you know what they did to me?"

"It was my other gift to you, but a selfish one. The other gods imbued you with blessings to extend your life, so that I don't need to mark you. I am not privy to the exact extent of power you were given by the other races, or exactly what the blessings do, but my own brothers and sisters each gave you a gift of their very essence."

"And your gift... the blade... you mean for me to do more with it than give you pain."

"I don't wish to master you by marking you, Nikhil. But..."

"You wish your master to mark you, don't you, little beast?" His eyes flashed with sudden understanding. "Of course! You crave being branded by me permanently."

Nikhil's entire body tensed around her and his aura swelled. He lifted her in his arms and stood her up, turning her to face him rather than the archway that led to the bedroom.

"No peeking," he said with a sly smile, producing a dry length of silk and securing it around her head to obscure her sight again. "You will see soon enough what I have planned."

Turning her, he pushed her forward. She knew the room well enough to stride confidently through, even blind, but he pulled her to a stop abruptly when she was about halfway in. Lifting her up again, he set her down atop a piece of furniture that hadn't previously been in the center of the room. This was the source of the cut-wood scent, she realized, and now that she was on it, she let her hands slide over the soft, cushioned surface. The smell and texture of fine silk surprised her and made her wonder to what lengths he had gone in such a short time to create whatever this was, or if this was something he had planned all along.

Nikhil urged her to lie back and she found herself prone atop something as comfortable as her bed, but barely as wide as her own backside. Her feet didn't find purchase at first, hanging down over the edge, as did her arms. There was nothing beneath the odd platform and she had the oddest sense of being laid down on a tree branch. Her limbs didn't dangle for long. Nikhil lifted one ankle and pulled it wide, resting it on a similar narrow, cushioned surface before binding it with ropes to the contraption. He bound her other ankle similarly, spreading her legs wide in the process.

Belah's pussy clenched at the gust of hot breath that preceded Nikhil's words, spoken within inches of her parted flesh.

"You are beautiful bound and ready for me, *Tilahatan*. I am going to enjoy fucking you tonight." With that, he pressed his lips against her slick folds, kissing between her legs so thoroughly Belah cried out in ecstasy.

With a reluctant groan, Nikhil pulled his mouth away from her, leaving her hot and dripping in the cool evening air. He stood again and moved around to her side, then lifted her arms and raised them above her head, binding each wrist on crosspieces that extended above her.

Nikhil disappeared for a moment and Belah could hear his footsteps move to the cabinet beside the bed. He was going for her oils and toys—or at least, that was what it sounded like. When he returned, the scent of sweet almond oil accompanied him. The warm oil landed between her breasts in a puddle reminding her of the times he had tormented her with hot candle wax, but she hoped he would go beyond candles tonight.

With both hands, he smoothed the oil over her breasts, working it in before spreading it down her torso. He took his time, drizzling more oil at intervals until he had methodically massaged it into every exposed inch of her body. He avoided her cunt this time, much to her discomfort—she craved his touch on all of her, and particularly in that spot.

Then he paused for what seemed like an eternity. Belah knew he hadn't moved away—she could still hear his heartbeat, could still feel the familiar tingling brush of his aura against her own, their magic twining together. Finally, she sensed the slightest movement, and his scent wafted to her nose. Pure arousal was what she smelled. She wished she could see him now. Was he still naked? She thought so—and how magnificent he must look with his hair unbound around his shoulders and his cock hard and thick, jutting out from the dark nest between his legs.

A weight rested against her breastbone and he stilled again. What was it? She inhaled deeply, letting her chest rise and fall as she tried to get a sense of the object. It was long and narrow, heavier at one end. It also seemed to possess its own faint aura, and she knew.

The dagger. He planned to tease her as unmercifully with it as he did with every new game he introduced her to. Her nipples grew harder and her clit throbbed at the thought of what he might do—what he no doubt was eager to do.

"I know you need pain as much as I wish to provide it, little beast. And I know there is another thing you wish for, too. That I will grant you eventually, but for now, I intend to indulge myself with your gift."

He traced a fingertip down the center of her belly, all the way to the apex of her thighs. He dipped between her folds, rubbing lightly with the pad of a fingertip against her aching clit. When she was panting with desire, he stopped. The dagger left her chest and the soft sound of the leather sheathe sliding off the blade caused her to tense.

Belah's breathing quickened, her body alight while she waited for the first cut, but for the longest time he simply kept teasing her. He rested his palm on her lower abdomen and slid it down over her oiled skin until his fingertips were threaded between the folds of her pussy again. He rubbed his fingers up and down in her hot wetness, avoiding direct contact with her clit but caressing either side of it with the length of his fingers.

The first cut was barely a nick, and she almost didn't feel it. The quickening of his heartbeat and the push of air beneath her breast let her know he'd done something different. A second later, the sharp sting blossomed through her from the cut on the underside of her breast, just beneath her nipple. While she was still processing the sensation, he made another cut in the same spot beneath her other breast.

"When I take a prisoner in battle, this is the treatment they get from me. They aren't honored with a bath beforehand, or bound to a cushioned cross, and I certainly have never used such an exquisite instrument as this to give them pain. How does it feel, little beast? Ready for more?"

The entire time he spoke, his fingers continued toying with her pussy, sometimes pushing deep into her, other times simply cupping her and letting his palm press infuriatingly against her clit without moving. He traced the edge of her jaw with the flat of the small blade. The knife itself was no longer than one of his fingers and as narrow as a reed, but both edges were razor-sharp. Both her breasts burned with the pain of those two small cuts, but Belah could feel them healing already, her body's natural defenses had sensed the blood seeping out and begun repairing the damage. Still, she could feel the trails of warm fluid making their way along the curve of the crease beneath her breasts and over her ribcage.

"More. I need more. And please, let me see it. I've never laid eyes on my own blood before."

The room tilted and the blindfold fell off. Belah found herself leaning at a diagonal angle against the platform, her bound feet resting on soft ledges. Nikhil stood facing her and she took in his tall, powerful shape. He was, indeed, naked and fully erect, the gold paint gone and his skin flushed with heat, in spite of the cool evening air that came in through the balcony doorway. His massive chest rose and fell with heavy breaths. The primal beast she loved was alive behind his eyes and he clutched the dagger in one hand, held as naturally as though it were an extension of his body.

He moved close, the contraption she was tied to offering space between her spread thighs for him to stand. The thick length of his cock brushed the very top of her aching slit and he pressed against her while he eyed her breasts.

Nikhil grazed the sharp tip of the blade over the upper swell of one breast, just hard enough for her to feel without actually breaking skin. Belah stared down, enraptured by the sight of the point and the pink line it left behind. He made another line on the top of her other breast, as though marking the cut before making it.

"Go slow," she whispered when he positioned the blade back at the start of the first line and pushed in, pricking ever so gently but enough for her to feel the skin break and see a tiny, crimson droplet rise up from beneath her honey-colored skin.

He pulled the blade back, his breathing ragged. Instead of cutting her, he kissed her, the hand holding the blade cupping her cheek while he caressed between her lips with his hot tongue. Between them, he gripped his cock and tilted his hips back, positioning his thick head at her entrance. He only pushed in a tiny bit, and when he pulled back from the kiss, raw, hungry need filled his gaze.

"Do you have any idea how you honor me by allowing this?" he said hoarsely. "*Tilahatan*, you are my heart. I would bleed a thousand men to make you happy, yet you only wish that I bleed you."

He pressed the tip of the blade back to her breast and exerted just enough pressure to pierce her skin again. As he drew the blade across her flesh, he pushed his cock deeper. Belah stared down, fascinated by the way her skin opened and her blood welled up from beneath. The scent of it startled her at first—it smelled nothing like human blood, but was both sweet and tangy like the juice of some exotic fruit. It mixed in her nostrils with the scent of sex when Nikhil pulled out of her again and pushed back in, just as slowly as before while he began the second cut.

These were deeper than the first two, and the pain dragged across, flooding her with sensation as exquisite as the stretch of his cock against the walls of her pussy.

With a groan, Nikhil jabbed the knife into the cushioned support beside Belah's head and cupped her breasts in both hands. He shifted his hips back, pulled out of her to the tip and slammed back in so hard he shoved her up the platform.

When he bent his head to capture her nipple in his mouth, the cut on that breast widened, more blood flowing slowly over the flesh and the stinging pain of it perfectly merging with the pleasure of his mouth suckling her hard tip. He tilted his head back and darted out his tongue, sliding the tip of it along the length of the cut and gathering her blood as he went. The sensation was as arousing as if he had run his tongue between her legs and Belah threw her head back with a groan of pleasure.

"Yes, Nikhil. Taste me." The words fell from her lips even as a niggling memory flickered in the back of her mind. Something she'd been told thousands of years before about the proper ways to transfer power to a mate. But she couldn't remember and didn't care. All she cared about was the exquisite pleasure he gave her now.

He continued pumping into her while he tongued her breasts, nipping at her nipples and sucking at the cuts on her breasts as though her blood were mother's milk. Each time he did, pain flooded her senses until she was nothing more than sensation.

Nikhil looked up at her after a moment, with beads of sweat covering his brow and glistening on his chest. His lips were red from tasting her and slick when they pressed against hers. Her own flavor hit her tongue and the taste was even more erotic than the flavor of his semen and her own sex juices combined. That it was his tongue transferring the liquid to her mouth made the pleasure surge even higher through her body.

His hips thrust his cock deeper, battering her insides repeatedly with each fresh thrust. She whimpered involuntarily against his mouth, overwhelmed by the combination of sensations.

"Does it hurt, little beast? Which hurts more: my cock, or the cuts I gave you?" He bent his head to bite hard at one of the cuts before gathering a mouthful of her breast between his lips and sucking hard. His tongue swirled over and over her nipple and around to both cuts that bracketed it top and bottom until the sensations became one, thrumming through her body to her core, where he kept fucking her harder and harder.

As amazing as he was making her feel in that moment, she knew deep down that this was more for him than it was for her. Even though he gave her more pleasure than ever before, he was reserving her true gift until after he'd had his fill of hurting her.

The thought of what was in store caused a sudden tremor to pass through her. She yelled out his name, the syllables broken by the pounding thrusts of his cock pushing air from her lungs. A second later he yelled hers in return and his cock throbbed and pulsed with his climax, his orgasm flooding hotly into her.

Belah could only lay back and take all he had to give, from the steady, wet heat of his semen filling her to the newness of his energy, now enhanced by the blessings he'd been given during their wedding ceremony. His energy tasted like life, like sunlight and rain and growing things, like air and water, earth and fire. She had reveled in it earlier in the day when they had first consummated their marriage along the streets of the city in full view of her people.

Something was different now, however. Like the dark threads she'd sensed in him months ago when she worried that his dragon blessing might be damaging his mind, a new thread was laced through the power with a frightening potency. It was something *beyond* simply life, and with a jolt she realized it was her own essence. But not the essence that a willing gift would provide its recipient. Her essence, taken directly from her body in a way that she could never willingly give except to her own offspring.

Nikhil had taken her blood into himself, and the shocking understanding of what that could mean terrified her. Never in the long history of her race had a human *taken* a dragon's blood, much less the blood of an immortal like her. The memory that had eluded her before came surging back—the warning from her mother that a dragon's blood should never be taken. Yet Belah had willingly orchestrated the taking of it, so surely that mattered? It must matter, somehow, because she could still sense the love in him.

With that exchange came a connection the likes of which she had never imagined. When Nikhil slipped out of her and strode away, his shoulders heaving from his exertion, every nuance of his thoughts were apparent to her, even down to the darkest wishes he kept locked deep inside his very soul.

What she saw beyond the very real and powerful love he had for her was something far darker. It lay dormant beneath the gifts he'd been given, subdued by the power of their love. Belah was comforted by that, at least. Everyone carried some amount of darkness in them, after all. But within Nikhil, it was like the sleeping leviathan that should never be awakened, lest you invite destruction upon the world.

That he was hers now meant she could at least control that darkness, to ensure it never saw the light. She alone had the power to provide him with the outlet he needed to keep his darkness sated.

She strained at her bindings, wanting to break them and go to him, to comfort the turmoil that raged through his mind. He wanted to cut her more, to see her blood flow. The ache was like a hunger inside him as strong as his desire to fuck her. That ache was tied to his darkness, and yet the part of him that rebelled against it was the part that wanted to please her.

He stood stock still a few paces away now, his entire body tense, and the knife still in his hand, its blade aimed at the floor.

"I need more of you, Belah," he said in a strained voice over his shoulder, somehow too unsure about what he was about to say to face her directly. "Your pain is perfect, and to see your blood flow, to *taste* it, makes me feel so powerful. Like I am truly worthy to be the mate of a goddess. Perhaps someday I will be your equal if I do this. If I take all you have to give. Will you let me take it? It is what you want, too, is it not? I won't waste a drop, I promise."

"What will you take?" she asked, sure she knew the answer already but hoping he would turn back and tell her directly.

His shoulders quivered and she wished she could touch him, but he'd bound her. She could have easily broken the bonds, as strong as she was, but to do that would negate her trust in him.

Nikhil turned to face her, his expression haunted. His hair clung to the side of his face and he pushed it back vehemently. The usual wildness she loved in him was present in his eyes, but something new had taken residence. A craving she didn't quite understand.

"Your life, my love. That's what you want me to take, isn't it?"

"You know it's only temporary. I can't die, Nikhil. I can never die. My life is infinite, and that infinite life I give to you. What you give me in return is everything I have always desired."

He shook his head. "Don't you see? What I have to give is no match for what you offer. No, you want me to mark you, remember? To brand you as mine. You would be mine for an eternity, but what good is that if I don't have eternity to spend with you? No, I will only give you tonight like this. When we are done and you wake up, I want you to mark me truly. I understand what it means, but it is my free will to sacrifice, is it not?"

"Please don't ask for that," she said. The cuts on her breasts still twinged with pain, though they were healing swiftly, but the pain within her chest came from a deeper cut—one he couldn't see.

"I have lived for this moment, *Tilahatan*. After I'm done, I only ask that you mark me, and then we can have an eternity together for you to remind me that you are my little beast. *Mine*."

Belah stared at him, shocked by the earnest look he gave her and the absolute desperation that flashed like a fresh bruise through his aura. Her heart ached and for the first time her resolve crumbled.

"My love, I cannot say no to you when I am at your mercy like this."

"Then it is settled," he said.

CHAPTER TWENTY

Nikhil picked up a small stack of clay pots with one hand and strode toward her. With a flick of the hand that held the knife, he turned it so the flat of the blade was in front of her mouth. "Open," he said. She did, and he rested the blade against her teeth.

Belah clamped down on the blade and watched him while he placed the ceramic bowls at each of the four corners of the platform she was bound to. Once he seemed satisfied with their placement, he took the blade from her teeth and kissed her with the slowest, hottest press of his mouth.

The kiss grew in fervor as his cock thickened between them, rubbing against the slickness between her thighs. He didn't enter her again, but kept his cock sliding up and down, spreading delicious sensation over her clit.

While they kissed he reached both hands out, sliding them up along the insides of her arms. When he reached her wrist, he pressed the blade's tip to the hollow of tender flesh, just beneath where her binding held her.

The pain seared her in a blinding rush that continued as he let the blade sink in, deeper than he had with the cuts on her breasts. The sweet scent of her blood rose again as the warm fluid trickled down her arm before a steady stream of it hit the carefully placed bowl beneath her.

Belah's clit throbbed and the sensation of his cock rubbing against her grew even slicker from the flood of arousal that filled her. Ecstasy overwhelmed her when he switched the blade to his other hand and made the cut to her opposite wrist.

"Will you come for me, little beast?" Nikhil murmured in her ear. He pulled his hips back just enough to let his cock dip between her spread folds and slide into her yet again. His shaft was every bit as hard and hot as it had been barely moments earlier, and the hot rush of pain thrumming down both her arms now made it impossible for her to hold back a cry when he settled in deep. He barely moved this time—he barely needed to, because she went flying the second his pelvis pressed against her clit and rotated just the tiniest fraction.

"Nikhil!" His name burst in a gasp from her mouth as her body shuddered with her orgasm. This time he pulled out slowly, sliding down her body and laying soft kisses against her skin as he went. He lingered at her breasts, which to her surprise still bled, though the sharp twinge of his tongue over her cuts lent faint pain in comparison to the cuts he'd put on her wrists.

When he knelt between her thighs, he gazed up at her, sliding his hands up and down, massaging the insides of her legs with one hand and caressing with the knuckles of the hand that still held the blade. He spread her open, pressing the cool flat of the blade to the top of her cleft and holding it for a moment without moving. The temperature shift indeed calmed her throbbing flesh, but he pulled it away only to replace it with the wide flat of his tongue, licking her entire cunt from bottom to top in one mind-altering sweep that had her throbbing and ready for more.

He held the blade loosely in his hands now, poised above her navel, which he eyed with a slight smile. Belah sensed him assessing her skin the way an artist might a canvas. She knew he had deft hands, capable of fine, delicate work. He had a reputation as a master torturer, after all. He also had a very keen eye, though she had no idea what kind of mark he might be inclined to make into her flesh.

The bleeding from her wrists had slowed, the upraised angle of her arms preventing it from flowing too freely, but it still ran in a steady, crimson trickle into the containers beneath. She watched, fascinated by the red ripples in the small container that captured her very essence.

Pain pricked her belly just below her navel, and she hissed, glancing back down at Nikhil. He gave her a slightly admonishing look, but it quickly shifted to his familiar wild lust when the blade pierced her skin just enough to draw blood and he drew it down in a perfectly straight line. The sharper pain the cut caused surprised her and made her gasp. Her reaction incited a rough growl from Nikhil, but he remained focused on his work. From there, he traced a perfect arc, describing a half-moon shape around one side of her belly before tracing a mirror image on the opposite side.

Blood welled up to fill the lines he cut and she closed her eyes, letting her mind follow the pattern of the pain he drew into her skin. It flared with white heat on the backs of her eyelids, the design gradually becoming clearer with each cut. When he was finished several minutes later, he called her name, urging her to open her eyes again.

He stood before her, his wide shoulders and beautiful face filling her field of vision. After a quick kiss, he moved to the side. Belah came face-to-face with her own reflection and inhaled sharply at the sight. A large scarab shape was etched into her belly, surrounding her navel. Its wings stretched outward from either side, but the wings resembled her own unfurled wings rather than that of a bird or an insect. The scarab itself was the seal and symbol Nikhil used, representing his family and his patron god, but the wings she knew were his homage to her.

With effort, she tore her gaze away from the image and met his eyes, unable to do more than smile with pure gratitude at his gift.

"I am not finished yet, *Tilahatan*. Now, I worship you before taking you to your heart's desire."

He fell to his knees before her and pressed his lips to the top of one foot where it rested on the small ledge of her platform, only a short distance above the floor. With slow, deliberate movements, he kissed his way up, to her ankle and then a little higher. He paused there, squeezed and caressed her lower leg in an odd fashion. Before she could wonder what he was doing, he brought the knife up and made a swift, sure cut on a diagonal into the flesh inside her leg. Blood flowed, landing perfectly in the center of the basin he'd placed beneath.

The pain spiked through her, but subsided quickly until he shifted to the other side. The speed with which he cut her told her that the pain wasn't his goal now, but the bleeding itself. The cuts to her ankles went deeper than the ones to her wrists and her blood flowed freely now, and so swiftly she felt a little drunk.

Nikhil rose up between her thighs and swept his tongue in a slow, languid lick around her soaked folds. He drew away and she could see fresh blood glistening on his lips.

"You taste like heaven, *Tilahatan*. It is my honor to kneel before you and worship you in your glory, to take your gift of blood while I give you the gift of pleasure. To take you into me the way I give my seed to you. I am your slave now, my free will matters not but how I can serve you. So you see, it will make no difference if you make me yours fully, for I am nothing without the taste of you on my tongue, the clutch of you around my cock, and the sound of my name on your lips. Tell me you will make me yours after I am finished making you mine."

"Yes, Nikhil. I will," she whispered, her lips and tongue feeling thick and sluggish. The ache in her heart lingered, but somehow what he said made sense now. It made more sense when he bent his head back to her pussy and covered her with his entire mouth.

He devoured her with a kind of hunger he reserved for the times he wanted to drive her mad to the point of begging to be fucked, his tongue sliding deep into her before slipping out and tasting every increment of flesh. She felt wetter than she ever had and looked down to see that the blood from the scarab sliced into her belly flowed down between her thighs, where Nikhil greedily lapped at it. He intermittently went back to her clit and teased and sucked until her hips began to twitch and the rising pleasure nearly went to her head. Then he would stop and simply lick like he were a child enjoying a sugary treat.

Over and over he took her close, each time looking up at her with eyes blazing. He was mad with his own need now, his aura a throbbing, pulsing cloud around him, deep red with the brightest threads of blue throughout.

In her muzzy mind, Belah thought the blue wasn't right, that it meant something important she should be wary of, but couldn't quite remember. Before she could reach deeper into memory to find it, Nikhil rose to his feet and leaned down to kiss her with both hands cupping the sides of her face.

He made love to her mouth, letting his tongue sweep inside in languid licks. The flavor of him was so unique it made her groan to taste. This was her very essence mixed with his and they were delicious together. What would a melding of their essences look like? If they could have a child, would the child's essence be as beautiful as the feeling that taste gave her? Dare she even wish for such a thing? But was it her wish or his? She wasn't so sure, now that his thoughts sank into her mind because she seemed to have lost the ability to control her power.

He slid one of his hands down over her collarbone, cupped her breast briefly, and teased at her nipple before coming to rest against her sternum. He pulled back from their kiss as breathless as she was, but his eyes were intent, concentrating on something.

Her heartbeat. She realized it without even meaning to read his thoughts, but in that second the heavy thud of his own made a quicker counterpoint in her ears. Her heartbeat was slowing, and with each beat she felt lighter and lighter and the love in his eyes was like the lightest breeze lifting her up.

"Stay with me, my love. Look into my eyes. I am the one giving you leave to fly, to release your tether to the world and set you free. Only I control that freedom, little beast. Little goddess," he said, though the words were barely a whisper.

His cock was at her core again, pushing deep. The pleasure of his fucking enhanced the feeling of weightlessness and she gave into it entirely. He was in control of her pleasure, of her power, of her very need to be released.

Belah's ecstasy peaked with the most exquisite surge of energy.

"Go," he said. He released her with that single word, his face still contorted with the strain of his orgasm as his semen pumped into her.

She let go, diving into the darkness of the abyss, her wings catching the wind. Elation filled her and she soared, buoyed up by her love and gratitude for the man with the strength to give her everything by taking everything she had to give.

CHAPTER TWENTY-ONE

NIKHIL

"Fly, *Tilahatan*," Nikhil whispered. He brushed his lips across his unconscious lover's, breathing her in while he recovered from another soul-wrenching orgasm shared with the woman he loved. The only woman he would ever love.

He was light-headed from the thrill he always got giving her the very thing that heated his own blood. Her pain gave them both so much pleasure, but while he could take pleasure in seeing the light and life fade from an enemy, the only pleasure he took from giving his lover that gift was in the act of fulfilling her deepest wish.

This was his gift to her on their wedding night. When she awoke, he would hold her to her promise to grant his wish. Nikhil refused to believe that her magic could be so powerful that he would lose his free will if Belah marked him. It was a risk he was more than willing to take if it meant spending eternity with her. Not that he feared death—not for himself; he feared it for her—but she had told him over and over again that death was not a friend to her. She only wished to experience that level of release, and he understood. As sexual a creature as she was, she fearlessly explored every avenue of pleasure to the extreme. He loved her for her sense of adventure.

At the moment he was conflicted, however, and forced himself to be comforted by the fact that he had succeeded in giving her the perfect gift—a temporary respite from the burden of her eternal life.

He reluctantly pulled his cock out of her and lowered the platform Belah was still bound to. Inside his belly burned an odd fire that surged when he laid eyes on her beautiful, serene face, as perfect as though she were a statue. Today had been a glorious day that had left him filled with a myriad of new sensations. All the gods had been present and had gifted him with their blessings—blessings that were meant to extend his life to give him more time with his bride. To him they were meant for something different—to ensure he was indeed worthy to be the consort of a goddess, regardless of the fact that she was more than willing to submit to him as his little beast. Now she was even branded as such, with the marks he'd cut into the pristine, fair skin of her abdomen.

Belah's debasing of herself honored him more than he could express, but it was still painfully apparent to him how much greater a creature she was than himself.

He swiftly wrapped a sarong around his hips before untying her. He carried her back into the still-warm bath and gently washed the blood from her limp body in the fragrant water, leaving it tinged pink. The first time she'd given up her breath to him to the point of total unconsciousness it had taken a couple days before she returned to him. He guessed that this kind of release would take her longer to recover from, but he would stay by her side until she awoke.

During that last, tortuous span of time when he believed her dead, she had never quite *seemed* completely gone. Her body never grew cold as a normal body would in death, yet her heart did not beat and her lungs did not breathe.

Even now, her skin carried a slight glow, which he'd only recently been able to see. She told him it was the magic of the Blessing he'd been given in his mother's womb that allowed him to see her aura—that it gave him the unique ability to recognize the magic of the gods once he became attuned to one of them.

Once clean, he carried her out of the bath, carefully dried her skin and hair, and dressed her in her favorite nightgown. He laid her in the center of her bed and moved around the room, first dismantling the elaborate bench he'd ordered built during the hours they were at their celebration, then moving the basins that held her blood onto a shelf beside the bed, believing deep in his bones that her essence was sacred and should not be wasted. He slowly lit more candles until the room was as bright as daylight. He didn't intend to sleep until she awoke.

A cold chill prickled the back of his neck as he lit the last candle. His body tensed, a sudden sense of dread encompassing him.

The room went dark. Nikhil blinked, a sense of vertigo over-taking him from the sudden, complete, loss of light—so dark he couldn't see the flame of the match he held, though the heat of it singed his fingertips.

"*What have you done!*" The angry voice boomed loud and deep, both inside his mind and so loud it left his ears ringing. The sound surrounded him so completely he couldn't even place a direction of origin for it, as though it erupted from the darkness itself. Nikhil spun unsteadily, hands outstretched.

Something hit him hard from the side, sending him flailing through the air. He hit a wall, his shoulder taking the brunt of the impact. His breath tore from him and he struggled to remain on his feet.

"Who's there!" he yelled into the pitch black. His own rage surged to match the palpable sense of animosity that surrounded him, permeating the shadows.

Belah. Her prone, defenseless body was his only thought and he ran in the direction he knew the bed to be. If he had to give his life to ensure her safety, whatever was in the room with them now would not harm her.

His thigh and shoulder hit the bedpost first, with a painful, cracking thud, and he rounded it to stand facing what his instincts told him was the direction of the dark threat.

"Who dares invade the goddess's chamber? Show yourself!" he bellowed. The more the rage in him grew, the hotter the strange burn in his belly became. He needed to *see* if he was going to properly protect her.

He couldn't tell anymore whether the heat that filled him was from anger over this unexpected attack—on their *wedding night*—or from the odd sensation that had been building inside him since he'd begun the ritual-like act of granting Belah's wish. His entire body flamed with it, inside and out, and he became acutely aware of another presence just opposite him on the far side of the room at the opening to the balcony.

A rage as potent as his own reached him from the darkness he faced, and along with it a mirror to his very need to love and protect the woman who lay on the bed. Nikhil's vision seemed to clear, though it appeared more like the darkness retreated from the force of his will to see his assailant.

"You have taken what was not yours to take. For that, you will pay." Belah's brother's figure loomed large on the balcony. He came forward, aiming toward the bed.

Nikhil stepped into his path.

Ked's expression hardened with disdain, his stride quickening like he was about to ram right into Nikhil.

Nikhil felt power bubble forth from inside him when the other man drew close. It began with that burn in his belly and rose with his rage, more potent even than the rush he felt on the center of a battlefield.

"Get away from her!" he yelled. His fist shot out at the moment Ked came into range. It connected with his jaw. Nikhil heard the clack of teeth and Ked sailed across the room to land in a heap against the far wall. The room instantly brightened.

Ked struggled to rise, blinking and shaking his head. He stared in astonishment at Nikhil.

Nikhil glared at him.

"How do you have the power to lay me down?" Ked asked. His amazement didn't last long. Before Nikhil could blink, his dark opponent shimmered and his body shifted its shape. The man became a scaled beast that resembled the beast his lover had shown to him, but much larger and with black scales instead of blue.

Sharp teeth snapped at him and he drew back.

"I will take her home." Ked said. "You are tainted now. Unworthy of her love."

"She's my *wife*. You will let me care for her."

"You destroyed her. You will die for this."

Before Nikhil could respond, black flames erupted from Ked's mouth and surrounded him. Pure agony bloomed across his entire body, his world growing blinding white from the heat a moment before darkness overtook him once again.

CHAPTER TWENTY-TWO

B elah dreamed of flying endlessly without tiring. The winds carried her, rendering her weightless and free. She flew among the whitest clouds and the bluest skies, the burdens of her world long gone.

She could breathe easily for the first time in thousands of years. Something itched in the back of her mind, but it was only the tiniest discomfort compared to the freedom of soaring aloft without end. Flying she could do for an eternity—being up this high left time irrelevant, left the world an inconsequential pinprick far beneath her. All that she needed existed among the clouds and the winds that kept her aloft.

Except for that tingle of awareness that she *did* need more, but not yet. Now she only needed to fly; whatever that other thing was could wait until she'd had her fill.

* * *

Belah, sister, wake up.

The voice was familiar, the deep, urgent voice of someone she loved. Around her the boundless blue sky filled with white mist that tingled when her wings flowed through it. Was it time to return? She circled around once, testing that tiny itch in the back of her mind, but it was too faint to worry about, so she flew on.

* * *

Belah, your baby is beautiful and healthy. She needs her mother. Please wake up, sister.

She had the clearest vision of a beautiful, fair-skinned woman with deep, compassionate green eyes. Yet she had no recollection of a baby. She hadn't had a baby in centuries. Someday maybe she would again, but for now she only wished to fly.

* * *

Belah, we tried to avenge you again, but he is more powerful than before. Not even the three of us together could overtake him. We dare not let our sisters near him—his Blessing is too much of a lure, even for males of our race. He has begun killing. He has corrupted two other Blessed humans and coerced them into hunting and killing for him, too. They are as strong as an army. The younger dragons are no match for them. You must wake up and help us convince him to stop—it is you he asks for. Only you can convince him to stop.

The smooth, deep voice sank into her mind like honey, reminding her of the warm, red gaze of someone she cared deeply for, once upon a time. All she cared about now was the push of the wind propelling her as she beat her wings, and the caress of the air sliding over her scales like silk. The North Wind was her only friend now, and his caress the only touch she needed.

* * *

Belah, we need you. Mother says you must make the decision for his punishment. Please, he is killing them. So many of them are suffering, forced into hiding. We must do something, but you are the only one who can calm him.

Another feminine voice this time, evoking an image of a bronze-skinned beauty with shimmering golden eyes and flaxen hair. The itch grew enough to make her slow and consider the words she heard. There was no suffering among the clouds and the sweet flow of the breeze, however; here, suffering was not her concern. She flew on.

* * *

Belah, we've been fools, but we know now it was your blood you needed to awaken. We convinced him to give it back to us, at least enough of it to revive you. He refused to relinquish it all—the only way to get all of it back is for you to agree to see him. You need to wake up and help us, sister. You must make him stop these horrible things he does to us—to all the higher races. He is too powerful for any dragon to slay now. Nikhil has become a monster. Please, sister. He has found our children and hidden them away from us.

Nikhil. The name echoed in the clear air around her. The itch became a buzz. Then a high-pitched scream. Pain erupted from her wrists and ankles, from her breasts and belly. The clouds around her began to swirl in a tornado of color, whipping violently until she had no control over her direction. The wind became a twisting vortex of red, green, and white. Instead of the slow, lethargic pull she'd felt when her blood flowed out of her body, she felt the piercing, burning surge of it being forced back in through the wounds it had left from.

Belah's spirit slammed back into her body with a sound as deafening as a thunderclap. Along with it came the memory and weight of all the things her siblings had told her while she lay unconscious, lost in her own world and oblivious to the time that had passed.

She lurched up with a scream that vibrated the air around her, found herself flailing and splashing in water with five pairs of hands struggling to hold her steady. A large pair of arms slipped around her from behind and pulled her back against a broad, strong chest.

"Sister, calm down, I have you," Ked said.

Belah stared wildly, kicking out at the other four who now stood back out of her reach, regarding her with worried looks. Nothing was right about this view. The last thing she remembered seeing was Nikhil's look of adoration as he made love to her, timing her climax so it hit her at just the right moment to send her flying into that glorious, vast nothingness.

"Nikhil," she said, though the word came as barely a whisper now, her voice suddenly used up with the scream of pain from her life's blood being forced back into her body. The torrent of emotion and sensation overwhelmed her now, all of it rushing back in a flood. Every stinging cut Nikhil had given her blazed fresh, as did the tingling afterglow of her orgasm.

But her surroundings didn't match her memory. She stilled in Ked's grasp, but remained rigid, uncertain. Slowly, the familiarity of this place sank in. The sights and sounds and scents were known to her because this was the place she'd been born. They were in their mother's Glade, the most sacred place for all dragons. This was their version of the Ursa's Sanctuary or the Turul's Enclaves, or the Nymphaea's Haven. They never came here unless they were in grave danger.

That understanding caused her to struggle against her brother's strong grip. Panic flared inside her as all the missives she'd heard from her siblings came rushing back.

"No, no, no. What did you do? Where is Nikhil?"

She clawed at Ked's arms, her talons manifesting from the tips of her fingers and raking down his flesh leaving angry red stripes.

"Belah, he has turned on us. He is our enemy now." Ked's voice was low and firm in her ear.

She shook her head, ignoring the hot rush of tears that flooded her eyes.

"No! He would never betray me. *Never!* Where is he? Why did you take me away from him?"

With one hand she reached back and swiped at her brother's face, caught the side of his cheek, and heard a harsh grunt of pain. She may not be able to draw blood, but she could make him hurt. At the same time, she released a lungful of her breath, filling the air around them and pushing the magic into his face where he would have no choice but to breathe it in, or else suffocate.

With a harsh curse, Ked released her. Belah shifted and launched herself into the air. She had to go to Nikhil now, to explain what happened, to beg his forgiveness. How long had it been since their wedding day? She had no way of knowing. She only hoped it hadn't been too long.

Above her, the idyllic blue sky split open as though sensing her need to depart, displaying a dark, cloudless, starlit night through a swirling portal. She flew through, ignoring the angry, desperate call of her brother and her other siblings. With a crack as loud as the thunderclap that returned her essence to her, the portal closed behind her.

She circled, disoriented for a moment until she caught her bearings by the light of a crescent moon. Beneath her was a mountain peak jutting up from the dense cloud layer. On the summit of the mountain was a stone structure built in the shape of a hexagon with an elaborate, glowing mosaic in the center.

Belah remembered the place from her childhood, but hadn't been back in thousands of years. She knew that beneath the cloud layer lay a monastery populated by a celestial race of humans who had served her kind since she and her siblings were born. Somewhere beneath her the monks kept records of her race's history, and the most valuable treasures that the dragons had created. The Monastery was the safest refuge for the younger generations of dragons, who were rarely allowed inside the Glade.

The Monastery wasn't where she must go, but it helped her choose the right direction. She flew west as fast as her wings could carry her, hoping it would be fast enough to outrun her brother, who she knew was already chasing her. She had nothing to say to him – not until she found Nikhil and let him know she was safe. That he might believe she had died after all her promises to the contrary left her with dark, twisting despair in her soul.

While she flew, her mind replayed the messages her siblings had given her while she lay unconscious. Each one had been more urgent than the last, and had made less and less sense. She had no daughter that still lived. All but one of the children she had borne in her life were now long dead after living their own long lives and carrying on her line. The one remaining son had been hidden away eons ago and likely lay in hibernation in some secret place even she and her siblings had no knowledge of, in spite of her brother's searching.

She had not even had the chance to mark Nikhil so they could breed. If she found him and he were well, she vowed she would grant his wish now. There was no need for him to be punished, as her sister Aurum had suggested, and she couldn't imagine him harming anyone without her orders.

The cloud cover burned away with the heat of midday and she dipped lower, recognizing the shape of the shoreline that drifted past beneath her. Close to dusk, her heart swelled with the familiar sight of the Nile Delta and its teeming life. It was just as she remembered, beautiful and green, with the mono-lithic pyramids standing guard in the distance. She picked up her pace, veering in the direction of the coast and the peninsula where her palace lay.

The closer she came to the city itself, the more pronounced the *wrongness* of the place seemed. She used to revel in the contentment of her people as she flew over, proud of how she ruled with love and generosity, how she protected them from the outsiders who wished to conquer and plunder.

Now, the difference was striking enough to cause her to falter. Strife and hunger were prevalent at the outskirts, only growing more concentrated in the densest center before fading to general dissatisfaction closer to the palace district. The city was visually different as well, though the differences were subtle. The buildings looked rundown, the walls crumbling in places. Some new ones had been built but without the care of the original structures.

With apprehension, Belah circled wide around the palace, remaining high in the growing dusk to avoid being seen.

The first skull she encountered mounted atop the palace walls shocked her and she slowed. Then there was another, unmistakable in its shape and size. They were the skulls of massive, horned creatures, with long, sharp teeth.

Sickness welled up in her gut. Disbelief urged her forward. Dozens upon dozens of dragon skulls adorned the rooftop of her former home, including two huge ones mounted on the wall outside her own chambers. The horror of the sight dimmed when she looked through the doorway into the palace.

She hovered in the air, staring into the well-lit interior of her rooms. What she witnessed made her heart lodge in her throat, so similar it was to her recollection of the last time she'd been inside that room.

The woman strapped onto the contraption that rested inside the opening of the balcony might have been Belah, based on her appearance. From her vantage she could tell it was a bronze-skinned woman with jet-black hair. The woman was both fearful and aroused, and just as blindfolded as Belah had been on her wedding night. But this was a human woman—Belah could tell by the clear, bright aura that surrounded her—and a virgin, no less.

Confused by the sight, she reached out farther with her mind, seeking out Nikhil.

Suddenly a dark cloud surrounded her, accompanied by a gust of wind.

"You must not alert him to your presence, sister. You'll endanger us all. Come away from here. This place is no longer safe for our kind."

Belah shrank from the presence, irritated at how well Ked held her encompassed in the dark cloud.

"Leave me be! He needs to know what became of me. I don't care who he's brought to our bed since you took me away from him. He deserves the truth."

Ked's power tugged at her mind, seeking to suppress the blaze of longing that burst from her soul when Nikhil's shape came into view. He was every bit as powerful a figure as she remembered, fully naked with a small, glinting dagger held loosely in one hand.

"He knows the truth already, sister." Ked's power tugged harder at her mind and a pair of strong talons clutched at her shoulders, pulling her back.

Belah resisted, her heart splintering when she watched Nikhil approach the female he had bound, murmuring soothing words and exuding a love that was too similar to what she'd felt from him herself. Was she so easily replaced?

She resisted Ked's talons, shrugging away so she could see what the man she loved would do to the woman who looked like her.

CHAPTER TWENTY-THREE

Nikhil bent to the female's breast, captured a nipple in his mouth, and sucked. She tasted of dirt, and he had to restrain the urge to let her go and rinse his mouth out. The female on his rack was no replacement for his *Tilahatan*, but he kept trying to find closure somehow.

He wanted nothing more than a child with her. A boy of his own blood to cherish the way he always wished his father could have cherished him. To teach in the ways of war he wished his father could have taught him. He had been the best warrior in his mistress's armies, but what kind of warrior would he have been if he'd had his father's wisdom on the battlefield, too?

Perhaps he would never have needed to take that wound while seeking *her* glory. Perhaps he never would have met and fallen in love with *her* when she came to save him.

Perhaps he could have turned around and truly conquered her, rather than living the rest of his unending days being conquered himself by his craving for a woman who left him.

He hated himself for that one weakness now. He had let himself grow to need her, to *love* her, and it had nearly destroyed him.

Somehow it hadn't, and for that, he was grateful. He could credit his absent wife for that, no doubt. All the rituals and blessings on their wedding day had made him strong, had set a fire alight in his belly. But the fuel that had kept it burning for the past two centuries was *her* blood.

He left the side of the virginal likeness of his lover and sipped from a goblet of thick, fermented liquid. Even as old as it was, it still made his blood sing. Her blood still tasted of her very essence and reminded him of the flavor of her sweet juices that would flood his tongue in the moments when he had his mouth latched to her nether lips, drawing her pleasure from her with his tongue.

He'd been beyond sanity after waking up alone in their chambers with her gone and nothing but her blood for his company. Being granted the throne in her stead didn't calm him. He could see them everywhere. Dragons were the ones who had taken her from him. They needed to suffer until she was returned.

He had no memory now of those times, only that he rabidly searched for her, interrogated every dragon he could find, using the knife she'd given him to torture them. The second they saw their own blood spill, they talked, but none of them had anything helpful to say.

Finally, he simply took to killing them outright. If he killed enough of them, the gods themselves would take notice.

And they did.

By the time her brothers came to reclaim her blood, he had lived on killing for decades. But they wouldn't return her to him. They made a deal—their useless blood for hers. "Because it is sacred to us," they told him.

"Is she dead?" he asked.

The three of them had stood around him in this very room while he asked that question and told him, "Yes, but her blood will revive her."

By their accounts, a dead dragon's blood was sacred. Nikhil didn't believe it. He'd killed enough dragons to know better. The Twins had taken to Belah's blood immediately, but after them, every single human he fed it to went mad and died within hours.

He hunted other dragons and tested their blood, both living and dead, on everyone he could convince to accept the test. Only the blood of the living dragons granted power to those who drank it, but never the level of power that he or the Twins had.

All he knew was that somehow *he* was special. Perhaps if he had a son or daughter, somehow his power would be passed on.

The nubile woman bound to his rack today was one in thousands. The only thing that differentiated this woman from all the rest was that she actually seemed to enjoy being terrified.

Nikhil's cock couldn't resist that combination of terror and arousal. He supposed he had his goddess to thank for that. Ever since their wedding night, he'd been acutely attuned to the hearts and minds of everyone he encountered. He could read thoughts, emotions, intentions. He could see things he couldn't see before, like shimmering clouds around people that he learned signaled their moods and desires.

This woman wanted him so desperately.

He wished he wanted her.

The people his *Tilahatan* used to rule now feared him as their devil. *Apophis*, they called him. He still lived, he still killed. He didn't care what they thought. He only wanted her, though now he wasn't sure what he would do with her if he had her back. If he had her back, he would never let her go again. He would leave her bound to this rack so he could drain her blood and teach her what it meant to truly be conquered every day.

Now he only wanted a child that looked like it came from her womb. The woman in front of him was nobody, but she looked like his love. If she bore him a child it might also look like *her*.

He swiped the blade of the knife across the underside of the woman's breast, but didn't dare taste her blood. Human blood tasted just as filthy as this woman's skin had tasted, but he relished the flash of pain that crossed her face and the resulting arousal. He only needed a little to help his cock rise. Another slice and she cried out. Then he was on her, shoving deep into her while he held the blade to her throat. Her fear kept him hard.

When he was finished, he called to his guards and ordered them to take her away. If his seed took root, he would wait and see what came of it. A son would allow the woman to survive. Anything less, and he had no use for her.

CHAPTER TWENTY-FOUR

Belah hovered, too paralyzed by the sight to do more than instinctively beat her wings to stay aloft. The aura of the man she viewed was nothing like the Nikhil she remembered. Not even a glimmer of that man remained.

Around her, the darkness thickened, obscuring the sight from her tortured gaze. With a swirl of dizzying movement, Ked transported them away. The air chilled suddenly, then warmed again and when the darkness abated, she found herself in the middle of a lush garden on a stone path that led down a hill to what looked like a small village.

"Where are we?" she asked, numb to any other thought but her present surroundings.

"At the Monastery. Things have changed since that day, Belah. I will tell you everything."

He shifted into his human form and clothed himself in simple robes. Reluctantly, Belah followed suit, though what she really wanted to do was fly away. If only she could return to the uncomplicated bliss of her slumber.

"Who was she?"

Without answering, Ked gently took her hand and led her up the path to a carved stone bench that rested in the shade of a large tree. They sat, and Ked's grip on her hand tightened.

"She is just a woman, his latest bride. If this one fails to bear him a son, he'll execute her. It's been the same, year after year. Sometimes he succeeds, but the child dies when he attempts to feed him your blood. Normal humans can't survive a taste of immortal blood. They go mad to the point of suicide. Some can accept a lesser dragon's blood, and those are the ones who follow him now."

"She looked like me," Belah whispered. She lifted her hand to her chest, wishing she could dispel the ache that had taken root there, burning like a hot coal.

"They always do. Sometimes he succeeds in capturing a blue dragon, as well. He does the same to them, but as you know he cannot breed a dragon without being marked by her."

"The skulls…"

Ked nodded and looked at her gravely. "He and his soldiers actively hunt us now. They have killed hundreds of our kind. The only way to make him stop is to return you to him, or so he claims, but we refused."

"You should never have taken me from him, Ked. We were in love. I trusted him."

"I protect what I love," Ked said hotly. A swift surge of darkness surrounded them, blotting out the idyllic garden along with every emotion Belah was experiencing save one: her shame. Shame for being so weak in the presence of a human man, for allowing him to overpower her so often. She hated her brother in that moment for holding the mirror up to her the way he did. As much as she had loved every moment of her time with Nikhil, she had let this happen.

"We must kill him. It's the only way," she said with forced conviction. As much as the idea destroyed her, Belah knew it had to be done.

"I wish it were so simple," Ked said. "Your fire is the only thing that has a chance of succeeding. I tried burning him the day I took you away. Our brothers and I have combined our three fires into one, but we weren't even able to subdue him. He can't harm us, but neither can we harm him. He's become too strong, but that's not the worst of it."

"So, I will go back there and take care of it. Now." She stood and prepared to shift.

"No." Ked grabbed her arm and pulled her back down.

Belah turned to look at her brother for the first time since they'd arrived here. Ked's brow was knit, his lips pursed. The expression alarmed her because for the first time in her life, he looked truly worried.

"Why not? What aren't you telling me?"

"Because he has our children, Belah. If we kill him, we will never find them."

"I have no children. None of us have any living children." Except for one son who their mother had hidden away. The son Belah wished she could find but knew better than to try searching for.

Ked's expression softened and he reached up to cup her cheek. He gave her a sad smile.

"You have two children, Belah. The son we made together, and the daughter Nikhil gave you. Your blood must have acted as a mark once he ingested it, allowing you conceive his child. She was born while you slept, and Mother promised her safe-keeping. We didn't believe him when he said he'd found them, and we have no idea how it happened. I confronted Mother about it, and she confirmed his story. They were hidden away in hibernation. Mother said only a pair of Blessed humans should have been capable of discovering where they slumbered, and only twins, at that. Such a thing would be so rare as to be nonex-istent."

Belah's eyesight dimmed and her world spun. Blood rushed to her head, causing a steady, painful throb at her temples.

Blessed twins. Sweet Mother, not Naaz and Neela.

She swallowed the lump in her throat and forced words out. "His soldiers… you said he has soldiers. They're just humans who follow him, right?"

"Mostly, yes, but there are two who are stronger than the others. The two are elites who are somehow able to lure any dragon and strong enough to kill them. I have never met them myself, but the tales I hear are of a brother and a sister who do Nikhil's bidding."

Belah crumpled against her brother, sobbing into his shoulder. The two precious children she'd cherished had been corrupted. This was all her doing—her cravings for an escape had left them vulnerable, had left her entire race vulnerable, and the very man who had granted her that escape upon the promise that she mark him had been the one to turn on them.

"Oh, Sweet Mother, what have I done?"

Once upon a time, she had been burdened by the responsibility of a slew of illustrious titles. Belah the Queen. Belah the Empress. Belah the Goddess.

She had lost the honor of any of those burdens.

Belah the Betrayer—that was the title that fit.

ABOUT OPHELIA BELL

Ophelia Bell loves a good bad-boy and especially strong women in her stories. Women who aren't apologetic about enjoying sex and bad boys who don't mind being with a woman who's in charge, at least on the surface, because pretty much anything goes in the bedroom.

Ophelia grew up on a rural farm in North Carolina and now lives in Los Angeles with her own tattooed bad-boy husband and six attention-whoring cats.

You can contact her at any of the following locations:
Website: http://opheliabell.com/
Facebook: https://www.facebook.com/OpheliaDragons
Twitter: @OpheliaDragons
Goodreads: https://www.goodreads.com/OpheliaBell

CPSIA information can be obtained
at www.ICGtesting.com
Printed in the USA
FSHW04n0848030418
46490FS